"I'm going

Claire's declaration was met by an equally defiant response. "I'll come with you."

"No, Tony. I need to find out for myself what's going on at Cauldron."

He pulled Claire toward him, despite her resistance. Folding his arms around her slim shoulders, he backed her up against the deck railing. "Claire, you're as much a victim as Patricia was. Don't push me away because you're hurting. I want to help. I need to help you. I care about you."

"I care about you, too. But this is a bigger issue than a passing attraction between two people—"

His fingers tightened on her arms. "For God's sake, stop that analytical distancing. I don't feel any 'passing attraction' for you. Let your guard down, woman. Believe in what you feel. Believe in me."

ABOUT THE AUTHOR

A native Californian, M. L. Gamble makes
her home in Mobile, Alabama, with her
husband and two young children. Her
fiction-writing career began a little over
three years ago, when she and her family
moved to Mobile, where there was little
opportunity for her to utilize her skills as an
advertising copywriter.

Stranger than Fiction

M. L. Gamble

Harlequin Books

TORONTO • NEW YORK • LONDON
AMSTERDAM • PARIS • SYDNEY • HAMBURG
STOCKHOLM • ATHENS • TOKYO • MILAN

For Philip Nuccio, with love

Harlequin Intrigue edition published March 1989

ISBN 0-373-22110-X

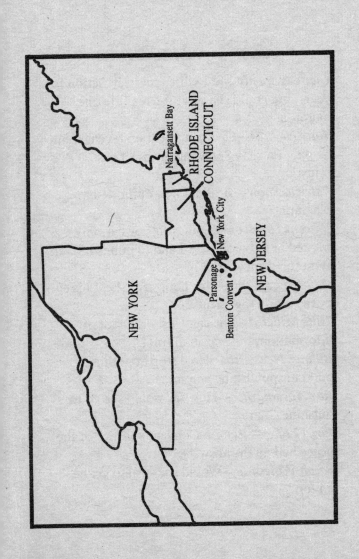

NEW YORK

Narragansett Bay

RHODE ISLAND

CONNECTICUT

New York City

Parsonage

Benton Convent

NEW JERSEY

CAST OF CHARACTERS

Claire Kennedy—She edited mystery fiction for years, but could she solve the real-life one haunting her?

Tony Nichols—He wasn't bent on revenge, but helping Patricia Snow might ease a past injustice.

Patricia Snow—Brilliant new author—or plagiarist?

Vincent Harrison—Cauldron's owner only wanted to know the truth and to publish Sarah Winesong's new book.

Damien Laurent—This book critic kept his eyes open . . . and saw plenty.

Tillie Millaird—She came up with a lot of information, but was it all true?

Billings Newcastle—He'd stop at nothing to build his publishing empire.

Roz Abramawitz—How far would she go to outshine Claire?

Pearl Loney—Benton Convent's justice of the peace had all the answers.

Sarah Winesong—Would she steal to get back on top?

Chapter One

Tony Nichols used both hands to push through the revolving door into the Waldorf Astoria. A second later he stood inside the hotel, his dark eyes methodically searching the throng of well-dressed guests.

The woman he sought was nowhere in sight.

Keeping his head down and his shoulders square, Tony walked through the richly paneled lobby. His demeanor was defensive, as if he expected to be asked to leave.

The people around him flashed discreet smiles, and their intimate conversations annoyed him.

Once he'd have felt right at home threading through this throng of professionals, greeting and being greeted affectionately. But today only disinterested glances were cast his way, the sour tang of insults too long held back burned in his mouth.

The person at the front desk directed him up to the third floor, where the socializing was now in full swing. Usually courteous, Tony snapped a curt no when a tray of canapés was offered to him by a gaping short-skirted waitress. With a deep breath he reminded himself to stay calm until he'd completed his task.

Everything was at stake.

Lengthening his stride, Tony reached the doorway of the main banquet room. A skinny redhead in a black sequined gown standing in the shadows took him by surprise.

"Why don't I fill out a name tag for you? We really aren't all that mysterious here."

Turning to her, the lean muscles working slowly in his jaw, Tony measured out his words. "Why don't you. The name's Poe. E. A. Poe."

The redhead smiled. "Poe. How appropriate. Any relation to *the* Poe?" Her black felt marker squeaked insinuatingly against the paper.

"Just in spirit." Slapping the white adhesive tag against his shirt, Tony walked over to the table bearing a Register Here sign. The chairs behind it were empty, but a banner tacked on to the wall behind it heralded the 45th Annual Mystery Writers Convention. He was in the right place.

So where the hell is she?

Turning back to search the now even more crowded room, his anxiety began to turn to anger. He fixed his stare on the groups of threes and fours moving into the room and studied each woman. Several, including a couple of blondes, returned his look.

But he did nothing to encourage any of them to speak to him. Only one woman interested him today. *Look for a tall blond woman about thirty with freckles. She's wearing a scarlet Karan jacket and miniskirt. With a croc belt.* Isn't that what the receptionist at Cauldron Press had said? Damn, every other woman here had on that color.

He discarded his original plan. He'd planned to confront the editor in her office when Cauldron's secretary told him the woman wouldn't be back until Monday. But

Tony now realized it might be impossible to find her in this crowd or, once finding her, to get her alone. But he had to keep trying. His business couldn't wait five days.

Tony was jostled out of his thoughts when a large group of Mystery Society members moved en masse in his direction. Backtracking to the banquet-room doorway, he noticed that the redhead was gone. Most of the people were sitting down at the round, pink-clothed tables inside as a battalion of waiters bustled around the room. He glanced at his watch.

It had been twenty-four hours since the phone call that had confirmed his suspicions. Time was running out.

He had to find Claire Kennedy now.

Find her. And convince her she'd be better off dead than publishing that book.

ACROSS THE ROOM, Claire Kennedy held out a graceful hand and, with a smile, accepted the sparkling champagne from the waiter. Taking a swallow, she closed her eyes to savor the tartness of the wine.

Five days off! And a surefire number-one bestseller coming out meant she should celebrate! With that thought, a smile played across her face. She sank into her chair and took a deep breath.

"Waiting for a kiss from Prince Charming? Or just sleeping, Claire?"

Claire's smile disappeared as the abrasive voice of Roz Abramawitz reached her. Opening her eyes, she nodded and extended her hand, praying she'd get all her fingers back. "Why hello, Roz. Nice to see you here today. How are things at the House of Usher?"

Roz, a woman whose small stature—she was four-foot-ten—didn't make her any less formidable an adversary, returned a tepid shake. Her tone made it clear she didn't like the pun on her company's name, and with narrowed eyes she studied the brown crocodile belt on Claire's slim waist. "Things are very, very good at Usherwood Publications. As they always are."

"Glad to hear. We all benefit when sales are up in the industry."

"In a pig's eye."

Taken aback, Claire lifted an eyebrow. She knew tempers were often short in the competitive field of mystery-fiction publishing, but Roz's was unusually so today. Even for her. "What's wrong, Roz? Having a bad time with one of your authors?"

"No. All my authors are top-notch and selling well. But I understand one of your people is big news today. Or is the rumor about Sarah Winesong's coming out of retirement with a book just wishful gossip?"

Bingo. That was what was ruffling her competitor's feathers. "How'd you hear that? I only sent galley copies and releases to the press a couple of days ago." Claire asked in amazement.

Roz sidestepped the question. "So you *are* pushing a new book from Winesong for September?"

"You know we don't 'push' books at Cauldron Press, Roz," Claire said, containing her temper. "We present them. We don't rely on hype, only quality."

Roz laughed without a trace of mirth. "Quantity is what you need. Your audience hasn't had a new book from Winesong for years."

"You're right. It's been five since we published the twentieth-anniversary edition of her work, which is why we're hopeful her fans will be very curious."

"You must be relieved."

"Relieved?"

Roz's face took on a sneer. "Of course 'relieved.' After all, I hear you rejected her last manuscript as unpublishable. I hope you haven't let some half-baked loyalty cloud your editorial judgment about Winesong's latest effort."

Cringing inside, Claire felt a blush color her cheeks. It had been the last *three* manuscripts from Sarah Winesong that had been rejected. The owner of Cauldron Press had warned Claire that Winesong would probably change publishers each time Claire sent the books back for more work, but luckily Claire's gamble had paid off. Winesong had stayed with them, and this latest book promised to be her best to date.

Despite the active grapevine in the publishing world, it rankled Claire that Roz had found out that any of Winesong's work had been turned down. "I'd have bought the *The Poison Pen Pal* if the author had been a librarian from Kansas City. It's written in a classic style, with all the wit and spirit of a brand-new author. It should outsell anything Winesong's ever done."

"Well, I hope it does. Did your boss tell you he had breakfast with mine this morning?"

At Claire's blank look, Roz straightened up. "No? Well, let me be the first to tell you that we're thinking of buying out Cauldron Press. If that happens, I'm in line to be in charge of acquisitions for all Usherwood Publications subsidiaries."

Claire choked down a gasp. Trading barbs with Roz had gotten to be an expected part of her job these past seven years. But the game Roz suggested now sent a shiver through her.

"I can see you get my drift," Roz added. "I'd be your new boss."

Her mind whirring, Claire again kept quiet. Cauldron Press was on the brink of turning its fortunes around by publishing Sarah Winesong's new book. Her boss would never sell now.

"Well, don't hold your breath waiting for that to happen, Roz. I'm sure Cauldron Press will remain as independent as ever." She stood, and before she could walk off, Roz grasped her sleeve.

"Don't let my boss's reputation scare you. After all, I thought Claire Elizabeth Kennedy had ice water in her veins. Except maybe when she's bidding against me for a book."

"That's a strange conclusion for you to draw, Roz. Considering the fact that the last book you outbid me on sank into anonymity without a trace."

"That's a lie!" A few strands of hair popped out of Roz's chignon.

"Is it?"

Roz chewed on her lip, calculating a response. "At least you've learned that there are no guarantees in this business, my dear Claire."

"That I have. Now, Roz, you must excuse me," Claire said. "I have to give a speech welcoming the new president of the Society in five minutes. But when I get back to the office, I'll be sure to pass along your best wishes."

"You do that." With a gulp, Roz downed most of her champagne, then tossed the remainder into a potted palm. "Oh—there's the group I'm lunching with. Sorry I can't ask you to join us, but we're going to discuss a new unpublished writer I'm really excited about. A college girl."

Before Claire could respond, Roz headed across the room toward a group by the door. Trying to calm her churning stomach, Claire crossed the banquet room toward the speaker's table. As she sat down, she suddenly felt self-conscious, as if hostile eyes were on her. Glancing around, she met only the smiles and nods of friends and colleagues. But as the lights dimmed and she heard herself being introduced, she couldn't shake the feeling that a problem awaited her. Just out of sight.

It was probably just her particularly unpleasant confrontation with Roz Abramawitz, she told herself as she stood to give her speech. But looking out at the sea of faces, a shiver of intuition chilled her.

Maybe today really wasn't a day to celebrate.

"LET ME BUY YOU a drink in the bar, Claire. It's only two-thirty and I'm dying to hear all about *The Poison Pen Pal*. Did you ever actually meet the reclusive author face-to-face?"

Claire patted Damien Laurent's silk-suited arm as they walked out of the deserted banquet room toward the elevators. She and the book critic had been held up by well-wishers after their speeches, and were among the last to leave. "No. True to form, Sarah Winesong's the same old hermit. I've never laid eyes on her."

"Aunt Tillie said she sounded good on the phone at Christmas." Deftly he twirled his walking stick in front of him, a habit that was his trademark.

"Tillie thinks everyone sounds good at Christmas. It's because she loves that time of year so much." Claire grinned when she thought of her editorial assistant, Tillie Millard. She'd been Sarah Winesong's first contact at Cauldron Press twenty-five years ago, and was one of the few to have the reclusive woman's confidence. Tillie took her job as chief messenger for the author very seriously.

"Did you have to edit her new book very much?" Damien asked. "I'd heard some rumors the old gal had lost her touch."

"No, I did very little. I sent her one chapter in the mail to restructure, and of course we used telepathy for some minor things."

"What?" Damien's eyes were alert. He was always eager to find a headline that would top his monthly column in *Cloak and Dagger*, a much read and respected industry magazine. And even though Tillie was his aunt, he'd never had any luck getting her to reveal Cauldron Press's inside operations.

"It was the wildest thing, Damien. Sometimes I'd be working on a certain scene or chapter, then suddenly, in the next mail, Tillie'd receive the exact same pages. Edited by Sarah Winesong exactly as if we'd worked on it together for hours."

"God, Claire, that's a great angle for my review. Have you got any psychic vibrations about her next novel?"

Claire shook her head as they walked, delighted that the influential critic was interested. "No, after all these years between *The Poison Pen Pal* and her last book, we decided not to push her at all."

"Except for a sequel."

Laughing, Claire squeezed Damien's arm. "I've got to run to catch a plane now, but let's schedule supper for early next week. I'm dying to hear what you think about the book."

"Fine. I'd love to have dinner. But don't torture yourself over my opinion, even if it is incredibly important." His laugh was intended to lessen the effect of his words, but Claire suspected he meant what he said. "I'll tell you this right now. Your book's a smash, Claire, an absolute ten. It's fresh, fun, yet vintage Winesong, all the i's dotted and t's crossed. A really good read. I'll tell you more when you buy me dinner.''

"Are you asking for a bribe?"

Now they laughed together. While Damien did expect her to pay for an expensive Manhattan dinner, they both knew it wouldn't buy his good opinion about the book.

Damien pressed the elevator button. "No one is happier than I am that this book will put Cauldron Press back on top. I've been so worried about Vincent—'' his expression softened as he mentioned Cauldron's owner, Vincent Harrison "—for the past year. But now that he has this book, I'm sure he'll be back to his old self. By the way, what's this I've heard about a buy-out offer from Usherwood—''

Before Damien finished his sentence, Claire was grabbed by a man stepping out of the elevator. "Ms. Kennedy, I need to speak to you. Now.''

Claire stared at the large hand aggressively clasping her arm. Silently cursing the name tag displayed so prominently on her sweater, she said, "I'm sorry Mr....'' She scanned his soft corduroy jacket and faded plaid shirt for some identification, then spotted the card pinned to his lapel. "Mr. Poe?''

Ripping off the name tag and balling it up with his free hand, he continued to grip Claire's arm. "My name is Nichols. Tony Nichols.''

"Really, Mr. Nichols, this is most rude.'' Damien's voice rose as he took a cautious step closer to Claire.

But Tony's frown only deepened. "Do we do this here, Ms. Kennedy, or shall we talk in private?''

Claire decided he was a writer and forced herself to feel a little sympathy. She knew that writers often waited for weeks, months even, while their manuscripts circulated through a publishing house. He'd probably sent in a

novel to Cauldron and decided to check on it in person.
"Mr. Nichols, if you'd like an appointment to speak to
me, please call my office and make one. Now if you'll
excuse us, Mr. Laurent and I were having a private conversation."

"I can't wait until next week."

Her impatience rising, Claire met Tony's dark unsmil-
ing eyes. Her bags were packed for a trip, and she wasn't
going to let this man ruin the first vacation she'd had in
two years. It would be just her luck if she'd already rejected his book and he wanted to argue about it. "I'm
afraid you'll have to."

But Tony Nichols would not budge. His voice took on
a nasty edge. "The only thing I'll have to do is send a
summons for you to appear in court, Ms. Kennedy. I
suggest you finish your private conversation with Mr.
Laurent and have one with me."

Damien stood very straight, glaring at Tony. "Mr.
Nichols, please take—"

Claire was horrified suddenly by the vision of Damien's being punched to bits by the muscular-looking and
obviously furious Mr. Nichols. "It's okay, Damien, I can
handle this. Go on down to the lobby. I'll call you later
to set up dinner." Claire leaned over and grazed the critic's pale cheek with a kiss, then pushed him into the
waiting elevator.

Turning back, she stared pointedly at Tony Nichols's
hand still on her arm. "You have five minutes, Mr.
Nichols. And please, take your hand off me. You're cutting off the circulation."

Tony stepped back. He was finding this much harder
than he'd expected. For one thing, Claire Kennedy was
fabulous looking. From the mass of wavy blond hair to
the bold cashmere jacket, she was a picture of loveli-

ness. Her brown eyes sparkled with energy, and her manner was brisk yet completely feminine. He nodded toward an alcove away from the elevator, deep in shadow. "Shall we?"

Following him across the plush red carpet, Claire had the odd feeling that she'd suddenly become a character in one of the hundreds of mysteries she'd read.

Heroine accosted by stranger. Handsome black-haired stranger. With a secret.

Well, he had the right looks for the hero. Or the demonic bad guy, she thought with a chill as she settled into the couch. Her heart beat uncomfortably fast as he sat down next to her and leaned toward her.

Claire inhaled deeply, hoping she'd be able to remember something about the manuscript she was sure he must want to talk about. "Well, Mr. Nichols, what exactly is this all about?"

He leaned closer, his olive complexion smooth under the well-defined stubble of a day's growth of beard. "You'll never get away with it."

Claire felt her skin redden with irritation. "With what, Mr. Nichols? Have we lost your book? Taken longer than you liked getting back to you on a proposal you've submitted? I'm sorry if you're upset, but we receive over a hundred unsolicited manuscripts a month from people and—"

"How many of that hundred did you steal this month?"

Claire recoiled in shock. Steal? "We'd never *steal* anyone's work. We're overjoyed to find publishable material, and more than happy to pay for it. Now, if you'll just tell me what's happened to confuse you..."

Her voice trailed off as she was distracted by the fragrance that emanated from him. The mixture of sandalwood soap and tobacco was so strong it seemed to be coming off her own clothes.

"What's happened to confuse me, Ms. Kennedy? 'Confuse' is the wrong word. When a book is attributed to one person even though it was written by another, I don't get confused. I get enraged. Because that is stealing. And I'm here to tell you I won't let it happen."

"Now look, Mr. Nichols. I appreciate your anger, but I guess I'm not following you. No one here has stolen any book."

His laugh ambushed her senses. It was rich, low and deep, enveloping her like warm fog. "You're really cool, Ms. Kennedy, I'll give you that. What is this? A trick? Have you signaled the house detective? Are you planning on accusing me of taking advantage of you so I'll get locked up and you can duck out and warn your cronies?"

Claire got to her feet. She had tried to get the truth out of this outrageous stranger, and now he'd proved offensive. She had to do all she could to muster her professionalism. "Call me if you're ever ready to talk reasonably, Mr. Nichols. I'll try to help you then."

He made no effort to move his feet, which were blocking hers. "You know what book."

"No. I don't."

"I don't believe you."

"Look, if you'll be honest with me, I'll try to find out what happened to your manuscript. But you really are going too far—"

"Okay, Ms. Kennedy. We'll play it your way. The book in question is titled *Letters in the Attic*. And it's not my book. It was written by a student of mine, Patricia Snow."

He waited for her response.

"Then I'll have to speak to this, er, Miss Snow about her book."

"Patricia asked me to inquire about it for her."

"Oh? Are you her agent?"

"No. I'm her friend."

Claire ignored the warmth she felt when he leaned closer. "I don't recall reading a manuscript with that title, Mr. Nichols. What was it about?"

"It's about deceit, and a lost love affair, and a girl's murder. But justice prevailed, Ms. Kennedy, just like it will in real life."

Though a warning bell sounded in a distant corner of Claire's mind, she dismissed it. The guy had to be a lunatic. A handsome, compelling lunatic, but a lunatic nonetheless. "I'm late now, Mr. Nichols. And I really have no more time for this, so if you'll excuse me..."

She stepped around his feet, but his hand once again grasped her arm. She winced slightly as he pressed on the exact spot he had earlier.

"How about *The Poison Pen Pal*, Ms. Kennedy? Do you have time to discuss that title?"

Suddenly queasy, as if she were on an airplane that had dropped a hundred feet, Claire stopped her resistance. "What interest do you have in Sarah Winesong's new book? How do you even know the title?"

"Getting nervous, Ms. Kennedy? Feeling guilty maybe?"

"This is a ridiculous game you're playing. If you want to discuss Sarah Winesong's new book—"

"Ah, but that's the point, Ms. Kennedy. *The Poison Pen Pal* isn't Sarah Winesong's book. She stole it, or someone stole it for her. From Patricia Snow."

Go slow, Claire. Go slow. Find out where the strength is. Then make your play. Her dad's words, spoken to her years ago while he taught her to play penny-ante poker, ran through her head. She took a deep calming gulp of air.

But before she could speak, a voice behind her almost shattered her last shred of control.

"Claire. Aren't you going to introduce me? Or are you hiding this man from the rest of us?" Roz's voice was sweet, and deadly.

Turning slowly, Claire wondered how long the other woman had been standing there. She let her breath out slowly and forced her words to sound friendly. "No, Roz, I'm not going to introduce you. This gentleman and I have private business. So, if you'll excuse us?"

Roz's face tightened and her white teeth glimmered in the shadowy light. She looked a little unsteady. Her black velvet bow had slipped over her right ear, and her lids hung low. She'd obviously entertained her guests to the limit at lunch.

"Certainly. Nice not to meet you. If you get tired of your present company, give me a call." Roz winked at Tony Nichols, then walked away as gracefully as she could manage.

Claire knew she'd have to pay for the snub, but she couldn't handle what this character might say in front of her rival.

"Nice job, Ms. Kennedy. But I wouldn't mind speaking to someone from Usherwood Publications." Obviously he'd made a mental note of Roz's name tag. "I might have to go to her if I need some expert advice."

"I don't know what your game is, Mr. Nichols, but I'm not going to play. If you have some legitimate complaint, or information about Cauldron Press or one of our books, call my office and make an appointment to discuss it with us. If you don't, I suggest you drop whatever game you're playing."

Tony stood straighter, balling his hands in anger. She was really cool. The straight freckled nose, tilted contemptuously in the air. Her wide-shouldered, slim body not shown off, but displayed to full advantage in the short skirt.

But what was most disconcerting was her honesty. It rang out like a bell every time she spoke. She must be a hell of a liar, or he'd misunderstood the implications of what little information Patricia had provided over the phone, concerning the theft of her manuscript.

Tony reached into the inside pocket of his jacket, noting Claire's tiny blink of fright. *What does she think? That I've got a gun?* The thought appalled him, but he did nothing to allay her fears. He withdrew the heavy parchment envelope and handed it to her.

"Read this. I'll be in touch. And by the way, I have no plans to drop this matter."

Outwardly registering none of the fear beginning to fill her, Claire didn't reply. She watched Tony saunter to the silvered elevator doors.

He'd lost a little of his bravado, but she saw from the set of his jaw that he'd lost none of his conviction. The envelope felt too heavy to hold.

She pulled out the contents and hurriedly scanned them. *I was right,* she thought. *This isn't a day to celebrate.*

Chapter Two

The elderly woman walked up the porch steps, looking around for her charge. Patricia Snow was nowhere to be seen outside, which meant the young woman was probably still sleeping off last night's bout of drinking.

The visitor leaned heavily on her cane and unlocked the front door. As she slid the key back into her dress pocket, the clasp of her Medic Alert ID bracelet got caught, and the copper chain fell to the ground with a dull tinkle. The woman stooped to retrieve it.

She walked through the door and down the dusty hallway, fiddling with the worn-out fastener. "Patricia? Are you still asleep? Patricia?"

The only response to her call was the creak of the boards beneath her feet. She stopped at the bedroom off to her right and opened the door.

Patricia Snow, looking twenty years older than her twenty-three years, was sprawled on her bed, dressed in yesterday's baggy shirt and jeans. All the outfits she'd worn the past week were heaped around the room. A pink bathrobe lay across a grease-stained pizza box. The shades were drawn tight, but several tiny holes let in baleful shafts of late-afternoon light.

The girl looked up. "Go away."

Her guest crossed the room and began sorting the clothes into piles. "Come on. Get up, Patricia. Come outside and do some gardening with me." Her shoe brushed against a bottle lying under the edge of the bedspread, and she leaned down to retrieve it.

The smell of cheap bourbon hung in the room like exhaust, stinging the elderly woman's eyes behind her glasses.

"Leave that bottle," said Patricia. "There's still some in it."

The woman eyed Patricia, then placed the bottle carefully on the cluttered bureau. "How's your writing coming? Have you put anything down on paper yet that I can take a look at?"

"No."

"It's been a couple of months since you've worked on anything, Patricia. Want to talk about it?"

"No. Just drop it." Patricia felt her head clearing, and she remembered what she had to do. Her plan. She deliberately altered the harsh tone of her voice. "I'll finish typing up that latest bunch of research tonight. Can you bring me some gas so I can drive into town tomorrow?"

"You were just in town yesterday. Two trips in three days. What's going on with you?"

"If you'd give me more money I wouldn't have to bother you every time I have to run an errand."

The woman shook her head in gentle rebuke. "No more money until you write another few pages. That's a directive straight to you from Claire Kennedy. You don't want to irritate your prospective editor."

"I think it's time I spoke to her myself. I don't need your help anymore."

"You know what happened last time you tried to negotiate for yourself, Patricia." The old woman reached out her dry hand and patted the girl's fleshy arm. "I don't mind doing this for you. It makes me feel part of things."

Patricia shrugged off the woman's hand. "I want to call and check on my mother. I've been worried about her," she lied. Aware that her guest was watching her closely, she looked away. It wasn't that she was scared of her go-between, but her call to Tony Nichols yesterday might unnecessarily irritate the older woman. No telling what might happen then.

Professor Nichols was so gallant and concerned. The news he'd had about *Letters in the Attic*'s being published under Sarah Winesong's name and a different title had come as no surprise. Even though Cauldron Press's editor, Claire Kennedy, had supposedly rejected the manuscript months ago as "too rough," Patricia'd had a hunch all along she'd not been told the whole truth.

She'd show them all, Patricia thought to herself now. Once she heard from the other publisher, it'd be Sarah Winesong's turn to be pitied.

"What are you thinking, Patricia? You look quite fierce."

The girl's eyes met her visitor's. "I'm thinking about what a fun and rewarding life writing has proved to be."

"Success will come in time. We all believe in you, Patricia, so cheer up. I'll take you into town tomorrow for your errands, then we'll have supper at the Benton Convent Grill."

"Fine." Patricia forced a smile. She couldn't remember what time she'd promised to call Professor Nichols, but the afternoon seemed good. "You'll come for me around three?"

"I'll be here. Now you try and write a little today." Patricia's visitor turned and walked back down the hall, the metal tip of her cane tapping lightly in the dusky quiet. She stopped at a cabinet in the foyer and took out a full bottle of bourbon. After loosening the top, she left it sitting there.

Patricia would find it. She always did.

The woman closed the door behind her, then walked carefully down the porch steps. As soon as she got back to town, she'd stop and call New York. Patricia Snow had been acting strange. Very strange.

With *The Poison Pen Pal* publication date so near, they couldn't be too careful.

CLAIRE SLAPPED fifty creased pages down onto the desk of her boss, Vincent Harrison. "It's our book. Not word for word. The characters have different names. And it lacks the polish. But it's the exact story Sarah Winesong sent us."

Walking to the window, Claire shook her head in frustration and stared out at the Manhattan evening. All energy had faded from her husky voice, mirroring the last cool shards of sun as they melted into the April sky.

"What do you think is going on? Is he a crook? A madman? Or do we genuinely have something to worry about?" It was Vincent's first question since Claire had entered his office a half hour before. He spoke with little inflection, as if he were reading from cue cards.

"I don't know exactly what he is. But if Tony Nichols repeats his accusations to anyone, *The Poison Pen Pal* will have to be withdrawn until all the legal battles are fought."

"And won."

"Or lost." Claire turned to meet Mr. Harrison's eyes. They were glassy with what looked like shock. "We'll have to ask Sarah Winesong to come in and discuss this. Immediately.''

"Good God.''

"I know she has a phobia about the city, and about people in general. We've never pushed her about it, Mr. Harrison, but this is so potentially damaging that—''

"That's enough!'' he interrupted. "I'm sorry to be so abrupt with you, Claire. But, please, let's slow down a little.'' Harrison's austere features were pinched. The crow's feet that marked his eyes with gaiety were drawn into tight lines of anxiety. "I know you feel I'm too indulgent with Miss Winesong, but I've dealt with her much longer than you have. I remember how horrible it was for her when we turned her work down, and how she suffered through writer's block and every other self-doubt that artists are prone to. Until we know more about this Tony Nichols person, I'm against confronting her.''

Claire crossed her arms. She seldom argued with Mr. Harrison, but when she was convinced she was right, she stood her ground. "Look, we planned on my meeting with her soon anyway. I can handle this tactfully. I won't make a big deal of it. Or you can go see her. Or we'll send Tillie.''

"No, not Tillie.'' His eyes issued a challenge, then he shook his head and backed off a bit. "Claire, we need to be very careful with her. What could we possibly ask? If she's stolen an idea—or more—from some unknown writer and sent it to us as her own? We'd lose *The Poison Pen Pal* and all future books she might write.''

Claire pointed to the offending pages lying on the desk. "That has to be explained somehow.''

"It will be. In time. For now, let's put our heads together and work this thing through. Did Tony Nichols tell you *how* he got a copy of Winesong's book to compare it to his student's manuscript? What's her name?"

"Patricia Snow. No, he didn't say how he got a copy of *The Poison Pen Pal*."

Harrison creaked forward in his swivel rocker, placing his hands on the pristine gray blotter covering his desk. "We need to find out."

Claire shook her head. "I'm sorry I didn't ask him more questions, but the whole thing was so unbelievable."

"You did just fine. Did he say when he'd call back?"

"No. But I had the impression it would be soon."

"Then we need to get started. We must be discreet, and thorough, in our investigation."

"Should we hire a private detective?"

"Good Lord, no. We can't risk telling anyone else about this. You know how rumors fly around in this business. We'll do the research ourselves. You'll have to find out where he lives, then go see him. Maybe you could follow him, see if he leads you to a meeting with this Patricia Snow person."

"Me?" Claire's doubts about her credentials as gum-shoe detective must have shown in her face, for Vincent Harrison got up and came around his desk to pat her hand.

"Yes, you. One of your greatest assets is your ability to judge the truth about these things. You can tell a promising writer or a market trend faster than anyone I've ever seen. Just believe in your instincts, and keep your ears open. Tony Nichols won't be able to fool you."

"I don't know, Mr. Harrison. We don't have long until the book is scheduled for printing."

Harrison shook his head with finality. "Which is why I'm counting on you, Claire. If word of this scandal leaks out, we'll be ruined."

"Well, okay. I'll give it a shot. I'm supposed to be out of the office for a few days anyway. I just hope he doesn't have a confederate working here at Cauldron."

"A spy! At my publishing company?"

Claire chewed on the corner of her lip as she began to think of things to add to a tablet of paper she'd pulled from her satchel, the top item of which read: cancel plane tickets. She'd checked that off before she'd left the Waldorf. "I've been worried we had someone with loose lips here all day. Roz Abramawitz knew we'd rejected some of Sarah's ideas."

This news made Harrison pale further. "Good Lord, if that's the case, Tony Nichols might be just the tip of the iceberg."

"What do you mean?"

"Maybe this scandal has been brewing for some time. Maybe there are several people involved. Several people who would benefit by the damage our company would suffer if this gets out."

Claire rubbed her long fingers up and down her arms as if trying to warm herself against a marauding Atlantic gale. In her mind's eye she recalled Tony Nichols, full of threats, not all of them yet revealed. "Mr. Harrison, I know competition in our industry has never been stiffer. But the publishing houses I know anything about would never deliberately sabotage—"

"We can't be naive, Claire. Usherwood Publications' new owner, Billings Newcastle, has been known to use every trick in the book to discredit a company he's interested in buying. Remember what he did in England?"

The events surrounding Newcastle's takeover of a conservative, two-hundred-year-old newspaper in London glimmered to the surface of Claire's memory. Something about call girls and a cabinet official. Newcastle money had arranged the scandal.

All the rumors about Vincent Harrison selling Cauldron Press rushed back to Claire. She sat down on the couch next to his desk and crossed her hands over her knee. "Not to change the subject, Mr. Harrison, but I understand you had breakfast with Newcastle today. Did he make you an offer for Cauldron Press?"

Harrison looked startled. "How do you know that?"

"Roz couldn't refrain from telling me."

The two regarded each other closely. Finally Harrison replied in clipped tones, "I was going to tell you. When it was all over. When I'd convinced that bastard corporate raider to go away. When I'd gotten the bank to—" He stopped and forced a smile. "Let's discuss this later. It's probably not relevant to Tony Nichols's charges at all."

Bile and acid mixed together in her stomach, and Claire reached into her pocket for her ever-present antacid. Mr. Harrison had been loyal and supportive to her these past few years, promoting her and raising her salary frequently. They had a relationship of mutual respect, and she thought she had his confidence.

But this trouble with Newcastle struck her as a complete surprise. She'd known Cauldron had come through a period of cash-flow difficulty, but his reaction now made it apparent that the future of the publishing company was in question.

Which meant her recent delight in looking forward to a solid future with Cauldron was fool's gold.

Well, time to dig in, Claire thought. While Tony Nichols's vile suspicions had hurt her pride, the precariousness of the company's future was what she had to concentrate on.

"I'll set up another meeting with Nichols as soon as I can, Mr. Harrison. Are you going to advise our attorney about the plagiarism accusations?"

"Yes. But we'll tell no one else, not even Tillie."

Swallowing her protest, Claire nodded. Tillie was her right hand. Damien's aunt knew everyone in the East Coast publishing business. If Tony Nichols was involved in a plot that was somehow connected to Billings Newcastle, Tillie would be able to track down the conspirators more quickly than anyone. Her network of editors, writers, ex-publishing friends and office personnel had legendary proportions.

But if Mr. Harrison was paranoid about anyone except her looking into this mess, she'd simply get Tillie working on it without telling her the whole story. *Ha,* Claire thought to herself, *and I was worried about the challenge of finding out about Nichols!*

As the chimes from the antique mantel clock signaled the half hour, Claire said gently, "I'll get right on this tomorrow. Why don't we both go home and get some rest tonight?"

Before he could answer, the intercom buzzer sounded. He pressed it. "Yes?"

It was his secretary. "Mr. Harrison? There's a Tony Nichols here to see you."

Claire's stomach lurched and her skin flushed at the mention of that name. Her eyes met her boss's. "How brazen can he get?"

"Shh, Claire. This is good. Let's invite him in. Maybe he's come to his senses and has decided to drop his phony charges. Don't overreact." Harrison pressed the talk switch. "Please send Mr. Nichols in, Tillie."

Tony's dark eyes bored into her own from across the spacious reception area. Leaning against the door frame for support, Claire felt her skin grow cold in anticipation of the coming verbal showdown with a man who seemed to enjoy them.

Though she'd grown adept at confrontations, the thought of them filled her with dread. As a small child, Claire'd always chosen to run and hide from her parents' nightly brawls. This impulse had finally been conquered during the last years she'd spent with her ex-husband. But only after she'd learned that silence and lack of passion were just as damaging as screaming insults. "Please come in, Mr. Nichols."

Tony Nichols walked toward her, not glancing into the office beyond. "Thanks. Let me forewarn you that I won't be bought off, Ms. Kennedy, no matter what the price."

"We don't pay for the truth at Cauldron, only fiction." Claire gestured widely with her arm. "After you."

His eyes traveled downward, but Claire ignored his glance. She turned abruptly and spoke in a too loud voice. "Mr. Harrison, this is Tony Nichols. Mr. Nichols, the president and owner of Cauldron Press, Vincent Harrison."

Vincent Harrison rose and extended his hand. "Mr. Nichols, please understand first of all that I am as interested as you are in seeing this matter cleared up."

Sitting down in a Chippendale chair facing Harrison's desk, Tony relaxed his muscles in a single breath, the way a cat does before it pounces. He saw that Claire was more uptight than she'd been when he'd first sprung the news.

Which proved nothing about the extent to which she and her boss were involved. Some people handled pressure better than others.

"I'm glad Ms. Kennedy had time to fill you in on the problem. I'm going to speak with Patricia tomorrow, and I hope I'll be able to give her some good news."

"News?" Claire didn't keep the contempt out of her voice.

Tony turned to her. "Maybe news is the wrong word. Information might be the better choice. Information about what Cauldron Press plans to do on her behalf. After all, I understand the book's about to go to press. You may be able to get a signed contract with Patricia before the cover's done. In which case you'll only have to change the author's name and the title."

Exchanging a look with Mr. Harrison, Claire pressed her lips together tightly. Her hunch about a leak had to be right if he even knew the printing schedule! She cautioned herself to remain calm, deciding to let Tony Nichols lay his demands on the table before she said anything.

"May I ask what your business connection is to Patricia Snow?" Harrison asked.

"As I told Ms. Kennedy, I'm a friend. A friend who discovered what you people were up to when I was given a book titled *The Poison Pen Pal* to review for the *Times*. I realized immediately that it's a ripped-off version of a book Patricia Snow worked on in my seminar last year at Immaculate Sisters College in Rhode Island."

Claire nodded as his name rang a bell, then quickly stopped for fear Tony would think she was agreeing with him. She knew his work as a reviewer; he was good—tough but fair. A very annoying recollection in light of the fact that she wanted to nail him as a con man. "So you called her to ask her about it?"

"Yes. It took me a few days to track her down, but she finally got in touch yesterday. She asked me to speak to Cauldron Press for her, since I know my way around New York publishers a little better than she does." Tony folded his hands and put them on his knees, a flush creeping up his neck. "But if you'd rather deal with a lawyer, that can be arranged."

This small misrepresentation of what Patricia had asked was minor, he thought. Even though she'd given him the go-ahead to confront Cauldron, her reluctance to offer a complete explanation about how she'd gotten herself into this mess made it clear there was something underhand going on. He just wasn't sure who the chief culprit was.

But if the rumor he heard last month was true—that Billings Newcastle was set to take over Cauldron Press— then he was ready to hazard a solid guess as to who the culprit was.

Having once experienced Newcastle's greed firsthand, he wasn't surprised to hear that Newcastle was involved.

"Lawyer?" Harrison replied. "No, no that won't be necessary. Ms. Kennedy and I can take your word for your relationship with Miss Snow, especially since you have these pages of manuscript. We're just very anxious to speak with Miss Snow herself."

"I heard Ms. Kennedy in action today. Great speech. No wonder you want to let her negotiate on Cauldron's behalf. She may be able to persuade Patricia to cooperate with keeping the plagiarism lawsuit out of the papers."

Claire could keep silent no longer. "I really resent your outrageous charges and innuendos. We will do whatever it takes to uncover the facts about *The Poison Pen Pal*. Including unmasking you for the fraud you are."

Vincent Harrison glanced quickly from Claire to Tony. "Mr. Nichols, forgive us for being somewhat brutal in our judgment of your character. But I'm sure you can understand our distress at being accused of a crime we are, in fact, quite innocent of."

Claire was appalled at her outburst, but felt even more remorse that Mr. Harrison hadn't used stronger language.

Of course Sarah Winesong had written *The Poison Pen Pal.*

She herself had edited it, line by line, and had even worked out a couple of bugs in the plot with Winesong through their weekly exchange of mail. Claire was proud of the book, and as possessive of it as if it was her own.

Tony's voice cut into her thoughts. "Someone is guilty of something, Mr. Harrison."

"Most assuredly, sir. Which is why Ms. Kennedy and I would like to work with you to discover just where the problem is."

Claire shuddered at that statement. She really didn't want to work with Tony Nichols. She wanted to punch him. For accusing her of being the worst kind of thief.

But she couldn't have him arrested, or sue him, or even slap him. Because despite his rudeness, two questions screamed for answers.

Was Sarah Winesong's book almost identical to a college student's unpublished manuscript?

And if it was, and that fact wasn't due to some hideous coincidence—the odds of which had to be a billion to one—which book was the genuine article?

Claire rose again from the sofa and walked closer to Tony. "I'd like to ask you a few more questions."

"Ask away." Tony settled back and watched her. For a moment he was struck by her openness, and her beauty. But he put those thoughts aside and listened.

"Did Patricia Snow say how Sarah Winesong supposedly got ahold of her manuscript?"

Tony was quiet for a moment. Patricia hadn't known that Sarah Winesong had submitted the work as her own. But she'd promised to fill him in tomorrow on the whole story. "I'd rather not reveal all the details until I know what Cauldron intends to do for Patricia."

"Without the details, we intend to do nothing," Claire shot back.

Tony leaned forward, patting his jacket pocket for his cigarettes. "I'll have to ask Patricia just what she wants me to tell you. I'm not really at liberty to tell you everything—for her protection, you understand."

"I assure you, Mr. Nichols, Miss Snow will not need protection from anyone at Cauldron if she's telling the truth," Harrison interjected.

"I think the quickest way to handle things is for me to meet with her," Claire added.

"Meet with her?" Tony raised his eyebrows and dug his hands into the pockets of his jacket. "That can probably be arranged."

"I'd like to meet with you both as soon as possible. I can come to Rhode Island tomorrow morning. Will that be convenient?" Claire spoke quietly, but a tangle of unspoken questions filled the room.

Instead of replying to Claire, Tony bent his head and lit a cigarette. He rubbed the thin tube between his long thick fingers as he dragged heavily and blew the blue smoke toward the ceiling. He'd not asked either of them if they minded if he smoked.

Claire couldn't move her eyes away from his mouth. She swallowed hard and looked at Mr. Harrison, who sat as if mesmerized by the smoke.

"Does this bother either of you?" When he looked up, Tony's eyes seemed to have gotten darker, his beard more pronounced.

"Yes. It does." Claire's skin blotched with nervousness. She wished she was anywhere but this place with this man. Not only did he threaten her job security, but he seemed to be always staring at her in a very intimate way, plucking personal facts out of the air around her.

"I'm sorry. I'll put it out right away." He crushed the burning end into the ashtray on Mr. Harrison's desk. "Now, that's terrific that you'll come to Rhode Island. Tomorrow will be fine. Do you have any more questions?"

"Are you going to be financially compensated for your help if Patricia Snow publishes?" Harrison asked.

Anger speared through Claire as the ramifications of Mr. Harrison's question sank in. A lot of money was at stake with this book. Hundreds of thousands of dollars. In her life she'd seen people gamble a lot more on a lot less.

"I edited Patricia's book as a favor to her. I have no monetary stake at all in the project," Tony said.

"But you wouldn't be adverse to her rewarding you, would you?" Claire's accusation landed like a slap.

"Truth has its own rewards, or have you forgotten *all* the basic tenets of the law, Ms. Kennedy?"

"Claire, Mr. Nichols, hold on." Vincent Harrison rose from behind the desk and stood next to Claire. "I think we need to look at each piece of this puzzle slowly and carefully. We have a book from a well-known and respected author. You have a manuscript from a student you know and respect. All we have to do is get together with Miss Snow and discuss how she came up with this material.''

"And when do we get to meet your Miss Winesong and see what she knows about all this?"

Mr. Harrison laughed easily. "As everyone knows, Mr. Nichols, Miss Winesong seldom sees anyone. Let's first concentrate on having Miss Snow meet with us. Claire will get to the bottom of things.''

Tony realized at this instant that he hadn't come to New York solely on Patricia's behalf. He'd wanted to erase his own blighted past the minute he'd realized *The Poison Pen Pal* was cribbed. He'd have to be careful not to let his own quest for vengeance ruin things for Patricia.

But it was time to turn the heat up a little. "Okay. I think it's great Ms. Kennedy is willing to meet with Patricia. Or should I say, meet with her again.''

Claire stared at Tony. "Again?"

"Well, I assume you've already met. At least on the phone or something. After all, Patricia Snow told me to contact you personally.''

"What?" Vincent Harrison's voice was filled with shock and disbelief. His gaze shifted from Claire to her accuser. "She specifically asked for Claire?"

"She mentioned my name?" Claire walked right up to where Tony sat, drawn like a moth to a flame.

"Yes. When I told her I was going to come and see Cauldron, she said to be sure and ask for Claire Kennedy. 'If anyone knows how Sarah Winesong got ahold of my work, she does.' ''

The three of them waited for someone to speak. Finally Claire broke the silence. "This gets more insane by the minute. I don't recall ever meeting her. And I've checked our files, called research, contracts and finance. We've never received any correspondence, or material, from her, nor have we ever sent her anything."

"Patricia gave me the impression you'd been interested in her book for several months." This was a small lie on his part. Patricia had only said "someone" had promised to show it to Claire Kennedy.

"I'm telling you, I've never even heard of this girl!"

"So you say." Tony Nichols's laugh closed over Claire like a blanket, smothering her. He stood and looked at her as if he was going to shake her hand, but stopped and again stuck his hands into his pockets. "I'll meet your train at Kingston Station, Rhode Island, tomorrow morning. Narragansett is just a few miles from there. Good night."

With a nod to Mr. Harrison, he stood and strode out of the office.

After a minute of silence, the three-quarter hour bells on the clock chimed. Claire's voice was thin. "Maybe we should find out more about this man before I go?"

Vincent Harrison went back to his chair and sat down, a muffled squeak of springs grating against the quiet of the deserted offices. "That's up to you, Claire. I doubt you have time. Do you think you can handle him?"

She blinked, filled with trepidation over the surprising implications of the question. "It seems I have no choice but to try."

"Catch them at their game. Call me as soon as they tell you how much they want, and I'll take it from there."

"When will you contact Sarah Winesong?"

Vincent Harrison's eyes clouded over, his jaw quivering with an emotion Claire judged to be fear. "As soon as we have to. If we have to. Please, Claire, be careful. Stay only long enough to find out the truth."

Fifteen minutes later, Claire stood on the sidewalk and looked for a taxi. Traffic was steady in both directions, and all the cabs were either in the lanes farthest from her, or they were occupied.

She pulled on her raincoat and started walking. It would be easier to catch a ride a couple of blocks away. Her satchel full of the night's reading material felt heavy on her shoulder.

The routine of eleven-hour days closing with three hours of reading manuscripts alone in bed didn't distress her. After her divorce two years ago, she'd decided she was lucky. Financially secure thanks to sound planning and a good lawyer, and really in love with her work, she didn't miss her husband at all.

She'd outgrown him, whatever that really meant, and she found that she liked her solitude, as long as she could socialize when she felt like it. But tonight her life as an editor held little charm.

The last thing she wanted to do was think about publishing anybody's new mystery novel. What she did want was to soak in the tub, drink a bottle of wine and watch something dopey on television. Or dance in a half-empty joint with a man who'd kiss her neck and not be around in the morning.

Or eat a pound of pasta.

"Claire?"

She jumped at Tony Nichols's voice.

He was walking beside her, a hint of a smile on his lean face. "Don't you have a car?"

"A car? In New York? Do I look like a Trump?"

He didn't answer, but from the look in his eye it was clear he was thinking about her looks. "Right. Too expensive for a working woman."

"Yes. Besides, in my neighborhood there's been a rash of car thefts. Three were hot-wired last week. One with a little boy in the back seat. New York's not the best place for cars.'' Feeling foolish over that little news report, Claire turned away and continued walking.

"Wait a minute.'' Tony caught up and fell into step with her.

She stopped. "What is it, Mr. Nichols?''

"I thought maybe you'd like to have dinner with me.''
He's a lunatic, she thought. After what just went on in Mr. Harrison's office, he thought they could dine civilly with each other? "I'm sorry, but I'm not very hungry. I'll see you tomorrow in Rhode Island.''

"I'm sorry you had to cancel your vacation. You must be disappointed.'' Tony watched her face carefully, ready for a scornful reaction, but willing to try to be friendly, anyway. Claire puzzled him the way a half-remembered song does. She nagged at him, resurfacing in his mind every time he thought about Patricia Snow's problem. He told himself now that was why he'd waited for her to come down from her office.

"How did you know I was going on vacation?''

"Your receptionist told me this afternoon.''

"Cauldron Press is staffed by people with big mouths.''

"Are you the secretive type?''

"I'm not a type, Mr. Nichols. But let me get this straight. You're sorry? You track me down at a luncheon to accuse me of felonious activities, then you want to take me to dinner and apologize about ruining my vacation? What's wrong with this picture?''

Claire started walking again, disgusted at the trace of hurt in her voice. After all, she had no reason to care what he thought of her personally. Before she took four steps, his hand closed over hers. It surprised her so much she let out a little yelp of surprise and dropped her valise.

"Let me help you carry this. It looks like it weighs a ton."

Claire whirled on Tony and grabbed the leather briefcase back. Glaring, she straightened to her full five-foot-nine height, helped by a pair of heels. "I'm a strong woman, Mr. Nichols. And I've carried my own books for years. Now let's say good-night."

"Are you a good judge of character?"

Claire sighed. This question was completely unexpected. "I'm okay. Why?"

"I'm usually pretty good. I've only been fooled once or twice in my life. That's why I wanted you to have dinner with me. So I could see if I was wrong."

"Wrong?"

"About you. As ticked off as I am about what I think you're trying to do to Patricia, I believe you think you're innocent."

The sounds of traffic faded, and Claire felt her anger dissipating. The first thought that came to her brain surprised her. *I believe him, too.*

Though she knew, from the moment he'd started talking to her this afternoon, that he couldn't have his facts right, she'd felt he was convinced of what he was saying. But what that meant was too complicated to sort out on a New York street corner. A cab roared up to the curb and let out three girls, and she moved toward it. "Taxi!"

Tony grabbed her valise and followed, holding the door open while she slid in. He tossed her bag onto the seat beside her. "Do you always have this much home-work? Doesn't leave much time for other pursuits, does it?" He stuck his hands into his pockets, the thick muscles of his arm bulging under the soft corduroy jacket.

"I take my job seriously, Mr. Nichols. Now, if you'll excuse me." She felt his eyes on her neck, and was glad for the raincoat, which she hugged to her. Goose bumps rose along the back of her legs as a draft blew through the cab.

"Come on, lady! Where're we going?" the driver snapped.

"Good night, Claire. I'll see you tomorrow." Tony shut the door and waved, a curiously appealing gesture from such a macho-looking type.

As the taxi pulled away, she craned her head to look out the rear window. He'd disappeared into the crowd, the place at the curb as empty as if she'd only imagined him.

But she knew she hadn't imagined him. Only a flesh-and-blood man could have provoked feelings like the ones she fought now. "Damn," she muttered as she sat back against the stiff seat. Just when she'd learned to excel at beating mystery novels into shape, real life decided to become even stranger than fiction.

It was going to be a long night. Even pasta didn't sound good now.

Chapter Three

Claire's night was nearly sleepless.

She finally gave up trying to banish dreams filled with black-haired men full of bizarre accusations and got up to fix tea at five in the morning.

Tillie Millard was not pleased with her wake-up call five minutes later. "Claire, have you lost your mind? It's the middle of the night! Why aren't you in the Bahamas?"

Claire talked fast to fill Tillie in on the events of the previous day. She'd decided to tell her assistant everything, despite Mr. Harrison's paranoia. Later she'd remind Harrison that if anyone could be trusted, Tillie could. "So that's it. I'm going to interview the girl face-to-face and find out what she wants."

There was a long silence on the other end of the phone. "How did Harrison handle this?"

"He's pretty cool. But he was adamant I don't let anyone, even you, in on the whole story. You know how protective he is of Sarah. And how this could hurt the company if a rumor got started."

"I can't believe this has happened. It could ruin us...."

Claire was surprised to hear Tillie, who usually had nerves of steel and wisecracks to match, sound so shaken.

"Come on, Tillie. You know it's a lie. I know it's a lie. I'll find out what the scam is and throw it to the lawyers. You just do the research I asked you for on Tony Nichols. And not a peep to anyone."

"If you mean Damien, my lips are sealed. That brat hasn't even taken me to lunch for months. What's this guy Nichols look like anyway?"

Claire gave a brief description, careful not to elaborate on how attractive he was. Tillie could be relentless if she sniffed romance in the air.

Promising to check back with her once she was settled in Narragansett Bay, Claire added, "Okay, Tillie. I'll get back to you by four. And thanks for feeding Woofer."

"That demented nitwit. I should stuff him and have him mounted when you get back. That would be a true act of friendship."

"Now be nice, Tillie. Woofer loves you."

"Sure he does, and I've got the teeth marks to prove it. You be careful with this Nichols. I really don't like you going alone. Maybe I should come, too."

"I don't need a chaperon, Tillie. I need you right here in New York, pursuing that background investigation."

"I'll be as discreet as the Queen Mum. Be careful, Claire."

"I will. By the way, check with the *Times* first to be sure they really did assign him to review our book."

Another uncharacteristic pause made Claire wonder if Tillie was worried about something else. "Tillie, are you there?"

"You're not thinking someone inside Cauldron gave it to him?"

"Lord no! I just want to find out if we can believe *anything* he says."

"But you only recently sent the galleys out. This Nichols character would have had to work really fast."

"It wouldn't take long to write a ripped-off fifty-page version if they had the whole book. If that's what she did."

"What do you mean, if? Is there any doubt in your mind, Claire?"

Claire blinked and looked down at the floor. Why had she said if? Before she had a chance to examine her mental lapse, her pet cockatiel, Woofer, began to bark like an irate Doberman pinscher. This was the bird's favorite trick at this time of the morning, or any time of day, if he wasn't fed. Claire promised Tillie she'd get back to her later and hung up.

She threw a black sweater on over her pink T-shirt and jeans, then fed Woofer. She finished packing and was out of the building into the cool moist April air by seven.

She snared a taxi, which miraculously appeared in front of her town house, threw in her canvas overnight bag and gave the driver her two-word destination: Penn Station.

As they lurched away from the curb, Claire wondered for perhaps the thousandth time what Tony Nichols was really after. Money? That obvious motive didn't seem to fit the man she'd spent the past twenty-four hours trying not to think about. He was too intent, the emotions too close to the surface, to be a person who was only out for a quick buck.

Claire wondered briefly if Patricia Snow was his lover. The idea made her uncomfortable, so she pushed it to the back of her mind, unwilling to examine it more closely. But it kept coming back again and again.

Okay, she told herself. Tony Nichols was damned attractive, very male and interesting. She was a woman who liked men and didn't have one in her life, or bed.

It was natural, she decided with a touch of guilt, to consider his personal motives. Natural, maybe, another part of her mind argued back, but totally unacceptable when done obsessively.

Claire leaned back and pictured Tony as he'd looked stepping off the elevator yesterday. Lean and smart, all that curling hair falling onto his forehead. Scorn, anger and something that looked like revenge had played alternately across his features when he'd talked.

Definitely not her type. She chose men with cool demeanors, steady-as-she-goes attitudes. This guy was unpredictable, passionate. He'd only prove a problem to a woman who valued stability over any other single thing in the world.

"You're boring, Claire," she said aloud, then opened her eyes and looked around to see if the cabdriver or anyone in a passing car was eyeing her. No one was. She gazed out at the morning traffic, but again saw an image of Tony, his head bent over a cigarette, avoiding her question.

Definitely a man with a secret.

Claire realized then, for the first time, that she was scared. What if Tony Nichols's accusations and her own "investigation" under wraps was dangerous? What if he turned out to be more madman than con man? Would he physically harm her?

Her intuition told her no, he wasn't violent. But he was complicated. Everything she didn't want in a man at this point in her life.

But he's not a man in your life. Crap! she thought. *Don't start that again!*

Hanging her head, she silently reviewed her plan of action. All she had to do was watch Tony Nichols and Patricia Snow closely, hit them with a million questions, and when they made the first move to ask for a payoff, she'd simply call the police and have them charged with blackmail. And fraud. And impersonating an author.

The last made her smile, but it quickly faded. There was nothing funny about this plot, and it was up to her to stop it.

LYING ON HIS STOMACH, Tony awoke with a start. The elusive dreams he'd had all night were fresh in his mind. A person he was following, a tall blond woman, with her back to him, kept moving away, always out of reach.

He closed his eyes, but opened them again quickly. It wouldn't take a psychoanalyst to figure out it was Claire Kennedy who'd made one hell of an impression on him, and was affecting his subconscious.

But dreams of her hadn't been what pulled him out of his deep sleep.

Dread and disbelief mixed for a moment, then a realization chilled his body. It was a noise, not far away, that had awakened him. Someone was in his house.

He listened, straining for another sound to be sure. It came. Outside the door the floor creaked with an intruder's weight. A second later, a murmur of wood sliding against wood, a tinny rattle.

A drawer being opened, he decided. The tension running wild through him solidified as he focused on the danger. The clock at his bedside said eight. He slipped from the bed, his nostrils twitching as he silently inhaled. He felt primitive and exposed. The disadvantage of being stalked by an unknown predator made his motions clumsy. He eyed his jeans lying on the floor, but decided not to risk the noise or time it would take to put them on.

Naked or not, he thought, it was time to get the jump on his uninvited guest. As the blood pulsed in his ears, Tony wondered if his visit to Cauldron Press yesterday had generated this little intrusion. There had to be a connection. He'd lived in his house for almost eight years now, and he'd never had any trouble before.

Slowly he crossed the room and leaned against the door frame. The door stood open a couple of inches, offering a view of his tiny living room and entrance. Nothing was amiss.

Easing the door open farther, Tony glanced out. The glass-paneled French doors, leading out to the deck, were still closed. Taking a step out of the bedroom, he shot a glance in the direction of the kitchen. He couldn't see around the corner to the sink and stove, but a burglar would have to be a complete fool to hide there. Tony'd have him trapped.

Him? his mind instantly threw back. What about a her? What if Claire Kennedy decided to come to Rhode Island a little earlier than expected to snoop around? The name Claire formed on his lips, and Tony grimaced. Boldly he walked by the closed bathroom door and out into the living room. The table was full of papers and notebooks on his current research project. Though they were orderly, he saw in a second they'd been pawed through.

Tony stayed near the wall, the hair on his legs full of electricity, which heightened his anxiety. It was time to confront the last concealed corner of the house. He lunged around the corner and looked into the kitchen. It was empty. For a moment he felt ridiculous and relieved at the same time. He'd been ready to fight, but was equally glad when he saw he wouldn't have to.

Had he imagined the whole thing? He made a 360-degree scan and picked out the small details that bolstered his supposition. His address book was lying on the counter, open, nearby. A drawer in the desk had been left ajar. His papers were askew. No doubt about it, someone had searched his apartment.

But what for?

He grabbed a clean pair of running shorts off a stack of laundry lying on a dining-room chair and nervously glanced behind at his bedroom door. Had the intruder been in there, in the closet? He took a step toward it, then stopped, exhaling. No one had been in the room where he'd been sleeping. Besides, his closet wasn't big enough to conceal a dwarf. "Cracking up," he muttered, then turned to stare out at the ocean.

The bay was gray and calm, although a few whitecaps foamed about a hundred yards out. The fact that someone had come to search his house proved to him that his old nemesis, Billings Newcastle, was probably involved. It was Newcastle's style to hire people for search-and-seizure missions. Was Newcastle the one who'd allowed Winesong to steal Patricia's book?

If the publishing magnate wanted Cauldron Press, the odds were that he already had an inside person on his payroll passing information and manipulating things to his advantage. Stealing a student's manuscript for a burned-out author could be one of those things. So could looking for evidence in the home of a man who was going to blow the whistle.

Either way, it looked like Claire Kennedy was involved.

Patricia was supposed to call him at ten, and when she did he'd have to get more answers. Tony had to convince her that whatever she was involved in—a shady deal she'd agreed to in order to sell her work to Winesong or Harrison and Claire—she had to tell him all the details. Because if Newcastle was involved, the kid was way outclassed.

Tony turned and walked toward the bathroom, reviewing his questions for Patricia. Something made him stop a few feet from the door and stare at the blank expanse of painted wood.

He never closed it, unless he had company. And he hadn't had company for weeks.

Grabbing a squat silver candlestick off the bookcase beside him, he continued toward the bathroom, anger clenching his empty gut. With a deep breath he threw back the door and lunged into the small, blue-tiled room. It was as dark as night, the shade pulled over the window.

An opaque, rubberized shower curtain was drawn completely across the rod. For a moment Tony stood still. Memories of every bad B movie ever made, as well as the A-plus *Psycho*, flashed through his head. Someone was hiding in the shower.

Without another thought, he grabbed the curtain with his left hand and lifted the candlestick above his head. At that moment the hidden assailant lunged at him, leaping out of the tub and wrapping the curtain around Tony. The action caught him completely by surprise. He struggled for, then lost, his balance, landing one ineffective blow before twisting and falling forward into the tub.

The next thing Tony knew, a thick, unpleasant-smelling liquid was poured over him, burning his skin and eyes. Instinctively he struggled to rise, rubbing his eyes against the curtain. As the pain escalated into agony, he realized that was the one thing he shouldn't do.

The smell registered. His homemade tile cleaner, a concoction of bleach, ammonia and soap, had been sitting on the window ledge. Not only had his assailant knocked him down, but he'd put him out of commission for several minutes by pouring the stuff over the top of his head.

Tony felt his way slowly out of the tub, wrenching his knee and cracking his shin as he fell twice. Finally he reached the faucet, turned on the water and stood for several minutes washing out his eyes.

Whatever he'd put in motion by calling on Cauldron Press yesterday had just escalated a notch. He wondered how rough things were going to get before it was all over.

THE TRAIN STATION at Kingston was not crowded. From her window, Claire noted two empty station wagons, parked side by side in the parking lot. A young woman with a sleeping baby in a cuddle sack stood by the bench waiting for arriving passengers.

At the edge of Claire's vision, an elderly woman, stooped and leaning on a cane, stood next to the ticket office. Claire watched as she tapped impatiently on the bars to get the clerk's attention.

A piercing whistle split the air, warning passengers that the train was preparing to continue on. Peering around the deserted coach, Claire checked back outside again. It was after eleven. Tony was nowhere in sight. She'd have to call him.

Call him where? Rats. I hope he's in the book.

Leaning over, she tugged at her overnight bag. It was wedged under the seat and resisted all her attempts to remove it. Claire kneeled on the horsehair-covered bench and pressed her leg into the cushion, gripping the leather handle with both hands, and pulled. As it gave way, she toppled backward. Her fall was broken by someone behind her who caught her shoulders in strong hands.

"Good morning, Ms. Kennedy. Wrestling with more than your conscience today, I see."

Tony Nichols's laugh poured over her like butterscotch. Claire flushed as the heat from his hands radiated through her clothing. "I really don't see the humor, Mr. Nichols."

He stopped laughing and stared at the woman before him. Her cheeks were burning pink with indignation, accentuating the freckles that scattered like wildflowers down her neck. Claire Kennedy looked younger and less imposing than the chic businesswoman he'd met at the Waldorf. But the independence and savvy were still there.

"Forgive my humor. But I have had rather a bad morning and don't feel much like arguing semantics with a pro."

Claire looked closely at him, noticing lines of pain around his red-rimmed eyes. He held his head stiffly, as if his neck were sore. "Too much partying in New York last night?" she asked.

"Too much stupidity in Rhode Island this morning. But I've learned my lesson. In future I'll not be so hasty to underestimate the strength of the enemy."

Unable to fathom his meaning, Claire shrugged and picked up her bag. "I'm ready."

Tony smiled, though all the humor had left his face. "Okay. After you."

Claire walked ahead of him off the train and across the wooden platform, worn smooth and silvery gray by years of rain. She was taken aback by his mood. He actually seemed hurt that she was hostile. What did he expect? A hug for trying to ruin her reputation? A kiss for accusing Cauldron Press of plagiarism?

As he came up beside her, she noted again how close they were in height. Which was nice somehow. She'd never been attracted to really tall men. She liked men who were solidly built and graceful.

That was a description that fit him. She matched his stride to the inch. Though his shoulders were wider than her own by nearly half again, and he outweighed her by a good fifty pounds, she liked the fact that she was at least able to look him in the eye.

Crunching across the bleached shells in the parking lot, Claire decided not to ask him any of the thousand questions rumbling around her mind. Mr. Harrison said she was a good observer. Well, it was time to observe.

An undergraduate student being ripped off by a successful writer was just the sort of story a newspaper reporter would love to expose. Shifting her bag into her other hand, she vowed to stop being so short with him. Like it or not, she had to at least appear to be keeping an open mind.

Tony stopped abruptly in front of one of the empty station wagons, a well-preserved green Volvo. The two front seats had faded gray college sweatshirts pulled down over them. He opened the door for her, but left it for her to close.

Claire sat down on top of Yale, he on Harvard.

The unusual seat covers gave her an opening for a little background digging. "Did you attend these schools?"

"What schools?" Tony's voice was distant, his dark eyes steady on the road as they pulled out.

"Harvard. Yale. You know, your seats."

"No, I went to U.C.L.A., but these shirts are easier to stuff than ones from Los Angeles." He laughed now with real humor.

Claire fought the urge to like the sound. "I'm from L.A. I went to school in Arizona, though, at Tempe. Are you from California?"

"Are you writing a book? Or are you just gathering intelligence to take back and check out?" He ground the gears of the car as his voice resumed its pique.

"Try to put yourself in my position, Mr. Nichols. I do need to find out as much as I can about you, Patricia Snow, about her alleged book—"

"Alleged book? Really, Ms. Kennedy, you've been watching too many Perry Mason reruns. Her book is real."

"Well, so is Sarah Winesong's. I'd say that certainly tips the balances on the scales of probability about who's stolen what from whom."

"I don't much believe in probability."

"Why is that?"

"It's misleading. People who look for the most likely thing leave themselves unprepared for the unexpected. And the unexpected happens to everyone."

"It does?" Claire had a moment's annoyance at her stupid question.

"Sure. Hasn't anything unexpected ever happened to you?"

You mean like meeting you? she wanted to say, but swallowed the question. Claire met his sideways glance. "I will have your credentials checked out. I'd be a fool not to." She crossed her arms defiantly, then uncrossed them and tried to relax. *Body language is tough to control.*

"You hate feeling foolish, huh? Me, too."

It seemed a strange remark to Claire. "Do you feel foolish often?"

"No. Though I did this morning."

"What happened?"

Tony applied the brakes and slowed at the signal. "Someone broke into my house, and I let them get away."

"What? Did they steal anything?"

"Yes."

Claire's mind raced. She knew he was baiting her, but she didn't know why. "Did you call the police?"

"No."

"Why not?"

"I thought you might have had an idea about who did it."

"Me?" Was this man going to do nothing but accuse her of criminal behavior? "I assure you I know nothing about it at all. If it even happened," she added suddenly.

"Oh, it happened." Tony's voice was even. "I thought maybe Cauldron Press had decided to check me out. But since it wasn't you, and you've just said you want to know more about me, let me tell you some things. I'm thirty-six. Never married, though I once lived with a woman for a year in Greece. I was born in Michigan, lived everywhere with my folks, who are both retired military. I still smoke, as you've seen, and know it's bad for me."

Claire repressed the urge to write all these facts down. "I moved a lot, too," she said, "when I was young, and hated it."

Tony registered the pain in Claire's voice and said, "I drink wine, particularly cabernet sauvignon with Italian food, which I have a passion for. I'm a great ice-hockey player, amateur league, love the Twins, and I can't swim.''

He was charming. And well-rehearsed. Claire made herself pretend to be impressed, which took very little effort. ''You look like you could handle just about any physical activity very well.''

''Thank you. So do you.''

Claire could never bring herself to tell anyone much about her life. Her ex-husband probably hadn't known that many things about her past, after four years of marriage. ''Thank you for being so obliging with the bio.''

''You're welcome. What did I leave out?''

A small laugh bubbled up in Claire's throat. ''Let's see, what brought you to Rhode Island?''

He didn't answer her for a mile or so, and Claire was content to wait. This exchange was far and away more enjoyable than yesterday afternoon's accusation trading had been. Nevertheless her stomach was knotted with tension, and she reached into her jacket pocket for an antacid.

Finally Tony answered, turning down the classical-music station. He'd gotten to the part of his life he wasn't about to discuss in detail. If she was working for Newcastle, she already knew much of it. If she was on the level, the facts of his past would only make her doubt his story more. ''Change of career. My folks have settled in New England. And so has my younger brother and his family. It made sense.''

''That makes sense.''

''I thought all you editor types never said anything repetitive.''

She raised her eyebrows at his remark and shrugged. ''We're not perfect. Like teachers or anyone else. We try to cultivate, encourage and help our writers if we can. But they're the ones with the creativity."

"I'll certainly agree that writers are creative, but the success of a book depends a lot on editing, promoting and marketing."

"And how well the editors steal?"

Tony blinked, but ignored the open invitation to resume the discussion of Patricia Snow's manuscript. "How long have you been at Cauldron?"

"Seven years. For the past five as an editor. I started as a reader, then jumped to copy editor, then got into acquisitions."

"It's obvious you like it. What do you know about Sarah Winesong, personally?"

Claire felt her wariness return. "I know a bit about her. But not much I feel like discussing."

"Just the facts, ma'am. Or don't you want to say anything I can use against you in a court of law?"

"Jack Webb, right? I'm not worried about court. It's just not very professional."

"Have you even met the woman?"

"No." Claire felt her irritation grow.

"Has anyone met her?"

"Of course. Tillie has, Mr. Harrison has, lots of people have. I myself was planning a trip to see her before *The Poison Pen Pal* hits the stores. What's your point?"

"No point. Just curious." Tony kept driving. Any lessening of antagonism between them was temporary at best. He'd had a brief hope the night before that she'd relax enough to take him into her confidence, but now he saw how foolish that was.

Particularly foolish if *she* was Billings Newcastle's inside plant at Cauldron Press.

He drove on silently, reflecting on Ms. Claire Elizabeth Kennedy. She did sound convincing. And sweet. Was she telling the truth? As soon as that thought formed, Tony's mind was jerked back in time to an incident that had changed his life.

He'd been fooled by another woman once, one he shouldn't have trusted for a second. That misjudgment had cost him everything he'd cared about. His reputation. His job. As well as most of his self-esteem.

It had taken him five years to piece his life back together. Pursing his lips, Tony knew he couldn't risk trusting Claire Kennedy. He'd get Patricia to tell him everything that was going on, then he'd hang the guilty out to dry, even if one of them was the dazzling lady beside him.

His hands tightened on the leather steering wheel.

Noting his white-knuckled grasp, Claire remained silent. Maybe now was the time to ask him about his relationship with Patricia Snow. Before she could come up with a leading question, however, Tony broke the silence.

"How about personal questions about you, Ms. Kennedy? What about your past? Why'd you come to New York? Wealth? Fame? Romance?"

"Self-preservation."

"Strange place to come for that. New York isn't known as the safest, or self-preservingest place in the world."

"I don't find New York nearly as bad as its reputation. It's hard living alone anywhere."

"You live alone?" He pulled up at a four-way stop, empty save for them. "I thought maybe you had a jealous husband, or live-in lover. You seemed rather eager to get home last night."

Claire looked at him carefully, then crossed her arms tightly as if to ward off an impending attack. "No. A jealous cockatiel, but no husband. I'm divorced."

"I've never been brave enough to marry."

Wincing at his use of that adjective, Claire fell silent. She hadn't been brave to marry Glen. Just scared. And she wasn't brave when she'd left him. Anger began to chip away at her nerves again. "I'm not brave, Mr. Nichols. Nor am I stupid. So why don't we knock off this chitchat and you can tell me where we're going."

In answer, he drove over a pothole, knocking her against the metal door.

"Will you please take it easy! I have enough bruises because of you already." Claire fingered her arm, glad of a concrete reason to shout at him.

"Sorry. I'll try to be more careful next time."

Tony's voice had returned to the cool, vaguely condemning tone of yesterday. Claire felt a loss that their camaraderie, however contrived, had disappeared. "I'd appreciate it."

"And I'd appreciate your thinking about the possibility that someone is setting *you* up."

Claire shook her head. "That's sheer speculation on your part. When I meet with Patricia, she'll set the facts straight."

Silence stretched between them. "Fine," Tony said at last. "How about if I give you some early drafts of her manuscript? You'll see how well she worked out the plot bugs from draft to draft. That would help convince you the book is hers, wouldn't it?"

"I'd be interested in seeing them." Claire clenched her fists.

"They're at my office at the college. We'll stop and get them later."

Claire leaned against the passenger door, aware that she was reddening again, her freckles blazing away is if he'd caught her naked. "Did you make an appointment for me with Patricia? Is that where we're going now?"

Without answering, he turned off the interstate highway onto Kennerly Ridge Road, a rutted two-lane strip of asphalt bordered by a few houses. Through hazy sunlight they passed crooked rows of maples and wild apples, draped in their first spring leaves. Storm clouds had begun to amass in the distance.

With a chill, Claire realized she hadn't a clue where they were. Huddling deep into her turquoise jacket, she was glad she'd worn tights under her jeans. Feeling Tony's gaze, Claire kept her eyes on the road.

"No."

"Why not? Isn't that the whole point of my trip?"

"I haven't been able to do that yet. I don't exactly know where Patricia is. You could say she's...missing." His words hung in the air between them.

"Missing?" Claire retorted and sat up. "I thought you talked to her the day before yesterday."

"I did."

"And she wouldn't tell you where she was?"

Tony sucked in a lungful of air. Claire's phrasing was uncomfortably close to the truth. "I didn't ask her. She made it clear she's kind of incommunicado."

"Isn't it rather convenient for you, Mr. Nichols, that the author of this so-called stolen book is now missing?"

A curtain of rain fell suddenly around them. Small drops exploded into large ones on the windshield while the rumble of thunder forced him to speak louder. "No, it's not at all convenient for me. Although it could be construed as rather fortunate for Cauldron Press."

"How?"

"I'll have a much more difficult time proving fraud and theft without the author to corroborate my story, won't I?"

The storm began to beat seriously against the car, but Claire's nerves remained unrattled. "I think it would certainly be much harder. Particularly since you've not offered me any evidence that Patricia Snow even exists, except as a figment of your imagination."

Tony Nichols craned his neck to the left, then right. "Go on, Ms. Kennedy. I have the distinct feeling you have more to say."

"Oh, I do. I'm not going to spend another minute dealing seriously with you until I get some proof." Claire crossed her arms again. "And I mean it. Take me back to the train station."

Tony stopped the car abruptly and turned to Claire. His eyes were completely opaque, giving no hint of his thoughts. "You're not going back to New York."

"If you won't take me, I'll get out here." She opened the door, but Tony reached across and slammed it.

His teeth gleamed against his dark skin. "I have someone I think you should meet." He nodded at the house outside.

"Who?"

"Someone who will vouch for the fact that Patricia Snow is real. Maybe then you'll give the truth a chance."

Chapter Four

Claire glanced up and down the narrow street. The neighborhood where Tony stopped was lined with box-shaped houses, their shutters touched with fresh paint. The lawns were all raked and perfectly manicured.

They'd parked directly in front of a brick dwelling whose shades were all drawn. Reaching back to close the car door, Claire jumped when Tony clasped her arm. His fingers held none of the steely strength of his other tactile encounters; they felt quite gentle now.

Her eyes met his. "I repeat, whose house is this, Mr. Nichols? Yours? Who's inside?"

"This is Jeanette Snow's house. Patricia's mother. Patricia didn't call back this morning as promised, and I thought maybe her mom could give me a lead on her whereabouts."

"Why didn't you just call Mrs. Snow and ask?"

"She doesn't have a phone." Tony released her, then swung the heavy car door shut. His arm accidentally rubbed against Claire, sending a confusing rush of emotion through her.

Claire averted her glance and stepped stiffly to the porch. "I see. You can't provide the author, so I get to meet a woman you say is her mother."

"Stop just a minute."

"What?"

Tony's voice was tight. "I was under the impression that you and Mr. Harrison agreed to meet Patricia Snow in good faith."

"That's why I'm here."

"I think keeping an open mind is part of good faith, Claire. If I'm mistaken, why don't you just go back to New York now. Cauldron can start 'investigating' this little stunt when Patricia's lawsuit is filed."

Claire had no doubt he'd leave her standing there while he drove off. "I'll go inside with you. But until I actually talk to Patricia Snow *in person*, I've accomplished nothing."

He seemed placated by her response and his voice dropped to a whisper. "I need to ask a small favor of you before we go in. I think it best if you don't mention your reason for wanting to meet Patricia. I wouldn't want to worry her mother unnecessarily."

A chill ran down Claire's back. She'd been ready to suspect Mrs. Snow of playing a part in the hoax, but the concern in Tony's voice put her off. What if Patricia Snow really was missing? This idea did little to cheer her up. "Of course," was all she said.

Tony rang the doorbell. "Thanks, Claire."

Jeanette Snow opened the door on the second ring. Through the screen, Claire saw that the woman was bound to a wheelchair. She lifted a skinny arm to the latch, her small features pinched, and accentuated by her wispy dark hair, which was pulled into a tight knot at the back of her head.

"Professor Nichols? How wonderful to see you again," she said in a reedy voice.

"It's good to see you, too. This is Claire Kennedy, Mrs. Snow. May we come in for a few minutes?"

"Certainly. This is unexpected, but so nice of you." She pushed on the screen door and Tony opened it farther so that Claire could enter.

It took several seconds for Claire's eyes to get used to the dim light. All the shades and draperies were closed tight. The only illumination was from a small, rose-shaded desk lamp in one corner.

Mrs. Snow wheeled herself into the center of the sparsely furnished room and nodded toward a well-worn sofa off to one side. Claire walked over and settled into it, waiting for Tony to join her. He did so, though he chose to sit as far away as possible. She felt her spine stiffen at this odd formality.

"Would you like some ice tea? Or some coffee? I have both ready."

Claire wanted to take some more antacid. The knot in her stomach threatened to explode into a full case of heartburn, her usual reaction when faced with overwhelming stress. Thinking she'd had enough of the stuff already though, she stifled the impulse and said, "Yes. I'd love some tea, thank you."

Mrs. Snow maneuvered herself easily out of the room, humming softly. When she returned with a tray balanced on her lap, Claire gratefully accepted the tea, which was served with a primly starched linen napkin.

As Claire sipped the lemony brew, Tony brought up the reason for their visit. "Mrs. Snow, do you have any idea where Patricia's living now? It's rather urgent I contact her."

"Well, Professor, Patty's been out of town for some time. She took a job as a researcher several months ago.

Saw an ad in the paper and got real excited about it because the job entailed working for a writer."

"A writer?" Claire's voice was louder than she'd intended.

"Yes. Patty said she was an elderly lady who didn't want her to receive mail at her house, so all I have is a post office box to send my letters to. Something of a privacy hound the lady is, according to Patty."

Claire kept her voice steady, suppressing a gasp. "What town is the post office box in, Mrs. Snow?"

"Well, let me get the letter for you." The wheelchair purred as Mrs. Snow turned away from them and rode off back through a low archway toward the hallway and out of sight.

Taking another sip of her drink, Claire avoided looking at Tony. Her mind whirred with Mrs. Snow's words. It had to be a coincidence that Patricia Snow worked for a woman with the same penchant for privacy that Sarah Winesong was so famous for. Either that, or Patricia Snow had intentionally misled her mother, to lend credence to her scheme.

Which would mean the girl and Tony *had* plotted this scam for a long time. But how could they have known about Winesong's book? Claire hoped none of her suspicions showed on her face.

Mrs. Snow was rolling back into the room, a pale blue envelope in her hand. "Let's see, this one was mailed about three months ago from Parsonville. But lately—" she came to a stop in front of the sofa, then fumbled with and almost dropped the envelope onto the floor "—the box she has me mail my letters to is Benton Convent."

"Is that near here?" Claire asked.

"No. It's up in New Jersey, about a four hour drive from Narragansett," Tony answered.

"Do you have a phone number where you can reach Patricia, Mrs. Snow?" Claire heard the relief in her own voice. Neither town was where Cauldron Press sent Sarah Winesong's mail.

"No, dear, I'm afraid I don't. I can't afford a phone on my income. If Patty needs me, she telephones my next-door neighbor and they come get me. But Patty and I write each other about once a month, and that's the way we keep in touch. Do you want me to write and tell her you want to see her, Professor Nichols?"

"No. No, I'll probably be up that way and look her up. If you'll just give me the name of the woman she was working for. . . ."

Mrs. Snow paused, a small tight frown pleating her brow. "A Mrs. Chancon. Mrs. M. Chancon. I don't have any address except the box number."

"Why don't you give me that?" Tony wrote it down on a small notepad and tucked it away.

Mrs. Snow studied him. "Professor Nichols, is Patty in some kind of trouble?"

Claire and Tony exchanged blank looks, neither willing to answer the question truthfully.

"No, Mrs. Snow, she's not," Claire answered. "I'm just eager to talk with her about a book she wrote. I'm an editor, and I'd like to see Patricia's entire manuscript." A faint blush warmed her cheeks as she realized Mrs. Snow would think she wanted to buy her daughter's book, when she really only wanted to prove her daughter guilty of a hoax.

"We both need to talk with Patricia within the next few days, Mrs. Snow. It could mean a lot of money to Patricia."

Slapping her glass down, Claire glared at Tony, who had a smug look fixed on his face. Couldn't the man see how needy Mrs. Snow was? It was barbaric of him to give her false hope.

The woman's face was glowing. "Well, that's wonderful news. If I hear from my daughter, I'll certainly have her get in touch with you, Miss Kennedy. Thank you so much for going to all this trouble on her account. You know, I used to write myself—just a little, you know. But anyway, with her ill... problems, she could really use some good news."

Mrs. Snow's voice trailed off and Claire shot a look at Tony. His usually opaque eyes seemed full of torment. Maybe he did feel some guilt, she thought. As she rose to leave, Claire took Mrs. Snow's frail fingers and squeezed them. "It's no trouble at all. Here's my business card in case you hear from her."

As they walked to the door, Tony turned back to Mrs. Snow. "Do you happen to have any copies of the manuscript, or correspondence regarding it, that Patricia may have left here, Mrs. Snow? Anything I could take and look through? I'm sure Patricia wouldn't mind."

Claire caught her breath. Mrs. Snow couldn't be in on a hoax. Was Tony duping her into being a part of it? At any rate, they had no right to look at letters and drafts of the book without Patricia Snow's permission. Before Claire could discourage Tony's request, however, Mrs. Snow had wheeled away, leaving them standing by the front door. Her thin voice floated from the back of the house.

"Professor Nichols, can you come in here and help me with this? I know there's a box here somewhere."

"Tony, I really don't think we should take anything out of the house until we talk to—"

"I do." He walked away from her. "The sooner we find more proof, the better. Time is running out, and we don't want to miss this chance of learning something more about Patricia's book. Unless, of course, you're worried there's a letter from Sarah Winesong or Cauldron Press in the other room."

"Don't pull that baloney with me, Tony. The only reason I'm here is to resolve any legitimate question about who wrote *The Poison Pen Pal*."

Tony turned back to her, and while his dark eyes held a smile, his mouth remained fixed in a hard line. "I'm really glad to hear you say that. Now if I can just get it in writing..." He left the room.

For several moments Claire waited, straining to hear their voices. A plunking noise behind her made her spin around.

Facing the front door, Claire watched as several envelopes fell through the tarnished mail slot onto the carpet. Without thinking, she reached down and picked up the assortment, then straightened them into a neat pile. As she walked toward the desk to put them down, her eyes widened.

The bold black scrawl on the top envelope sent a chill of recognition down her spine. It was addressed to Patricia Snow, but it was the return address that horrified Claire.

Above the words Usherwood Publications, New York City, Roz Abramawitz's name stared up at Claire like a cobra daring her to make the slightest move.

CLAIRE ROLLED onto her stomach, shutting her eyes against the light filtering in through the west window of the hotel room. Tony had dropped her off at the Woodbury Inn, a quaint old place on the water.

He was headed for his office at the university to make a few more calls. He thought he might be able to locate

Patricia. Claire had agreed to be ready in two hours to go out again with him.

Finding no copies of Patricia's manuscript in the things Mrs. Snow had let him go through, Tony had ushered Claire quickly out of the house. Too quickly, she thought now, for if he'd given her a little more time, she might have put the letter back on the desk.

Instead she'd stolen it. She'd slipped it into her jacket pocket before Tony and Mrs. Snow had come back into the room. Now her guilt ate away at her, even as she told herself she'd been driven to take it out of fear it contained more bad news for Cauldron Press.

Besides, if Tony Nichols saw a letter from Roz for Patricia Snow, Claire thought now, this mess would surely become even more complicated.

A tiny, inner voice interrupted and seemed to sum up her action. *Now he's right. You are a thief.*

Claire bolted off the white chenille bedspread and grabbed her jacket. *Well, if I am a thief, I better at least see what I've stolen.* She'd always heard that people under pressure did abnormal things. Claire had always managed to stay in control. Until now.

Pulling the crumpled envelope from the side pocket of her jacket, she tore it open. Unfolding the single sheet, she read:

Dear Ms. Snow:

Thank you very much for the recent submission of your novel, *Letters in the Attic*.

We are very pleased to tell you that we're interested in purchasing this manuscript. However, we do need to talk with you about several possible revisions first.

Would you please contact me at the number below at your earliest convenience.

Very truly yours,
Roz Abramawitz
Usherwood Publications

Nausea built up in Claire's stomach and throat. She tossed aside the letter and hurried into the bathroom. Running the icy stream of water on her hands helped, as did dabbing the cool washcloth across her face. She returned to the bedroom and sat down at the desk.

Of all people! Patricia Snow had sent her Sarah Winesong lookalike manuscript to Roz Abramawitz, the one person Claire knew would take great joy in making any similarity between her book and Sarah Winesong's a national scandal.

Tony must not have known anything about this submission to Usherwood, Claire decided. Unless they'd done it hoping it would increase the pressure on Cauldron by involving another publishing house.

But he didn't know Roz. He hadn't acted at all odd when Roz accosted them at the banquet. As her stomach lurched even more, Claire tried to deflate the fear that grew with each new conclusion.

There *was* a Patricia Snow. And she *had* written a book, and sent it off to Roz Abramawitz. A book that resembled—more than resembled, *duplicated*—Sarah Winesong's.

With a sinking feeling, Claire dialed a number. She sat back and asked for Vincent Harrison without enthusiasm, knowing full well how hard he'd take her news.

"This is Vincent Harrison. Are you there, Claire? What have you come up with?"

Briefly she related the news.

"How did you find out about this? Did you hear from Roz?"

Recounting how she'd stolen the letter was an uncomfortable experience for Claire. It was made worse somehow by the fact her boss didn't seem to notice she'd committed a crime.

"So maybe they think if Usherwood is involved," Vincent suggested, "we'll be more eager to bargain with them."

"I thought that, too. But the timing really bothers me. Roz must have received the query and manuscript from Patricia Snow at least six weeks ago. No one gets back to a new author quicker than that, even if the book is brilliant. How did they get Sarah's book that long ago?"

"It makes your fears about a leak much more credible, doesn't it?"

"If someone stole one of our author's manuscripts," Claire almost yelled, "it's a great deal more serious than a leak!"

"I still can't believe someone on our staff would be capable of that kind of treason."

"I think it's time we considered going right to Sarah Winesong, Mr. Harrison."

"Claire, I agree she might have the answers we're searching for, but you're going to have to interview that Snow girl first. We need to know what her story is, then I'll arrange the meeting for you."

"So far I haven't even been able to find Patricia Snow."

"You will. Keep me posted. I have to be out of the office the rest of the day, but my secretary will patch your call through to my car phone. Don't worry about Roz. I'll call Usherwood myself and explain the situation once we've dealt with all this. Roz will appreciate our keeping her from being involved with Nichols."

Remembering the hungry gleam in Roz's eyes when she'd seen Tony at the Waldorf, Claire doubted that. "Okay."

"They're going to back down. You'll see, Claire. Be sure and let me know the instant they mention a blackmail figure."

This willingness on Vincent Harrison's part to listen to a plan for a payoff chafed at Claire. It might be necessary to avoid dragging the whole mess through court and the newspapers, however. She knew of several cases where publishing houses had settled plagiarism suits that way to get their book in the stores without delay.

Hanging up the phone, Claire paced the room for a few minutes. As soon as Tony arrived, they'd head up to Benton Convent. Time was slipping away, and along with it her confidence in quickly resolving this mystery.

PARKING THE VOLVO behind the Humanities building, Tony turned off the car and sat for a moment.

Claire Kennedy puzzled him. He didn't know if it was her insistence that Cauldron was innocent or her antagonism toward him that bothered him most. *Oh, hell,* he thought, *admit it. It's Claire's fabulous legs, that shining hair. Her soft mouth that looks like it would bruise if kissed properly.*

Which is what I've wanted to do for about twenty-four hours now!

Angry with himself, he yanked the keys out of the ignition. He couldn't let himself be attracted to Claire. Even if she was personally innocent, which probably wasn't the case, she was dedicated to shielding whoever at Cauldron Press was trying to take advantage of Patricia.

Patricia Snow. The troubled young woman who'd haunted his classes the past two years. A student with real talent and, sadly, a self-destructive urge.

He'd been supportive of her when she revealed to him she'd begun a book. And he'd encouraged her throughout the previous year to finish it. She took his advice and more—until he recommended she polish it more to get it in shape for a New York publisher.

Despite her laziness, Tony stuck by her like a big brother, trying to persuade her to get help for her drinking problem. He coaxed and pleaded, telling her he knew she could do it.

Tony knew firsthand how cutting the professional publishing world would be to her if she hadn't given her book her best effort. The pros in the business always worked sixteen-hour days and still took work home to read. Last night he'd seen Claire's valise full of manuscripts. All the editors he'd known were ethical and caring.

It still shocked him senseless to think Cauldron Press was going to publish Patricia Snow's book under another author's name. The minute he'd started to read the galley copy he'd been sent to review, he'd known it was her book.

At first he'd been elated. He thought maybe Cauldron Press had bought the book from Patricia and released it under the pen name Sarah Winesong. A lot of houses owned author's names, and used several writers to turn out work under one identity.

But when he'd verified that the real Sarah Winesong was the author of the book, his sense of justice was enraged. He knew Winesong hadn't been published for the past five years. It looked like the classic rip-off; all he was lacking were the particulars of how Winesong had obtained Patricia's work.

Patricia's phone call two mornings ago had galvanized him into action. As he sat staring out of the Volvo, he went over their conversation for the umpteenth time.

He'd answered curtly, "Yes?"

"Professor Nichols? I understand you're looking for me."

The woman's voice was familiar, but too indistinct to identify. "Who is this, please? Speak up."

She'd spoken a fraction louder, her voice slurred. "I'm afraid of being overheard. This is Patty. Patricia Snow. Someone told me you've been trying to find me. Why?"

"Patricia! I've been looking for you. I need to see you as soon as possible. It's about your book. Where are you calling from?"

"My book? What do you know about my book?" The girl's voice had become frightened, anxious. Tony realized she'd been whispering before, because she'd screamed the last question at him.

"I've just seen your book with another author's name on it. I want to know how this happened, Patricia. Did you sell the manuscript to Cauldron Press?"

"I can't talk about all this. Oh, no."

"Tell me where you are, Patricia. I'll come and get you."

Patricia had started to talk in a torrent of uneven, booze-roughened sentences. "I've been working for someone who showed it to an editor at Cauldron. They gave me some money for it to tide me over while I worked on it some more. Then they said they weren't going to be able to use it, but that they owned the rights. They said if I tried to get any more money from them, they'd sue me."

"They? Who? Give me some names, Patricia."

She seemed not to hear him. "I didn't really know what to do then, but I'm going to get even with her...."

"Did you sign anything?"

"What?"

"A contract?"

"No. I think it was an IOU for the money."

"Why in the hell did you get involved in something like this?"

"My mother's sick. I needed money. I never realized this would happen."

"We need to go to the acquisition people at Cauldron and check this out, Patricia. What was the name of the person there you got the money from? Where is the IOU?"

"I can't talk about this," she sobbed. "I can't. But go see Claire Kennedy. I'll call you back tomorrow at ten."

The click in his ear had signaled the dead line.

As the conversation ended in his head, Tony got out of the Volvo. Until he sat down with Patricia and filled in the missing pieces of information, he'd be no closer to getting the whole picture. Confronting Cauldron Press had been a gamble, one based on emotion, when he'd heard the rumor Newcastle was ready to take them over.

This morning's break-in told him he hadn't made the wrong move.

Hurriedly, Tony climbed the stairs to his office. The campus was deserted, because everyone was away for spring break. With Claire at the inn, he'd have some time to get a lead on the Chancon woman's address. Maybe he'd get lucky and find a phone number. He needed to talk to Patricia at least once more without Claire, if he could.

Unlocking his heavy oak door, Tony reached for the light switch to counteract the darkness inside his office. Someone had been in and shut the bulky vinyl drapes against the daylight. The cleaning people? As he fumbled for the switch, he dropped his car keys.

Leaning down to retrieve them, Tony didn't see the cane raised behind him, only felt its heavy silver handle crash down on his skull.

Chapter Five

Feeling antsy, Claire picked up the phone and redialed her New York office. It was almost two, and she was sure Tillie would have found out some things about Tony Nichols by now.

Tillie was in a dither about not being able to come up with anything on Tony Nichols but the basics. "He's a professor. And the university where he works is a private, well-regarded women's college in Narragansett. He's single. And he's currently on sabbatical."

"Does he know how to swim?"

Claire's caustic tone earned a chuckle from Tillie. "Why? You planning on drowning him if he doesn't drop his charges?"

"No. But it's a tempting thought. This kills me. He told me more about himself today in one minute than you've been able to dig up all morning. I thought you'd have all this great news proving every word he'd uttered so far was false. It would make it easier to believe he was lying about Patricia Snow and her damn manuscript."

Tillie was silent for a second. "Why won't you admit to me you really have doubts about who wrote *The Poison Pen Pal*, Claire?"

"Because I really don't," she answered quickly, before Tillie asked any more impossibly loaded questions. "Look, I'll call you tomorrow. I don't know what time. Keep working on it. Try to find out what Tony Nichols did before he became a professor. I'm sure he's hiding a past of crime."

She hung up and rummaged in her overnight bag, pulling out a pack of cards. Playing Solitaire always calmed her down, but after five minutes, she'd lost three games.

She seriously considered cheating just to win. Frustrated, Claire put the cards away and grabbed her jacket. "I'm not waiting for you another minute, Tony Nichols. I'll just damn well track Patricia Snow down without you."

While shouting her words to the empty room did release some of her pent-up tension, the prospect of sending him completely out of her life did not fill her with joy.

At the front desk, Claire ordered a taxi. The library at Brown University in Providence would have access to phone directories for the whole country, but unfortunately it was too far away. Today she'd have to settle for the local library.

The cabby took her to Narragansett's public library, an old limestone affair. She forced herself past the shelves of hot new bestsellers and headed for the reference librarian.

The only directories they had were local, but amazingly to Claire, they had computer hookups to Brown. For the next hour and a half she pored through phone books, finding no listings for current years. Methodically she went backward on the microfiche, hoping that Mrs. M. Chancon hadn't always been such a "privacy hound."

The microfiche ran out in 1980, with no listing for M. Chancon. "Can I help you find something more, dear?"

Claire chewed her lip. "I hope so," she answered the bubbly blond woman who's pin-on tag read, Anne Hebert, Head Librarian. "Is there any chance of another program that could pull up older phone directories? This microfiche only goes back to 1980."

Miss Hebert frowned, then tugged at her denim skirt. Her blue eyes shone with determination. "I'll check. Wait right here." Ten minutes later, Claire was accessed into New Jersey Bell's records. In the 1973 edition of northeast New Jersey, her work yielded pay dirt.

Marielle Chancon was listed, at 2011 Cherry, Benton Convent. Claire copied down the address and phone number excitedly. Her instincts told her the number might have been changed by now, but at least she had a real lead. She added other information to her list, such as the current numbers for Benton Convent's only listed hotel—the Convent Garden—and its justice of the peace.

After thanking the librarian, Claire hurried outside to a pay phone and started calling. Her heart pounded as an elderly female voice answered the Chancon number.

"Yes. May I speak to Mrs. Chancon, please?"

There was a heartbeat of a pause. "I'm sorry. You must have the wrong number."

"Don't hang up, please. Have I reached a residence in Benton Convent, New Jersey?"

"Who is this, please?"

Claire debated what to answer. Her story was so convoluted, how could she get a total stranger to understand? "My name is Claire Kennedy. I live in New York and I'm trying to find an, uh, elderly cousin, a Mrs.

Chancon. This was an old number my mother gave me, and I thought I'd give it a try."

On the other end of the phone, Claire heard the woman choke or cough, then apparently drop the receiver, for a metallic clatter rang out. There was a muffled clearing of the throat. "I'm sorry, Miss Kennedy. Got something in my throat. I don't know your Mrs. Chancon. I'm afraid I don't know anyone by that name here in Benton Convent. I'm glad I could save you the trip. There's not much for a young person to see in our little town."

Sighing, Claire pursed her lips. "Thank you, ma'am. I appreciate your help." She hung up the phone and turned back to the street. Despite her lack of info on M. Chancon, she was determined to visit Benton Convent. As the chilly wind picked up, tickling her neck uncomfortably, she called for a cab to take her to Immaculate Sisters College.

A surprise visit to Tony Nichols might be just the thing right now. And if he was willing to drive her to Benton Convent, they might be able to resolve this whole thing tonight.

The grounds of the stately university were almost completely deserted when she got there. Claire wondered how she'd find out which was Tony Nichols's office.

"Well, lady? Is this where you're getting out?"

Handing the taxi driver some bills, Claire stood beside Tony's empty green Volvo. She'd told the man to pull up and stop behind it, hoping she'd find Tony at the wheel. Only his corduroy jacket greeted her, tossed across the Yale sweatshirt.

Shaking off her nervousness, Claire headed for the main entrance of the Humanities building. As she walked, the massive clock atop the building began to strike the half hour. It was already three-thirty. After a whole day away from her office she wasn't much closer to finding out the truth. But she had come up with another name to check with in Benton Convent.

While waiting for the cab, she'd called the office of the justice of the peace. A woman by the name of Pearl Loney held the job, as well as several other positions. She was the town's tax assessor and unofficial mayor. Claire hadn't been able to talk with Pearl herself when she'd called, but had been promised by the youthful-sounding clerk who'd answered the phone that Miss Loney would be glad to see her that evening. She gave Claire Pearl's home phone number.

Claire glanced up at the clock's heavy black hands, then looked away. The chimes echoed gloomily as she pulled her jacket snug around her and reached for the door. Vibrations from the clock tingled through the steel door handle just as a breeze whipped up behind her.

Had she heard someone call out? Looking behind her, Claire saw no one, but she could have sworn there'd been a faint cry carried on the gusting wind.

Tony had not shown up to get her at the inn, nor had he called with a message. She'd checked the inn not more than a half hour ago. Was his lack of punctuality further proof of his criminal makeup? she wondered.

Her determination not to be manipulated propelled her up the stairway to the second floor. The lighted hallway was empty of any security guards, secretaries or students to direct her.

Turning away from the stairs, Claire walked toward a closed office with English Department stenciled on the frosted glass and knocked.

There was no answer. A lectern stood next to the door, and the black notebook on it listed the instructor's office hours. Turning hastily to the *N*s, Claire found the entry Nichols, A.A. (Tony), Associate Professor, Creative Writing—319.

The space for appointments was crossed through with a large black X.

She ought to just go see Sarah Winesong, Claire thought as she hurried down the hall. If Mr. Harrison and Tillie hadn't babied the author all these years, Cauldron Press might not have been in this predicament. And she wouldn't be chasing around after Tony Nichols.

Claire took the stairs up to the third floor, pausing out of breath on the landing. A black arrow with the numbers 311-321 led her to the left.

That hall was dark, the only illumination coming from the gray sky visible through a single window at the far end of the corridor. All the offices appeared locked and unoccupied.

There was no lettering on the frosted glass of room 319 other than its number, and the small metal nameplate holder above it was empty. Claire's stomach churned. She rapped loudly and waited. Nothing. "Tony? Are you in there? It's Claire."

Her inquiry was met with silence. Rubbing one hand with the other, Claire looked around. Though everything was silent, she had the feeling that someone was nearby. Gingerly she put her hand on the brass doorknob and turned it. It opened easily, into almost complete darkness.

"Tony?"

The instant she spoke his name, the shrill cry of the telephone rang out like a startled sentry's gun. Clutching her chest, Claire gasped and stepped back.

Nearly laughing, she decided to answer it and groped for the light switch. As she did so she noticed the room was dense with the odor of Tony's tobacco. Inhaling, she tried to ignore the vivid pictures that rose to mind. Suddenly she found the switch and flicked it. The room lit up.

The first thing Claire saw was the blood pooled on the dingy carpet just inside the office door.

She froze. Dully she realized the phone had stopped ringing. Then her ears picked up a new sound. In the hallway she'd just vacated, the creaking of a door hinge was followed by footsteps.

Footsteps that were coming closer.

Frantic, Claire snapped off the light and moved deeper into the small office. Her hands groped in the dark for a weapon.

Heavy, leather-bound books were everywhere. Gripping the smooth surface of a large, anonymous text, Claire raised it above her head and waited.

A bulky silhouette filled the doorway as the hallway light tumbled into the room. Though Claire had made no sound, it was clear she'd been spotted. Without a word the figure lunged across the small office at her. She brought the book down squarely on the intruder's face, the corner stabbing into his cheek.

She was tackled and thrown against the edge of the desk while her attacker howled a curse at her blow. Claire struck him again and again with the book.

As they both crashed to the floor, Claire beat him with every bit of adrenaline pumping into her body. Then, quite suddenly, she knew who it was cursing her in the dark. She recognized the strong hands that hugged her waist, the wavy hair brushing against the tender skin on her arm.

Her body identified her captor even when her terrified mind had not. "Let go of me, Tony. You're hurting my arms."

He was straddling her hips. She could now clearly see his eyes in the dim light from the hall.

"Claire! Holy cow! What are you trying to do, kill me?"

His face was inches from hers. He'd relaxed his grip on her arms, but she wished he hadn't. She fought an insane urge to hug him in relief. Before she could answer, the phone renewed its jangling.

Tony got up and grabbed the receiver. "Yes. Hello?"

Claire stood and switched on the light as Tony sucked in his breath.

"Patricia, don't hang up. Just tell me where you are."

As their gazes locked, Claire noted with shock the extent of the damage to Tony's face. A red, swelling welt and a trickle of blood had turned his handsome features into a scarred battleground.

Guilt over the blows she'd administered flooded her, and Claire saw Tony's eyes fill with fear. But the fear was for the person on the phone, not for himself.

"Patricia, listen to me! I've got Claire Kennedy with me now, and she's very eager to straighten all of this out. She wants to meet—"

He stopped again and listened, patting his handkerchief against his forehead. "Just tell me where you are and I'll come and get you right now."

Tony paused, then, "Patricia, don't do that—"

He slammed down the phone and said, "Damn. She hung up." A flush of anger colored his strongly corded neck, turning the glowing olive skin the color of desert clay. When he turned his head to face Claire directly, she saw a gash at his left temple. It was dark and swollen, and there was a flap of jagged skin.

That explained the pool of blood at the door. "Dear God, how'd you get that?" She pointed to his temple.

His voice was flat. "That one is from an anonymous donor. I guess you did the rest, Claire. But you're going to have to find a different method of mayhem to get rid of me. Mugging someone with a book is not incredibly effective. Though your choice of weapons was witty."

Claire looked down at the blood-splattered book clutched tightly in her hands, her heart doing a flip as she noticed the cover.

She'd beaten Tony Nichols over the head with the twentieth-anniversary edition of the collected novels of Sarah Winesong. She dropped the book onto the desk as if it were alive, then turned her full attention back to Tony. "Sit down," she said. "Tell me where the first-aid kit is and shut up for a while."

A few minutes later, with a gauze bandage over the gash on his temple, Tony resembled a pirate. *A very attractive pirate.* Claire frowned at this latest comment from her libido and snapped the first-aid kit closed. "You'll be all right. Although your head needs to be stitched, I'd say."

"I'm sure I'll recover."

Whirling to face him, Claire saw Tony staring at her. "I'd get a second opinion if you don't want a scar. How did it happen?"

His eyes were impassable closed doors of steel. "You don't know? I thought you might have an idea."

"Like you thought I might know who broke into your home this morning?"

"Exactly like that."

Claire crossed her arms. "I have no idea who attacked you today, other than me. I've been busy."

"So has someone else. I was whacked over the head the minute I arrived, around two. I came to as the chimes were striking three."

Claire was stunned. She'd had her doubts about his story of someone breaking into his house. But the gash proved someone was stalking him, and growing bolder. "I was at the inn at two, waiting for you to come back."

The question of who else could have, and would have attacked him waited on both of their lips.

"Can you prove that?"

"Do I have to?" She waited for his answer, which didn't come. "If you think I'm guilty, why don't you just call the police?"

"We'd both have to explain a lot of things about the past couple of days. We don't want the police, or a news reporter, to get involved in this, Claire." He got up and started putting books back on the shelf.

Claire leaned down to help him. "But that's ridiculous. Someone tried to kill you!"

"I doubt that. If they'd wanted to kill me, they would have. I think this is a warning to me, a second warning, to back off."

Claire crossed the room and sat in a gunmetal-gray chair. "So you think it was Sarah Winesong who hit you? Did you see her?"

"No, to both questions. I only caught a glimpse of the person who hit me when I fell. Bigger than the person at my house today, and I'm fairly sure it wasn't a woman."

Claire's brain was spinning. She looked around the office. "This place looks like a typhoon passed through."

Tony nodded. Through the aches and pains of his injuries, he watched Claire carefully. She had to be one hell of an actress to pretend ignorance to this degree. Not that one woman he'd known wasn't capable of that, and more. But again he was struck by the ring of sincerity in Claire's voice.

He was ready to bet she was as much in the dark as he was about who'd struck him. It was obvious, however, why someone had. "Why didn't you wait for me at the inn like I told you to?"

"I'm not accustomed to doing what you tell me to do, Mr. Nichols. I'd still be there if I'd listened to you. I left the inn and checked around to get a lead on the Chancon woman Patricia went to work for. She's not currently listed in Benton Convent, but I got the name of a woman there who can help us."

Tony tensed. "Someone who knows Patricia?"

Claire's eyes followed his to the phone. In the excitement, she'd forgotten to ask him about the call he'd just received. "That was Patricia who called. What did she say?"

Patricia's voice had been booze-slurred and hysterical. Tony felt a flush of anxiety. She'd sounded scared. "She didn't stay on the phone long enough for me to find out where she is." Pulling his keys from his pocket, he winced slightly and rubbed the back of his head. "So, let's go to Benton Convent."

"Not until you tell me what she said." Claire kept her voice steady, wanting to show no trace of the concern she felt.

"I'll level with you, Claire. Patricia sounded pretty upset, and she told me to lay off. She doesn't need my help anymore."

For a moment neither of them spoke. Claire realized that she could go back to New York now and wait for the other shoe to drop when Patricia Snow called. If she called. Or when Roz Abramawitz linked Snow's book to Sarah Winesong's. If she did.

For a moment she felt dizzy with relief. But only for a moment. The immediate threat of Tony's pressing a lawsuit might be over, but a hundred mysteries remained about *The Poison Pen Pal* she couldn't let go of now if she tried. "I take it you're not going to do what she asked."

"No. I'm going to do whatever it takes to find Patricia and her manuscript, Claire. I told you I'm going to prove to you that she wrote that book, and I always do what I say. So, tell me about this woman you mentioned." He leaned over and took a deep breath, his skin pale under all the bruises and scrapes.

Claire told him about Pearl Loney, then asked, "Why is this so important to you, Tony?"

"Personal reasons."

"Personal reasons?" Claire knew she sounded mocking, but if she was close to finding out what was really motivating Tony, she couldn't stop now.

"Things are heating up, Claire. When I came to, I looked around a bit. Whoever was here stole a few things that are going to make it tricky for me to prove my case."

"Things? Like what?"

"Like Patricia's drafts of her book. Like some notes I had on an article I was researching on Billings Newcastle."

Her stomach contracted as if she'd been hit. "You're doing a piece on Newcastle? That's why you jumped all over Mr. Harrison and me. You've heard the buy-out rumors."

"Yes. And my sources say they're a lot more than rumors."

"But what does this have to do with Patricia Snow's book?"

Tony decided he'd said enough. He now fully believed Claire wasn't part of the plot to rip off his student, but she was still a loyal employee of a crooked company, and he wasn't bound to tell all. "Let's go see Patricia and find out. Are you coming?"

She walked through the door he held open. "Yes. Whatever awaits in Benton Convent I need to see with my own eyes."

"Seeing is believing, huh?"

Claire thought of the fifty pages of manuscript he'd given her yesterday. "Not necessarily. But it's our only shot."

"Good choice of words, Claire. Let's just be sure to make this shot count. It might be the last chance we'll get."

Chapter Six

"Give me your keys. After all your cracks on the head I think it'd be safer for both of us if I drove." Claire held out her hand as they stood beside the Volvo.

Tony gave them to her, then went around to the passenger side and got in. Leaning back in the seat, he closed his eyes and tried to sort out the events of the day.

Patricia Snow was in danger, of that much he was certain. From what, or whom, he wasn't sure. He was glad Claire had agreed to come along. Maybe Patricia would open up to her.

If we ever find her.

It was obvious there'd been someone with Patricia when she'd called. Someone she was afraid of. Her voice had the edge of a hostage whose words were being monitored. He had to find out how that someone was connected with Claire.

"I think it's time you leveled with me about everything, Tony. What exactly has Patricia Snow told you that you haven't shared?" Claire asked softly. She didn't turn to look at Tony's bruised and swollen face. Even though the man posed a threat to Cauldron, and to her job security, her guilt was as intense as ever over his injuries.

Opening his eyes slowly, Tony regarded Claire in the fading light. Her skin had a translucent sheen, and her hair glowed against the dark interior of the car. He wanted to wipe away a small smudge—blood?—on her knuckles, but he didn't trust himself to touch her.

His instincts shouted that Claire was as honest as she claimed. But he'd paid the price once before in his life of trusting when he shouldn't have, and he was damned sure he was not going to do it again until he was one hundred percent sure.

Until he knew the name of the person Patricia had been working with to sell her novel to Cauldron, he couldn't let his guard down. "She said she was going to destroy all the copies of her manuscript. She wanted me to stop trying to convince you *The Poison Pen Pal* was her story."

The impact of his words nearly sent Claire veering off into the dense forest bordering the highway. "Why? Why did she change her mind?"

"I'd say she's been threatened. She sounded very frightened."

"Frightened? Of what?"

"Or whom?"

Their separate theories regarding Patricia Snow's torment were like two silent passengers sitting in the back seat, waiting to be introduced.

Finally Claire spoke. "If someone has threatened her, she needs to go to the police."

"Maybe she's afraid to, because she's done something wrong herself."

"Which is what I've said all along." Claire regretted the I-told-you-so sound that clung to her words, but couldn't stop it.

"She still needed one or two conspirators to get the book passed off as Winesong's, Claire. Do you trust everyone you work with at Cauldron?"

"You keep asking me leading questions, Tony. Can't you even consider the possibility Patricia Snow fabricated this whole story?"

"No. She didn't fabricate her work. I saw it, edited it, helped her with it for a year. *The Poison Pen Pal* is her story, Claire. There's no disputing that."

Claire sighed and glanced at the sky. It was overcast and gloomy. And hopeless. She fully understood Tony's tenaciousness. It came from that shared sense of creation she knew so well from her own editing experience. "But there's no real proof. No complete copy of the book. No Patricia Snow."

"We'll find her. Even though whoever hit me today stole the manuscripts, I'll get them back. Give me a little more time, Claire. I'll show you."

Claire didn't seem completely convinced, but her voice was firm. "Okay, let's go see Pearl Loney."

WHEN THEY ARRIVED in front of the Convent Garden hotel, it was after eight. Claire pulled up to the curb and turned off the ignition. She was exhausted. Tony's estimation of four hours had been almost on the dot.

She turned to Tony. He'd slept for the past hour, his breathing ragged with fatigue. He woke up as she pulled the keys from the ignition.

"Shall we go in here and get something to eat? Then we can check around to see if anyone knows Patricia or this Mrs. Chancon. Or should we phone Pearl?"

"Let's get you something to eat," Claire replied as they entered the small neat lobby. "If you'll excuse me for a minute, I'm going to wash my hands."

"Claire? Can we get something straight first?"

"Sure."

The two of them looked at one another, as uncomfortable as a pair of fifteen-year-olds on a first date. "It can wait," Tony said. "Go ahead. I'm just going to ask the clerk a couple of questions."

"Fine. I'll be back in a minute."

Claire was relieved to get physically away from Tony and think for a minute. Hurrying into the rest room, she spotted the pay phone. At this hour she could catch Tillie, who never went anywhere but to work and home. Stopping in mid-dial, Claire realized she really didn't want to hear Tillie say she'd come up with proof that Tony Nichols was a con man.

That's ridiculous. I do want the truth. Her lack of conviction tightened her stomach muscles painfully, but she dropped in the quarter and read her credit-card number aloud.

Tillie didn't answer. She tried again. Still no answer. With a sigh of exasperation, Claire hung up. If she was honest with herself, she thought, she'd acknowledge that she felt a little relieved.

Turning to the sink, Claire ran the tap, soaping her arms up to her elbows. The warm water soothed her nerves, making her feel in control.

After she dried herself, Claire brushed her hair with long calm strokes and reran the day's events through her head. She berated herself for not insisting that Tony call the police from his office and report the attack on him, even though the inevitable questions would have been most uncomfortable.

Wincing at the thought of how interested the police would be to know she'd stolen a piece of United States mail, she pushed that anxiety aside. The biggest mystery was, who'd knocked Tony out? Someone who knew about his accusations? Or someone who wanted to stop him from proving them?

Either way, it was difficult not to speculate that the interests of Sarah Winesong and Cauldron Press were being served by the attack—

"Cut it out, Claire!" she yelled at her image in the mirror, angry that her subconscious seemed intent on proving the truth of what Tony said, instead of the opposite.

Throwing the brush and lipstick back into her bag, Claire hurried out into the lobby, determined to demand that Tony call the authorities. If any negative publicity about *The Poison Pen Pal* was generated because of her actions, well, so be it.

Too many little crimes were being committed, too many conflicting axes were grinding against the facts. Claire wasn't going to be a party to concealing the truth, no matter whom it hurt. Even if it damaged Sarah Winesong's precious reputation.

An empty lobby greeted her. Claire glanced back toward the rest rooms, then down at her watch. She'd been gone about ten minutes, more than enough time for any man she'd ever known to freshen up. Where was he now?

Crossing the small room, she sat on the sagging couch. It smelled of soap. It's cabbage-rose upholstery was faded but clean. There was no clerk behind the desk, no guests milling around. She couldn't see the lobby-café door from where she sat, but she'd seen a sign indicating it was closed.

"Miss Kennedy?"

Nearly jumping out of her skin, Claire turned at the sound of the question spoken so quietly behind her and stood up.

A small, dark-skinned woman in a maid's uniform smiled at her. She looked at Claire, then repeated her question. "Are you Miss Kennedy?"

"Yes. I'm Claire Kennedy."

"Mr. Nichols asked me to tell you he's across the street at the diner."

"Oh, thank you," she said, trying not to sound impatient. Quickly she scurried across the street and into the diner. Immediately she saw why Tony hadn't waited in the lobby. He had hurried over to catch the elderly woman who was now paying her bill, looking impatient with his questions.

The short, frail lady was leaning on a cane. She had a paper sack in her hand. Claire caught her softly spoken words as she approached.

"I'll be tied up for a few minutes, but I've given you my address, so you folks come on over when you're done with supper. Just give me a half hour."

"Of course, Miss Loney. We'll say about nine?"

Pearl Loney! How had Tony gotten ahold of her so quickly? Claire cleared her throat. "Hi, Tony. Miss Loney. I'm Claire Kennedy. I left a message with your assistant today."

Tony turned and smiled at her, but something was wrong. He was ill at ease under the surface of his cheery facade. "Claire. Sorry to leave you like that, but the hotel clerk told me Miss Loney eats here every night at eight, so I rushed over to catch her."

"Nice to meet you, dear," Pearl added. She put her change into a deep pocket of her coat and moved toward the door. "I really do have to run. But I'll see you two in a bit."

Claire watched her leave, a pinprick of worry in her mind. There was something vaguely familiar about the woman, but she couldn't put her finger on it.

Tony directed her to a booth and they ordered. When the waitress walked off, Claire studied her surroundings for a moment. Red leather booths, clean picture windows, a beige linoleum floor. The Benton Diner, as the menu proclaimed, was nondescript but nice. Her attention focused on Tony.

In the fluorescent light, the bruises and cuts on Tony's face looked even worse. The purple contusions on his unshaven face gave him a desperate air. "I'm surprised Pearl talked to you. You look like an escaped criminal."

Tony studied her, not smiling. "Thanks."

"Come on, I'm joking. What's wrong with you?"

Tony's dark skin burned, contrasting with the whites of his eyes. "I may have found out a clue to Patricia's disappearance."

Her stomach flip-flopped. "How?"

"Claire, I think it would be best if you went back to New York. We can get a cab, and I'll take you to the train. I'll send your clothes to you."

"Have you lost your mind? I came to see Patricia Snow, and I'm not leaving until I do."

"Things may be getting dangerous."

"Dangerous? Come on, Tony, don't make me laugh. We were supposed to be working *together* to find your little student-author and her book, remember? Do you think I'm going to forget all your accusations now, because you think you've found out something dangerous? Do I look stupid to you?"

Tony's answering look was cold fury, tempered by what Claire thought was pain. But she decided immediately that couldn't be. She'd been a fool to let her guard down with this man, but she wasn't about to fall for any more of his tricks.

"I don't think you're stupid at all."

"So what's so dangerous?"

He waited to answer until the waitress finished bringing their dinner, which neither of them even glanced at. "Miss Loney knows where Patricia Snow is staying."

"Where?" Claire was breathing hard, angry at this slow-motion delivery, which was making her feel vulnerable.

"A small house out of town, about twenty miles into the country. Pearl said for us to come by, and she'd draw a map for us. She knows the property well. It was owned by an M. Chancon, according to Pearl. Though she never met Chancon."

"She's met Patricia, though?"

"She thinks she has. Wasn't sure of the name. Said a young woman has been living on the property 'doing some writing.'"

"Well, let's go out there."

Tony was silent for a moment. When he spoke, it was in carefully measured words. "I think it would be better if we didn't go together."

"I disagree. And furthermore I fail to see how this information is dangerous. Unless you're intimating that what I may find out from Patricia will be."

Tony remained imperturbable. "Miss Loney told me something else. She said Chancon died about six years ago. But her heir kept the property."

"And?" Claire's annoyance was clear.

Tony kept his voice low. "When I said dangerous, I wasn't really worried for your sake, Claire. I'm concerned about Patricia's safety. You see, Chancon's only surviving relative is named Winesong. Sarah Winesong owns the house now.''

The implication of this statement was clear. Tony was afraid to take Claire along, because he thought he now had indisputable proof of his case against Cauldron. And her.

She stared at his well-sculpted profile, the long lashes framing penetrating eyes now squinted with fatigue, the face battered and bruised. Claire felt angry, but also kind of relieved.

This news proved something to her, too. Tony wasn't lying. He wasn't a con man. He really had grounds for believing *The Poison Pen Pal* was stolen.

And for the first time, so did she.

PEARL LONEY walked slowly across the room, her sensible, thick-soled shoes making little squeaks.

"Here's your coffee. You better hurry, though. They'll be here in about twenty minutes."

Her guest sipped the coffee, then stood. "I'll go now. You understand what I want you to do?"

"Don't I always?"

"You try, but—"

Pearl placed her hand on her guest's soft jacket. "Please, don't be angry because I didn't get the drafts from his apartment this morning."

"Stop it, Pearl. You should have taken care of him like I told you to, but don't worry about it now. I got the drafts from his office myself. This has worked out much better than I expected."

Pearl studied her guest, absently turning the bracelet on her wrist. "They're going to go out as soon as I give them the directions."

"Good. That's what I want them to do."

"I told Nichols about Chancon's heir. He nearly fainted."

Her visitor walked to the door, then rummaged in the hollow brass pot of umbrellas and walking sticks. Withdrawing one, her guest murmured a few last words. "You handled Claire Kennedy's call in exactly the right way this afternoon. Thanks again. I'll be in touch."

"We've been together for twenty-five years, do you know that?" At the casual nod, Pearl forced some cheer into her voice. "Drive carefully, Sarah."

Their eyes met and smiles were exchanged. "Good night, Pearl. Be sure the directions are clear. We wouldn't want the poor dears to lose their way."

Chapter Seven

Tony pulled his car alongside a broken fence bordering the unpaved driveway and stopped.

Through the windshield Claire saw a small brick house. A barn and garage were shadowy companions in the distance.

No lights could be seen from outside. The windows reflected no clue about the inhabitants, only the starless night. Claire felt as if the velvety darkness was pressing against the windshield.

Though unwilling to trust her voice since Tony's revelation of the solid link between Patricia Snow and Sarah Winesong, Claire had not come undone when they'd gone to see the proof. Pearl Loney's property-assessment records were kept in a small office in her home, and she'd shown them the title transfer.

The description Mrs. Snow had given them of the woman her daughter had gone to work for reran through her mind. "Something of a privacy hound," she'd said. Claire berated herself for not realizing there were only so many coincidences.

But she realized it now. The world's most successful con man couldn't have arranged these interconnections. The letter from Roz seemed even more proof that Sarah had stolen the girl's book. This news would kill Tillie, and Mr. Harrison, Claire found herself thinking. Winesong was more than a claim to fame to those two; they ran their lives on the basis of her reputation.

"Watch your step—the ground's full of ruts."

Tony's whisper broke into her thoughts. "Do you think she's inside?" she asked.

"Ssh. Who? Patricia? I hope so."

"No. Sarah Winesong." Claire lowered her voice as she felt Tony's strong hand on her arm. His touch gave her some comfort.

It pained Tony to see Claire so anguished. But he knew how it felt to be lied to by someone you had faith in. It took time to believe it had really happened. And even more time to put it behind you. He wanted to hug Claire, tell her that he'd be waiting for her when she was ready to trust again, but her brittle posture stopped him.

Instead of a hug Tony offered more information. "I doubt if Sarah Winesong lives here. Pearl said she knew of Sarah's work when you asked her, but she's never met her. Said none of the townfolk had, either. Didn't you hear that?"

Claire chewed up her last Tums as a shiver tingled down her back. "I guess I did. Let's go in. Now."

Shoulder to shoulder they walked to the front door, the wet grass squishing beneath their feet. The floorboards creaked the length of the porch as they went up the three steps. Claire cringed when Tony's knock resounded through the stillness of the night.

No one answered.

Squinting in concentration, Claire leaned her ear against the door. Just like in the movies, she thought. All she could hear was Tony's measured breathing next to her.

Moving away from him, Claire walked toward the large front window of the house. Heavy curtains covered the six-by-nine paned window, but she detected a small bluish light behind them.

With a flutter of hope, and apprehension, she surmised the glow was from a television set. "Someone's inside."

"I'm sure it's Patricia. I think that's her car." Tony's voice rushed toward Claire from the other end of the porch where he stood, his arm pointing to a bulky shape near the barn.

"Maybe she's asleep and didn't hear our knock. These old houses have thick walls. Should we wait and come back in the morning? It's almost eleven."

Walking back, Tony stopped just a few inches from where Claire waited by the door, her freckles like pin-pricks of worry against her pale skin. Tony silently considered the possibility that Patricia was asleep, but decided to keep knocking. It was more likely she had passed out.

Or someone was keeping her from answering the door. That worry prompted him to action. "We have to see her tonight. Tomorrow may be too late to do any of us any good." He saw the question, and the fear, in Claire's eyes about what lay behind his remarks. Turning, he grabbed the doorknob and rattled it. "Patricia? Open up, it's Tony Nichols. Wake up!"

Though the knob moved easily, the door itself was stuck, warped at the bottom. After a few pushes with his shoulder, it gave way.

A vision leaped at them out of the blackness of the foyer, a two-headed monster with gleaming eyes and white skin. In a blink Claire swallowed the scream in her throat as she realized it was only her and Tony's reflection in the dusty mirror hanging opposite the door.

"Well, now I can add breaking and entering to my list of criminal accomplishments," Claire muttered.

Stepping inside, they faced the dust and gloom of the house. The rooms off both sides of the center hall were cluttered, full of bulky shapes unrecognizable without light.

But neither felt inclined to turn on a light. It seemed too intrusive an act. After all, they were trespassers in what was an obviously lived-in home.

As her eyes adjusted to the darkness of the front parlor she'd stepped into, Claire located the small television set. It sat on the floor in the far corner of the room, the volume turned off. A mute Johnny Carson was interviewing a guest who wore heavy makeup.

Claire caught a distinct stubble of beard on the guest's jaw. A female impersonator? The incongruous image seemed to fit the bizarre evening.

"Patricia?"

Tony's voice distracted Claire from the flickering television. As spooky as this place was, she realized her jittery stomach was due more to an intuition that something was amiss. As her eyes grew used to the darkness, she saw piles of papers strewed around, a stool on its side, books in a heap by a corner bookcase.

"Look, Tony. Do you think someone else has been in here, searching?"

He eyed the mess and shrugged. "I doubt it. Patricia's never been known for neatness."

"Is there any sign of her?"

"No. Stay there, Claire. I'm going to check the bedrooms."

Somewhere in the darkness she could hear a clock ticking.

As Tony's broad back disappeared farther down the hallway, a hollow pop like a car's engine backfiring, made her jump. Willing her legs to walk, Claire crossed the room to peek out of the sagging curtains. No glimmer of headlights verified what she'd heard. Nothing moved on the road.

Turning back into the room, Claire confronted Tony, who seemed to have materialized out of the velvet darkness of the hallway.

He had an unlit cigarette in his mouth, a burning match in his hand. As their eyes met, she grabbed away the cigarette and stuck it in his pocket.

Tony shook out the match. "Sorry. I forgot you don't like smokers."

Claire's throat constricted. She was alone in someone else's house, uninvited, in the dead of night. "Did you find her?"

"No. But the bedroom doors are closed. I think I'll go back and knock. I hope she's alone." Tony tossed the match into a small bowl on the coffee table in front of him.

Embarrassment rolled through Claire, bringing a kind of relief. Of course, Patricia Snow was just out of college, not some gothic recluse. Her lover was probably here with her. "No, don't go in there, Tony. We'll come back in the morning. Let's go now. No one will even know we've been here."

His olive skin seemed to have paled in the ghostly blue light. "No. I'm not leaving until I know if Patricia is all right. Stay here and wait. Remember, Claire, I promised you proof, and I plan to give it to you."

"Then I'm coming with you." She pulled herself into action, and followed him down the hall, softly calling Patricia's name. A glimmer of light from a high window—a skylight?—caught Claire's attention. Turning, she spied a towel lying crumpled in a heap just inside the bathroom door to her right. The air was scented with a faint aroma of lavender soap. Someone had showered. And dressed for bed?

As Tony moved into the room on the right, Claire opened the door of another room and stepped into a deeper darkness. She made out the shape of a dresser, a narrow bed and, in the corner farthest from her, a pile of clothes on the floor. "Patricia?"

Feeling like a Peeping Tom, she turned to call for Tony. Before any words came out she froze. A small red glow flickered at her from across the room, the acrid smell of burned paper and cotton assailing her nostrils.

A cigarette filter? Had someone left a cigarette burning?

While she stood there attempting to sort out this new information, Claire was seized by a terror unlike any she'd ever felt. There was a new shape, a human figure sharing the quiet darkness of this strange bedroom.

Someone was sitting across the room, next to the burning glow, apparently staring straight at her.

"Is she here?" Tony bumped against Claire as he came up behind her in the bedroom.

Pointing toward the corner, she whispered. "Patricia. Is that Patricia?"

In a flash, Tony's hand found the wall switch, flooding the room with a glaring, too bright light.

"Oh, my God!"

"Patricia!"

They spoke in unison as the figure in the chair came clearly into view. A young woman in a pink terry bathrobe sat with an empty bourbon bottle clutched in her hands. Her eyes stared straight ahead.

In the middle of her forehead, a smudged round hole neatly marked the entry point of the small-caliber bullet that had killed her.

THE VOLVO FISHTAILED violently as they raced around the corner and through the only stoplight in Benton Convent. Accelerating to fifty miles an hour down the slick, two-lane road, Tony floored the gas pedal, urging the Swedish engine to propel them as fast as possible away from the horror behind them.

Claire sat motionless against the door, her face white, her brown eyes huge with disbelief.

"Claire? Are you okay?"

"Okay? Of course I'm okay. Shouldn't I be? After all, I live in New York City. Breaking into a house and finding a dead body is something I've become accustomed to. What do we do next? Stop in and see *Psycho 15* at the movies?"

Slowing the car, Tony ordered his own breathing to steady. He knew Claire was in shock, her bitter retort only a defense. With alarm he noted she was shivering despite the heater's steady stream of warmth. "I'm sorry, that was a dumb question. Let's stop and get something to eat. Then we'll go report Patricia . . . uh, the body."

The memory of the poor girl sitting drunk, and dead— dead drunk, her mind ghoulishly offered—clamored back into Claire's thoughts. Shivering uncontrollably, she fought back the tears that burned in her eyes. "We shouldn't have left her there, Tony. We should have called the police and waited for them."

"I don't think that would have been a good idea, Claire."

"Why not?"

Tony didn't answer, and Claire's voice rose in anger. "Who would do such a thing? Why did someone murder her?"

The last question tore Tony's returning calm asunder. His hands felt disconnected from his body as he gripped the steering wheel. *Why indeed?*

"I don't know, Claire. But I do know it's crazy for us to get involved with the police now. We'd have to tell them about the manuscript, Sarah Winesong, the criminal activities you've been advised that Cauldron Press might be responsible for."

"Oh, don't not call the police to spare me any trouble. You're the one who's been implying I've been behind this all along. Why stop now?"

Tony fell back into silence, knowing his suspicions could send Claire over the edge.

"How can you even worry about a damn book at a time like this, Tony? Some lunatic murdered a girl in cold blood. In cold blood!" Tears ran down her cheeks, and Claire began to sob and shiver even more violently. Her husky voice broke with every breath.

Nearing the edge of town, Tony pulled the car into a small lot. He parked it away from the white light pouring out of the twenty-four hour doughnut shop. With great care, he folded Claire into his arms, rocking her while her sobs increased, her arms clutching him tightly.

After several minutes she stopped shaking and, with a final sniff, accepted his handkerchief. Uncontrollable hiccups punctuated the silence as Claire moved back into the seat.

Tony brushed away a tear-dampened strand of silky blond hair and waited. He had an overwhelming desire to kiss each of the freckles sprinkled across her nose until her skin regained its normal rosy blush.

But he didn't. "Let's get some coffee. Then we'll go back to Narragansett Bay. I have a house on the water. It's quiet, and you can rest while we sit down and decide what to do next."

Claire stared at this man she'd known for such a short time. Only two days, but so much had happened. Tony had sparked something inside her the moment he'd jumped out of the elevator and demanded she speak with him. He'd gotten under her skin.

Though a physical pull of attraction was significant, it wasn't only his body she craved. A bond had formed between them in those first few seconds, a bond rooted deep inside of her.

She cared about Tony, even though she knew little about him. With all that had happened, she thought, she still had no good reason to trust him.

But I do. "I'll take some milk. And about half a dozen buttermilk doughnuts."

With a gentle caress of her chin, Tony hopped out of the car, but turned and stooped back inside to give her a smile, his black eyes glittering. "Okay. Now we're getting somewhere. Lock the doors. I'll be right back."

THE MORNING LIGHT scratched her consciousness like a lover's day-old beard. Pulling herself awake, Claire opened her eyes and saw she was still in Tony's car. And the car was still moving.

Around them the sky was red and raw-looking, gray clouds streaked across it like claw marks, lacerating the glow of a hot-pink sun on the horizon.

Though she had slept several hours, she was exhausted. Her bones were sore, her muscles cried out to walk, run, anything. Tony had taken the Harvard shirt off his seat and covered her legs with it, but that protection did little to dissipate the cold knot inside of her.

Flexing her toes, Claire sat upright, not risking a look at Tony. She wasn't ready to meet his eyes. She knew they'd hold the proof that Patricia Snow's murder wasn't a nightmare.

The car turned down a narrow dirt road, sending pebbles flying. The pinging noise they made against the wheel wells jarred Claire's nerves.

Scruffy sea pines and bare cedars, with white trunks stark against the marshy ground, blinked by her like a skeleton crew of guards. A mile in the distance, Claire saw a house perched on a sandy knoll above the beach. As they neared, she realized it must be Tony's house.

She was surprised by how fresh and cheery it was. White shutters sparkled with new paint, and a well-polished brass lantern gleamed beside the front door. "This is where you live."

"Yeah. Coffee awaits."

"It's been so long since I was at the beach." Claire leaned forward slightly, running her hand through her tousled hair.

"I love it here. Even though I've only had the place eight years, it feels like home."

"Only eight years—that's an eternity to someone from California. I moved twenty times in eight years when I was a child." The memory of the rundown duplex in El Monte where they'd lived for two weeks when she was nine rose to mind. Her dad had made them move in the middle of the night. The poker parlor he'd been working at had caught him betting against the house, causing the record short stay.

"What did your folks do?"

The Volvo creaked to a stop. "They followed Lady Luck. I can't wait to get out of this car."

Before Tony could move, Claire jumped out onto the sandy walk. Facing the sea, she stretched her arms above her head and inhaled the tangy air, reveling in the salt sting against her face. The water rocked gently for miles in front of her, brown-gray calm at low tide.

"You'll have to tell me more about your family's pursuit of Lady Luck some day. I could use some help from her myself."

Claire turned to Tony with a rueful smile. "Daddy said no one could ever run fast enough to catch her. It's much wiser to make your own luck with hard work. Let's go get that coffee."

While Tony began making comforting sounds in the kitchen, Claire locked herself into the tidy blue-and-white tiled bathroom. She felt grimy and hot, so she peeled off all her clothes.

Eyeing the shower longingly, she opted instead for a soapy washcloth. Running it over her arms, neck and face, Claire wondered if Tillie had called and left a message at the inn.

The inn! She'd better call Tillie and Mr. Harrison and let them know... Let them know what? That she'd discovered Sarah Winesong was involved in...what? A book theft?

Murder?

Should she even tell them that Patricia Snow was dead?

Claire shuddered, refusing to let her mind dwell on the image engraved on her brain.

Pulling her jeans on over her bare body and tucking in her pink shirt, Claire decided that before she could come up with any plan of action, she'd eat and talk to Tony. Together they could make sense of what to do next. Despite the girl's death, Claire still had to track down the truth about *The Poison Pen Pal.*

And pray that neither led back to anyone she knew.

The sound of crackling bacon met her as she walked into the compact kitchen where Tony stood at the sink, peeling potatoes. Claire sat down at the breakfast bar watching him toss the chopped pieces into the hot cast-iron skillet, adding onion and diced green pepper by the handful.

In no time she was enjoying a plateful of scrambled eggs, whole-wheat toast and a heaping mound of potatoes *au* Nichols. Tony matched her forkful for forkful, watching her discreetly. With her pink scrubbed skin, her blond hair sleekly brushed away from her high cheekbones, she looked like a teenager.

Except for her eyes. The shock from last night still lingered there, clouding the clear brown irises.

"You're a fabulous cook, Tony. You said you love Italian food. I bet you make great spaghetti."

"Actually I don't even try to cook Italian. I go to Mama Vincenzo's. She's in town, three miles down the beach. She's the best."

"You're one of the best. This is some breakfast."

"Thanks. I do okay when I'm in the mood."

Claire wondered about his moods. There was so much she didn't know about him. So much she didn't know about a lot of things. As she looked out the French doors toward the bay, she knew it was time to get back on track. The food had given her some strength, enough at least to call the authorities.

"We have to call the police. Now, Tony."

Tony paused, his last bite of toast inches away from his mouth. Claire noticed for the first time how his beard was filling in. She could see patches of his smooth skin underneath, the bruises already fading, only hinting at yesterday's scuffle.

"I already called them, Claire. About four this morning, when you were asleep in the car. I stopped for gas and coffee. I let you rest. They have all the details."

"You should have wakened me. They could have interviewed me. We could have gone back and met with them."

Tony finished the morsel of bread, then took a long drink of coffee. "I didn't give them my name. Or yours. We still can't get involved, Claire. Until we know who did it. And why."

"Get involved? We *are* involved! For heaven's sake, we're the ones who found her body. We couldn't get much more involved than that."

Tony had put off pursuing the matter until he was sure Claire was over the shock of finding Patricia. It looked like the time had come. "We could be a lot more involved. Which is what I suspect the police would think when faced with the facts."

"What facts?"

Claire had finally gotten up the nerve to ask the question. Tony took a deep breath. It was time to tell her the whole story.

Chapter Eight

"Now wait just a minute." Claire marched around the bar stool to stand beside Tony.

He ignored her.

"Are you implying someone at Cauldron Press planned that girl's murder, intending to implicate you?"

Tony brought the coffee mug to his lips, slowly draining the cold remainder. He faced her. "There's no escaping the facts, Claire. The day after I came to New York, my house was searched, the manuscripts were stolen from my office, and now Patricia's dead. And after we took a very high-profile tour of her town, complete with telling Pearl Loney and a couple of others of our intentions to go see her, I might add."

"Why would anyone go to all that trouble, Tony—especially murder? To protect Sarah Winesong's book?"

"There's a lot of money at stake with that book, Claire. Don't be naive about the suitability of greed as a motive."

She clenched her fists. "Don't be condescending, Tony. And speaking of greed, what about Patricia's? Or yours, even? We still haven't proved that *The Poison Pen Pal* is her book."

"She told me someone gave her money and promised to show the book to you. She said she was given a retainer, or some 'help' money she signed an IOU for. She implied it was Winesong."

As Tony talked, Claire's brain felt frozen. His words bounced off instead of being absorbed. "I just can't believe what you're telling me now. How much money? Did she get a check? A contract? Where's the IOU now?"

"She didn't tell me."

"But you're convinced Sarah Winesong killed her."

"I don't know who pulled the trigger. Or who paid Patricia off. But Winesong has to be involved somehow."

"And Cauldron Press, too? Particularly the acquisitions editor? Is that what you're thinking?"

"No. I mean...no. I don't honestly know what to think, Claire. My heart tells me you're honest and caring, but—" Tony walked back to the counter and poured more coffee into his mug, pain tightening his mouth "—it's just that I've been wrong about people in the past. So wrong that it cost me everything that I had. I can't let my feelings for you cloud the evidence."

Tears of frustration welled in Claire's eyes. She rubbed them away fiercely. "I've never gained anything in my life illegally, Tony Nichols. My hard work, sweat and eighteen-hour days for the past seven years pulled Cauldron Press out of a terminal slide. Can't you see that I'm as appalled at what's happened to Patricia Snow as you are?"

"Claire, I'm sorry, it's just—"

"No. Let me finish. You asked me to tell you about myself yesterday. Well, my dad was a penny-ante poker shark. My whole childhood was spent on the run because he was too selfish to change. He wasn't strong enough to change. But I have that strength. When things have gone wrong in my life, I've done whatever needed to be done. If someone connected to Cauldron Press has done something illegal, I'll see it's made right."

Tony stared at Claire. Her impassioned speech, and its painful revelations about her past, convinced him completely she was telling the truth. "I believe you wouldn't willingly have gone along. But if you were tricked...?"

Shutting her eyes against the bright morning light, Claire turned away. She knew exactly what he was implying. Someone at Cauldron had betrayed her. "Did Patricia tell you why she agreed to sell her manuscript that way?"

"Patricia was an alcoholic," Tony said quietly, knowing the impact of his words. "The funds seemed like a windfall, a month of drinking money too tempting to pass up."

His revelation was met with silence. Suddenly Claire's eyes brimmed again with tears. It hurt almost beyond bearing to think someone could be so exploitive of another person's weakness. "Why didn't you tell me this before?"

"What difference would it have made? If I'd told you she was a drunk, you'd have disbelieved my story even more." Tony could see the pain Claire was in, but he made no move to comfort her. She had to reach within herself to weather the betrayal of those around her.

Blinking, Claire walked through the French doors and out onto the deck. Tony followed her. He put his hands on her shoulders and pulled her back toward him, kissing her hair.

Claire moved away, then turned back. Her voice was strong again. "I'm going back to New York."

"I'll come with you."

"No. I need to find out what's going on at Cauldron for myself."

"Don't be hurt by my suspicion. I had to assume you were the one who'd paid her off."

"It wasn't me." Claire clutched the deck railing more tightly, her eyes aching with held-back tears.

"I know that. Now." Tony pulled Claire toward him again despite her resistance. Folding his arms around her slim shoulders, he backed her up against the deck railing. "Claire, you're as much a victim of this hoax as Patricia was. Don't push me away because you're hurting. I want to help. I need to help you. I care about you."

"I care about you, too, Tony. But this is a bigger issue than a passing attraction between two people—"

His fingers tightened on her arms. "For God's sake, stop your analytical distancing, Claire. I don't feel any damned 'passing attraction' for you. Let your guard down, woman. Believe in what you feel. Believe in me."

For a moment Claire allowed herself to revel in the feel of Tony against her. His chest was broad and strong, his manner reassuring and caring. But the caution she'd built up in herself for the past twenty years was too hard to overcome.

Claire pushed away, breaking the embrace. "I really think I need to do this on my own. Two days ago I said I'd come here to find out who wrote *The Poison Pen Pal*. Despite all that's happened, I'm no closer to proving anything."

"I see." Tony's black eyes took her in. "Do you think the fact that Patricia Snow was murdered has no connection to her claim that Cauldron Press stole her book?"

"It could be just a tragic coincidence." Claire diverted her gaze. She had to get her equilibrium back and not jump to any conclusions yet. "But until I have solid proof, I'm going to work on the assumption that Sarah Winesong is innocent."

"I see. Shall I disappear into thin air now? Or drive you to the train station first?"

Claire turned back toward the ocean. The sight of Tony, his arms crossed angrily across his soft white cotton sweater and his dark eyes blazing, was too painful.

It made her wish she could put *The Poison Pen Pal* out of her life entirely. Then she could concentrate on getting to know the man behind those eyes. Find out what made him laugh. Why he'd never learned to swim.

But as she gazed at the choppy water, Claire saw clearly that getting to know Tony was a selfish luxury she had no time to indulge in. Ugly accusations had been made, and a young woman was dead. The future of everyone at Cauldron Press was at stake.

"Claire, if you'd just rest for a while—"

"There's little time for that." She turned her brown eyes to meet his. "Take me to the police before I go back. They can start trying to find the murderer."

"You can't go to them." Tony's chin was set in a stubborn pose, his arms crossed tighter against the now chilling wind. Above them the sky began to darken.

"Why do I get the feeling you're still holding back some facts from me, Tony?"

"Because I am." Uncrossing his arms, he searched fruitlessly for his cigarettes.

"Well. Get to it. What else is going on?" The anxiety over what other facts Tony was concealing was getting to her.

"I haven't told you everything. Yet. But I will, as soon as you look me in the eye and agree to work this mess out with me."

Claire's stomach burned with pain. "I can't, Tony. Please, just leave me alone for a while." Brushing past him, Claire hurried down the stairs of the deck and out onto the beach below.

Tony watched her for several moments as she ran from him, her slim body pounding against the packed sand and her blond hair a silk wedge against her neck.

He'd give her a couple of hours alone to sort out all that had happened these past two days, then he'd tell her about his missing gun. And about his personal grudge against Billings Newcastle.

Turning on his heel, Tony rushed back into the house. He scribbled a note, then called Jeanette Snow's neighbor and asked her to meet him at Jeanette Snow's house in a few minutes. He had to take care of this last sad duty before he could think any more about Claire. But as soon as he could, he was going to come back to her.

If there was any justice at all in the world, it would be for good.

As FAST AS SHE COULD, Claire ran from the dark-eyed man who had upset all of her priorities. She wasn't one to duck out on decisions, but the ones he was forcing on her were too fraught with complications.

Finally short of breath, her lungs bursting, she stopped and kneeled on the sand. She could no longer put off facing the fact that she was falling for Tony. For a few moments she felt nothing. She listened to her breathing, tasted the tears and salt spray on her lips.

"Great timing, Kennedy," she muttered, then lay back on the sand. Despite the horror of the past twelve hours, she felt a tiny wave of joy. Love popped up at inopportune times in her books, and her fictional heroines always coped with it.

Life didn't imitate art, she thought, not without plagiarizing. Which led her right back into the puzzle of *The Poison Pen Pal*. Claire decided to make a mental list of what facts she knew were true.

Sarah Winesong said the book was hers.

Patricia Snow said the book was hers.

Tony said Patricia Snow claimed to have received money from some unnamed person who was going to show it to Cauldron.

Patricia had been living in Winesong's house.

Tony had been attacked twice.

Patricia was dead.

Patricia got a letter from Roz Abramawitz.

What was the common thread that would tie all of these facts together? Claire sat up and brushed the sand off her hands. There were some real possibilities. Mr. Harrison himself had wondered if Patricia Snow was part of a much bigger plot to ruin Cauldron Press.

What about Billings Newcastle? Had he set this whole thing up to make it easier to take over Cauldron? The notes Tony had made for his article had been stolen. Was Newcastle the key?

Beginning a slow jog back to the house, Claire was exuberant. Maybe Roz Abramawitz was the culprit. She'd been jealous of Claire for years. Maybe she'd planned this whole thing on Newcastle's behalf.

Wait till Tony heard her idea, she thought as she sped up the beach. As she approached the deck stairs, she saw that Tony wasn't on the deck.

The next breath brought Claire a much more worrisome realization. His driveway was empty. The Volvo was gone.

There was a note on the kitchen bar. "Claire, I've gone to see Mrs. Snow. I'll be back in a couple of hours. Get some rest. When I get back we'll work everything out. T.''

Mrs. Snow.

Claire's stomach contracted at the poor woman's grief upon learning of her daughter's death. Her momentary annoyance and anger at Tony for leaving her stranded vanished. Despite his own fatigue, he was going to help someone in need.

Grabbing the kitchen telephone, she dialed the Woodbury Inn and requested that they hold her room for another day. Once Tony got back, she'd go get some fresh clothes. Then they could map out a way to trap Newcastle.

It was only a little after eight, too early to catch Tillie in the office. She'd wait and call her in an hour or so. By then maybe her thoughts would be clear enough to tell them about last night's events and today's revelations.

One thing was obvious to Claire. Her boss had to set up a meeting in the next couple of days with Sarah Winesong. Then another possibility occurred to Claire.

Maybe Newcastle had stolen a copy of Sarah's work and paid Patricia Snow to concoct this whole thing.

That theory brought a rush of hope. If she could just prove it, *The Poison Pen Pal* could go to press as scheduled.

Light-headed with fatigue, Claire unplugged the coffeepot that Tony had left on for her and ran her hand along the painted tile counter. She hadn't noticed before how professional the kitchen's design was. It was tidy and well-equipped, awaiting only the sure hand of a serious cook.

Was this a woman's touch? ''No,'' she said aloud, unable to deny the happiness that answer gave her. Anyone could see Tony lived a solitary existence in this small house. Everything had a masculine stamp.

A small copper pot, filled with riotously colored tulips, sat on the counter where he'd served her breakfast. Smiling, Claire thought how nice it would be to be in love with a liberated man who cleaned up his own dishes.

Slow down, she cautioned herself. But the thought of being in love thrilled her as she fingered the hammered design on the side of the vase. It portrayed a lion whose head was thrown proudly back. Claire pressed her hand onto it, liking its cool feel.

Weighted down with a longing for a nap, she left the kitchen and walked toward the bedroom where she stripped off her jeans and crawled under the quilt that covered Tony's bed. She'd take his advice and rest for an hour. When he got back, they'd "work everything out."

His remembered promise worked like a sleeping potion, and Claire was gone, dead asleep, in less than thirty seconds.

A SMOKE ALARM? Was her apartment on fire? Claire tensed, her mind fighting to wake up. The bell's insistent warning continued. Sitting straight up in bed, she realized the noise was a telephone.

Glancing around, she finally remembered where she was. Tony's. Jumping from the bed, she ran across the bare wood floor toward the corner desk, noting with alarm the darkening sky outside. How long had she been asleep?

The digital clock on the desk read twelve-eleven. Twelve-eleven? Could she have been asleep for four hours? She grabbed the phone and ran back to the bed. "Hello?"

A quick intake of breath, followed by a familiar nicotine-roughened laugh greeted Claire. "Well, I'll be damned. Answering the hunk's phone already? You two must have had some night together."

"Tillie. How did you find me here?" Claire smiled and sank into the fluffy pillows behind her, covering her chilly legs with Tony's sheet. "Didn't you trust me to call in?"

"Yes, Ms. Kennedy, I surely did. But since all hell has broken loose around here today, I thought I'd try to get through before anything else happens. Finding you where Mr. Nichols hangs his hat was my first guess after the inn said you'd stayed elsewhere."

Though Tillie's tone was joking, Claire sensed her friend was worried. "What's happened, Tillie? What's wrong?"

"Wrong? What's right? Starting with Roz Abramawitz, who parked her irate fanny in front of Mr. Harrison's door this morning at eight o'clock screaming for blood, and ending with two New York City cops who are looking for you, everything is wrong."

Hopping back out of bed, Claire held the phone against her shoulder with her chin while she wiggled into her jeans. The mention of Roz filled her with dread.

What if the letter Roz sent to Patricia Snow was legitimate? Had Roz found out that Patricia's manuscript was a virtual duplicate of Sarah Winesong's?

As upsetting as these questions were, they were pushed aside by a bigger worry. "What did the police want?"

"They wanted Tony Nichols."

"Why?"

"Seems one of his students was murdered at her home in New Jersey yesterday. They didn't give me her name, but the cops said Nichols's name and phone number were found at the scene of the crime in a lovely little place called Benton Convent. They showed up here because his secretary at the university said he'd visited you at Cauldron Press in New York. I'm sure they'll turn up at his house next. What's going on?"

Her anxiety fast returning, Claire winced as lightning flashed, followed by a crack of thunder. As the storm lit up the room, Tony's digital clock blinked out altogether. "It was Patricia Snow."

"Who was?"

"The girl who was murdered, Tillie. Patricia Snow, the same person I came down here to interview about *The Poison Pen Pal* thing. We found out where she was staying, but when we went to see her, she was dead."

There was a long moment of silence. "Whoa. That complicates things quite a bit. Is Nichols there with you now?"

"No, darn it. Tillie, what time is it anyway?"

"What? It's ten past four. You don't know what time it is? Are you sure you're okay?"

Ten past four. The electricity must have gone off and on during the storm, switching the electrical clock back to twelve each time it surged back on. She'd been asleep for more than eight hours! "Yes, I'm okay. Now look, Tillie, I'm going to find Tony. And don't tell Mr. Harrison about Patricia Snow just yet. I'll do it soon enough."

"Okay. But I have some things about Tony Nichols I think you'd better know."

Claire fought to keep her voice noncommittal, but she could hear the bad news in Tillie's voice clearly. "What?"

There were sounds of Tillie scrambling through a notebook, then her puffing her cigarette into the phone. "Let's see. Well, out of the blue this morning I got a call from Damien. He wanted to talk to you about Mr. Nichols. Seems he thought he recognized him during the chat you three had in the hotel the other day. After checking with a friend over at another publisher, it all came together. Turns out Damien's friend edited one of Nichols's books.''

"One of his books? What are you talking about? Tony Nichols is a teacher, not a writer.''

"Have you ever heard of A. A. Nichols, Claire?''

She blinked, and a faint memory stirred in her head. "Yeah. No. I don't know. Who's A. A. Nichols?''

Tillie laughed. ''The *Good Food from a Good Guy* author. A handsome, bearded young man who roamed the continents looking for the perfect meal. *New York Times* bestseller list in the late seventies. I remember he was a darling of the talk shows, *Cosmopolitan* bachelor of the month, all that.''

"You're telling me Tony Nichols is A. A. Nichols, a cookbook author?''

"Yeah. Only it's ex-cookbook author now. He made a small fortune, which was quickly used up when he had to defend himself a few years back against a lawsuit involving a European publisher. Seems our boy was sued by a Greek woman for plagiarism. Damien said the last his friend heard, Nichols got out of writing after he lost the lawsuit and dropped out of sight. No one in publishing has seen him until he walked into your life at the Waldorf.''

Claire could hear the rain pounding furiously against the shake roof. Staring out the bedroom window at the swollen sea, she shivered. It was as if the same wind that bent the pliant sea grass against the wet sand was blowing inside the house as well.

"Claire?''

Tillie's voice tore her away from the view outside, forcing her numb mind to draw the obvious conclusion. Tony had been involved in a plagiarism suit and lost! The odds that he was doing the same thing now began to multiply. "So Mr. Harrison's suspicions about Tony Nichols were completely on target. He *is* a con man."

"He was involved in a lawsuit, Claire. Doesn't make him Al Capone."

"He was convicted, Tillie, for heaven's sake. How much proof do we need?"

"Whoa. Hold on Ms. Kennedy. I haven't been able to substantiate all this yet. And you know what a gossip Damien is. Besides, all the folks I talked to at the university where Nichols teaches think very highly of him."

"Did any of them mention the plagiarism conviction?"

"No. But where's your famous wait-and-see attitude? Or better yet, what do your own instincts tell you after spending a couple of days with him?"

Before she could reply, the phone went dead in Claire's hands. A tremendous clap of thunder shook the small house, and the shutters flapped against the windows. Placing the lifeless receiver back on the desk, Claire blinked back tears of humiliation.

Tony really could be a crook. Not the principled man standing up for a friend in trouble. But maybe a fraud who'd arranged a series of happenings to suit his own nefarious scheme.

Could he also have "arranged" Patricia Snow's death?

Too filled with hurt to feel as scared as she knew she should, Claire laced up her shoes, then zipped herself into her jacket.

Grabbing her purse, she went into the living room. With a shock, she saw the door was standing wide open.

The storm must have blown it open, she told herself as she crossed to peer out.

The rain was falling in torrents, obliterating all vision. She had to get to the main road and find someone to take her back to the Woodbury Inn. She had to go to the police, confess her amateur attempt at sleuthing and turn the whole mess over to them. If it meant trouble for Tony, well, he'd have to talk his way out of it, she decided.

Damn. Why am I always wrong about men! With that curse, Claire raced out into the storm. But she didn't get five steps away from the house before she saw a car turn into the drive, its twin beacons of light heading straight for her.

STOMPING DOWN on the gas pedal, Tony chewed on the thick filter of his cigarette. His eyes were bleary, and the sheet of rain falling on the windshield obliterated his view. Still it wasn't fatigue or fear of veering off the road that made him grip the steering wheel so tightly.

Roz Abramawitz's letter to Patricia Snow lay on the dashboard, its black ink stark against the refracted glare of his headlights.

The maid had given it to him at the Woodbury Inn checkout counter. ''This was in Ms. Kennedy's room, sir. You wouldn't want to forget it,'' she'd said, handing the envelope to him.

He'd intended to surprise Claire with her clean clothes and a special dinner. Then he'd fill her in on some news he'd learned during a call to his friend at the *Times* about the Newcastle buy out of Cauldron. But now that he had the letter, he realized Claire probably knew full well that Vincent Harrison had agreed to sell.

As the groceries clinked together in the back seat, Tony's scowl became full-fledged. If Claire had stolen this letter from Jeanette Snow's house the other day, the only conclusion possible was that he'd been duped.

She had to be in on the scam up to her beautiful little neck.

Skidding to a stop beside the dark house, Tony slammed the door of the Volvo and threw his cigarette to the ground. In three steps he was inside. His empty bed mocked him, the soft impression of Claire's body a further insult.

There were no clues to her whereabouts. The only note he found was the one he'd written to her hours ago. When he picked up the phone to call the Woodbury Inn, Tony found it dead.

How long had it been since she'd left? Had she taken a taxi, or had one of her coconspirators picked her up?

Racing out into the rain, which had slowed to a misty shower, Tony scanned the stretch of beach below. It was empty for miles in both directions. "Dammit." His curse died in the heavy air.

A figure, bundled against the rain in a black coat and hat, materialized out of the mist to his left. Then suddenly he caught a glimmer of blond hair in the distance.

Claire was running at the far end of the drive, turning left onto the two-lane highway. She appeared to be running for her life.

Then something else caught his eye. For a moment he didn't move, but then understanding dawned. The figure in black clutched a gun, a silver job that glinted even in the haze and gloom. With a yell, Tony took off in a dead run.

Chapter Nine

Struggling to keep her footing, Claire ran to the end of the muddy drive and out onto the two-lane highway. Though the rain had slowed considerably, she shivered in the damp heaviness of her clothes. Her jeans were soaked through, and she cursed the fact that she'd not put on her tights.

The thought of Tony sent more anger coursing through her veins. She increased her speed down the road toward the small town of Narragansett Bay. A quick glance over her shoulder told her his house was still dark. No headlights glared through the deepening evening.

Was he still inside looking for her?

A knifelike pain tore at her left side, and Claire slowed down to catch her breath. After seven years of late hours and New York taxis, she'd lost the endurance for running she'd built up in California.

How far away did Tony say the town was? Three miles seemed the right answer, and she began to run again, toward help and away from a confrontation that would break her heart.

Though she ordered herself to think of any subject but Tony, her mind strayed. She shook her head to banish the unsettling memories, and her anger helped her put another half mile between herself and Tony's house.

There were no other cars on the road. As the twinge in her side worsened, Claire slowed her pace to a walk, moving off the paved surface onto the dirt shoulder.

All around her, the marshland rolled away from the road down to Narragansett Bay. The water's surface sparkled, the oily blackness reflecting the retreat of the storm. Stars began to blink overhead, and Claire's temper cooled.

Abruptly she looked back toward Tony's. Maybe she shouldn't have run away before asking him for his explanation regarding Damien Laurent's story, she thought. After all, Tony didn't kill Patricia Snow. There were still no lights at his cottage, which was now just barely visible atop its elevated knoll two miles away.

Suddenly Claire turned away. She had to stick by her instincts and her resolve to tell her story to the police. They'd be able to find out what was going on without being sidetracked by the sexiness of Tony's laugh.

Straightening her back, Claire marched down the highway. After twenty or so steps, an insidious crackling noise behind her caused her to stop cold. Turning, she saw nothing against the silhouette of scraggly cypress. The night was now bereft of all sound, too. Nothing moved. No wind blew, no night animal cried out, no insect buzzed. Beginning to run again, Claire kept her eyes straight ahead, trying to concentrate on the comfortable rhythm of her rubber soles.

Then she heard it again. Louder. A sort of crackling behind and to her left—the unmistakable sound of branches being thrashed by arms—and the thud of running feet.

Someone was chasing her.

Fear, sudden and potent, seized her as she kept her eyes glued on the road ahead. Last night she and Tony had discovered a body, and her only thought had been escape. The fact that there was an unknown person, a cold-blooded murderer, on the loose, had not really sunk in.

Until now.

Her throat constricting with a silent scream, Claire took bigger strides, trying desperately to outrun the unseen menace. Out of the corner of her eye she detected movement from an ominous form about fifty yards away, slightly ahead of her and crossing at an angle to intercept her course.

With a cry, Claire pushed her lungs and aching legs. Now a new noise bit into her mind. A pop. Followed in rapid succession by three more. Pop, pop, pop. The last generated a whoosh of air to the left of her face, followed by a decisive splat as the lead of the bullet flattened itself in a tree across the road.

Someone is shooting. At me! Oh, God! The adrenaline pumped through Claire, and she thought she'd pass out from the fear. Smack in the midst of this panic, her terrified mind picked up a new threat.

Lights, car lights, were coming right at her, less than a mile down the road.

Was this gunman's cohort arriving to assist? As the car ahead hit a dip in the road, another set of headlights was revealed behind it!

Desperately Claire crossed away from the gunman to the other side of the highway, and sobs broke loose from her aching throat. But she wouldn't surrender. She scrambled through the muddy vines, tripping but keeping herself upright as she tore through the underbrush deeper into the copse of trees.

She'd give whoever was out there a run for their money, or die trying. Another burst of adrenaline sent her crashing deeper into the woods just as the cars skidded to a stop.

THE RHODE ISLAND state troopers were making no effort to hide their doubts about Claire's story. They'd seen her duck into the woods and had surrounded her within minutes. When she'd realized who they were, she'd been delirious with relief. But her anxiety was beginning to build again as they continued to question her account of the gunman.

"Now tell me again what happened, miss. Someone was shooting at you and you thought my officers were the perpetrator's reinforcements?"

Claire rattled through the whole thing again, letting herself sound as if she was about to cry. Maybe that would move them to do something. "I'm sorry I didn't recognize your cars as police vehicles. I never would have run away. Now please, can you start looking for him?"

With an indulgent edge to his voice, the trooper gave the order to his men to start searching the area.

Several minutes passed but they found nothing. The tall young policeman told to keep an eye on Claire peered at her intently. "Sure you heard gunshots, ma'am? The woods are full of funny sounds at night. Might've been an animal."

"I'm sure, officer. Unless the squirrels around here spit lead projectiles. There's no sign of anyone?"

The trooper looked out to where his partner and the two cops from the other cars were searching the marshy woodland. They'd pointed their car's headlights toward the woods, creating an eerie moonscape of monster shadows.

"Not so far. But there's plenty of footprints leading to and from the cottages and the boat houses down by the bay. Might've been a couple of people running around out there. There are lots of fresh prints. I've called in for more help, but those prints might belong to some locals. Don't worry, though. No one can hurt you now."

With a flash of new fear, Claire suddenly remembered that Tony was back at his house, alone.

What if the murderer had gone for him?

Panicking, Claire grasped the trooper's arm. "Please, could you drive me down the highway about two miles? My friend is there, and I need to check if he's okay."

"If you've got a friend around these parts, what were you doing running down the road at night by yourself?"

Flushing at the cop's increased scrutiny, Claire chose her words carefully. Despite her plan to let the authorities handle things, she didn't want to waste the time filling them in on all the events of the past two days. "I was out jogging—I do it every night. Please, can we go?"

"Just a minute. What's this friend's name?"

"Tony. Tony Nichols. He's a professor at the university and—"

"I know who he is. I know real good who he is. As a matter of fact, that's who we were coming to see when we spotted you."

Claire blinked. With a quick flash of insight she remembered Tillie's warning that the police were looking for Tony. "Why? Why were you going to see him?"

Before he could answer, the other policeman started shouting. Ignoring the young trooper's directive to stay put, Claire ran alongside him across the muddy land, down toward a boat shed that sat half-concealed behind a thicket of trees.

The three other cops stood in a half circle outside the dingy shack, staring at the closed door. "Police. Come out with your hands up."

The young trooper pulled Claire away, shielding her with his body. All four of the cops had their pistols drawn. Her heart beating wildly, she wondered if she was on the verge of finding out who'd been chasing her, who'd fired the shots.

Who'd killed Patricia Snow.

"Come on out, or we're coming in."

Cringing with anticipation, Claire held her breath as the sagging wooden door swung open. The shock of recognition almost made her faint.

As soon as TONY regained consciousness, he heard the voices. Rising unsteadily, he peered out the dust-caked window and saw the glaring headlights aimed down from the road. He now had another bump on the head, this one an egg-size lump at the base of his skull.

As he stood fingering it, two tall uniformed figures were walking about a hundred yards up the hill, flashlights aimed down, as if they were tracking an animal.

Frantically he looked around the small boat shed. He'd followed the crazy who'd been chasing Claire. Thanks to a padded jacket and ski mask, he hadn't been able to tell if the person was a man or a woman. Which made the fact that the bozo had crept up behind him and knocked him out with the butt of the pistol even more infuriating.

He kicked a rotting fishnet out of the way, then tried his strength against the tiny window at the back of the shed. It was nailed shut, and a helpless rage swirled in his gut. *I suppose I should be glad the bastard didn't shoot me.*

When the cops found him in here with the gun that lay on the floor next to him, it'd be impossible to explain.

At least Claire was okay. Tony was sure she hadn't been hit by a bullet. Even though anger at her flooded through him, he didn't want her to get hurt.

Besides, there was still a possibility she had only stolen the letter in a fit of panic, a way to protect her precious Cauldron Press, no matter what it cost Patricia Snow, or him.

Whatever the deal was, it now looked like one of the conspirators had decided to cut Claire permanently out of the picture. Just like they'd cut Patricia out.

The voices were closer. He heard victory in their tone and knew he'd been spotted. Flattening himself against the wall, away from the window, Tony made a jerky move toward the gun. With this motion the room spun and his eyes felt as if they'd roll out of their sockets.

He slumped to the floor, hands on his temples. It was useless to try to hide the gun. But maybe if they took his wounds into consideration, they'd believe him. Even if he were arrested, with any luck he'd be out of jail in a couple of days.

He glanced up as the spotlight beamed through the dirty pane of glass. When he did get free, he had one plan of action. He was going to interview Sarah Winesong himself. In the flesh.

Following the cops' orders, Tony stepped from the murky darkness of the boat shed with his arms up. He scanned the assembled group. His eyes stopped dead when they met Claire's.

On her face warred two emotions: shock and betrayal.

"OFFICER, HOW MANY TIMES are you going to ask me the same question?" Claire's voice was weary and beginning to sound antagonistic.

She'd been over the events of the day at least ten times and was ready to sign her statement, but still the trooper pushed on.

"As many times as I need to hear the answers. I think you're leaving certain things out of your story, Ms. Kennedy. May I remind you again that concealing evidence is a felony?"

Claire stared evenly at the police captain across the scarred metal table in his office. "Am I under arrest?"

"No, of course not." The trooper smiled. "And I apologize for keeping you so long, after your ordeal. But I'll ask you again, did you know Patricia Snow?"

"No. I never met her."

"How long have you known Tony Nichols?"

"Two days."

"And you've been staying at his house?"

Claire banged her fist on the table. "No. I have not been staying at his house. I visited his house for the first time today. I'm registered at the Woodbury Inn in town."

"But you didn't sleep there last night? Where did you sleep last night, Ms. Kennedy?"

Claire bit her lip. Overruling her conscience, she'd chosen not to admit that she and Tony had been driving from Benton Convent and sleeping in parking lots all night. Claire knew it was a crime not to confess that they'd been the ones who'd found Patricia Snow's body, but she couldn't bring herself to open that can of worms right now.

All she wanted to do was talk to Tony. The police had recounted Tony's story to her about the figure in black, and she believed it. But the cops didn't. The only way out of this mess was for her to get back out there and find out who was trying to destroy them all. "I did not sleep at Mr. Nichols's house last night. Now may I go?"

The captain tipped back in his chair, his belly overhanging his belt. "Okay, Ms. Kennedy, but you're going to have to come back. As soon as we catch that person who was shooting at you, there's going to be a trial."

"Fine." Claire stood and walked toward the door, then turned and said, "I'd like to talk to Mr. Nichols."

The captain laughed, then settled his chair flat on the pockmarked linoleum. "Well, until we get a ballistics report on that gun we found in the boat shed, I guess that would be okay. We can't charge him until we've got more evidence he was lying. Unless you have some reason we shouldn't believe him?"

Claire's mind raced through the doubts she'd had about Tony these past few days, her certainty he was a con man. But all her fears about him were now gone. "I believe him completely, and you should, too."

Shutting the door behind her, she sighed. Then she saw Tony. The troopers had left him handcuffed by his left hand to one of the chairs bolted to the floor outside the captain's office.

He didn't meet her eyes, but turned away to fumble in his pocket. He took out his cigarettes and matches, clumsily managing to light one with one hand.

The tobacco smoke burned Claire's chapped nose. She stared at him and felt irrationally miffed that he was smoking. Her reaction made her grin. People were trying to kill them and she was worried about his dying early from smoking.

"What's funny?" He didn't look at her.

"Nothing. I told these guys I believed your story, Tony. I'm sure they'll let you go, once they verify where you were earlier today."

Tony still didn't look at her, just blew three smoke rings toward the peeling green ceiling. "Thanks."

His single-word response was full of poison.

"I'm sorry I ran away from your house when I saw you. I was mad, and hurt that..." Claire's voice trailed off. She didn't want to tell him about Tillie's phone call and Damien Laurent's revelation about Tony's life as a cookbook writer. This wasn't the place for a heart-to-heart about his past.

Tony turned his dark gaze on her. He dropped the cigarette onto the scuffed floor and ground it out. "Why don't you stop the act, Claire. You guys are going to pull this off, there's no need to keep pretending."

"Pull what off?"

His laugh had a jagged edge. "The scam. Winesong's reputation will be restored, you guys will give Newcastle a good deal on the company, and everyone will be happy. Except, of course, Patricia Snow."

"Tony, what—"

"That's enough, Claire. Don't lie to me anymore. I've been set up once before, but that gal was an amateur when it came to a frame."

Claire's mind was spinning. His bitterness shocked her, scared her even more than the gunman had. She swallowed back fresh tears. "I need to talk to you about Billings Newcastle as soon as you get out of here. I've got a couple of theories that might explain *The Poison Pen Pal* fiasco."

For a moment Tony just stared at Claire. His cheek quivered as he clenched his jaw, then relaxed it. His eyes were unreadable. "I found the letter from Roz, Claire. I know you stole it from Mrs. Snow."

"Tony, it's not what you think...."

"Give it up, Claire. Just tell me something. Did you know it was coming? Or was it just luck that the one piece of solid evidence that Patricia's book was real fell into your hands?"

Claire crossed in front of Tony and sat beside him. Her heart was pounding. She couldn't stand for him to think she'd lied to him. Used him. Her control was slipping and her voice shook. "It *was* luck in a way. I did take it, but I was going to tell you about it as soon as I talked to Mr. Harrison."

"Sure. Mr. Harrison would have been delighted to let me in on Abramawitz's letter, right? Please, don't insult me any further."

With a wrench of understanding, she saw she was losing him. She'd broken the law, and now it seemed as if she'd broken any chance she had to ever really reach Tony's heart. "You don't understand. When I saw that letter from Roz, I just reacted."

Tony turned away from Claire. "You're the one who doesn't understand, Claire. The police have a lot of evidence against me. According to the captain here in Narragansett Bay, the cops in Benton Convent are going to put out a warrant for my arrest for the murder of Patricia Snow."

Blinking several times, Claire tried in vain to swallow. "That's...that's ridiculous. Didn't you tell them I can give you an alibi for that hour?"

"No, I didn't. Because you can't. You were with me, and you've just given sworn testimony that I'll bet didn't say a word about our activities last night."

"I'll go back in and explain everything."

"Give it up, Claire. They'll never believe you now."

The truth of his words hit home. "What time did the police say she was killed?"

"About ten."

"Well, tell them to check with Pearl Loney. We were with her. She'll vouch for that. Then they'll let you go."

"Right. Except that Pearl Loney has conveniently disappeared. I tried to reach her earlier today at the hotel in Benton Convent, and they said they hadn't seen her all day. Her office is locked up tight."

Claire got up and paced in front of Tony. She had to do something, anything to regain some control. "I'm sure she'll turn up. And once the troopers check all the facts, you'll be free. You can come to New York and we'll find out who's really behind all this. Together—remember what you said in your note?"

His eyes narrowed as he shook his head. A part of him believed her, but a tiny doubt clung stubbornly. He decided to let the last bit drop. "You've done your job of sidetracking me and muddying the trail long enough. They've got the gun."

"What gun? The one used to shoot at me?"

He nodded, waiting.

Claire stopped pacing to stand with her hand poised just above the sleeve of his sweater. "So? They'll trace it and find out who owns it. Once the ballistics tests are back, the police will probably give you a medal for recovering it from that nut."

"No, they won't. Because it's my gun. It was stolen from my office yesterday."

"No! Are you sure it's your gun?"

"Yes, and it's got five bullets missing. Since you've told them you heard four of them tonight, what do you want to bet the fifth is the one in Patricia Snow's brain?"

It was back. The mistrust she'd seen in his eyes when their glances met as he walked out of the boat house. Claire now fully understood Tony's sarcasm and anger. He thought whoever had framed him—and she fervently believed he was being framed for Patricia Snow's murder—was working with her.

"Tony, I know you don't want to, but you have to trust me. I'll go back in there and tell them everything about Patricia Snow's manuscript, and Sarah Winesong's book, finding her body—"

He lashed out. "Then what? Offer me a deal? My silence about the Snow rip-off for your alibi? That duck isn't going to fly, Claire."

Claire backed away, shocked at the extent he doubted her. "Why not, Tony? They'll believe me, and we can tell them how we found Patricia's body, how you called in the anonymous tip, then they'll know you're innocent—"

"Do me a favor, Claire. Don't help me anymore. Besides, you've got your own problems to deal with. Someone's trying to kill you, remember?"

Claire suddenly felt faint and would have fallen but for Tony's quick reflexes. He reached out and grabbed her with his free hand. Her arm tingled at his strong touch.

But before Claire could lean down and wrap her arms around him, and convince him to trust her, his jailer walked in.

TILLIE MET the five-thirty train on Saturday as it pulled into Penn Station. If she was shocked at Claire's appearance and weary greeting, she kept her feeling to herself.

"Well, Ms. Kennedy, I presume. How you holding up, kiddo?"

Claire rolled her eyes and pushed her bedraggled hair off her forehead. "Great. Rhode Island will be my first choice for a vacation spot next year. What have you been up to? I tried to get you late Thursday night."

"Thursday? I was, uh, out. A lady in my building was ill. I took her soup."

Everyone was acting abnormal, Claire thought to herself. Tension unhinges the strongest. "How's Mr. Harrison doing?"

"He'll survive. He always does. Sometimes I think none of us really knows just how strong he is, Claire. He tore out of the office yesterday morning after he threw Roz out and said he was going to take Newcastle head-on. Maybe he's found out something that will end this mess." Tillie pulled her car into the traffic, heading in the direction of Claire's place. "Do you want to stop and eat before I take you home?"

"Thanks, no. I just want to get home and shower and sleep. The police kept me up all last night."

"Are they going to charge you with stealing the mail? They hanged Jesse James for that, didn't they?"

"Very funny. I don't know what they're going to do. I admitted to Tony I took the letter, but I don't know if he told the police about it or not. They never mentioned it."

"You said on the phone they're going to charge him with murdering Patricia Snow?" Tillie asked the question quietly, but Claire cringed as if she'd shouted it.

"I thought so. But I really don't know what the police are going to do. I feel so guilty for not telling them we were the ones who found Patricia's body...but that would have opened a whole new can of worms."

Tillie frowned. "Maybe you should have."

Something in the older woman's voice unnerved Claire. "What is it, Tillie? What's wrong?"

"Nothing." She pushed in the rusty chrome lighter on the dash and rummaged for her cigarettes. "I just don't want anything to happen to you, Claire. Things have gotten too dangerous for you to keep poking around. Didn't your close call make that clear enough?''

''The only thing that's clear is that I'm going to try to reach Sarah Winesong first thing tomorrow. It's time I sat down with her and asked her point-blank about *The Poison Pen Pal*.''

Tillie increased her speed, inhaling deeply. ''That might be unwise until you speak to Mr. Harrison.''

''Tony needs my help now, Tillie, but I have to make sure Winesong's involved before I can be of any good to him.''

''Do you think she'll stay with Cauldron Press after you talk to her?''

''I hope so, but that's not the biggest issue here, Tillie.'' Claire's voice was steely. ''There's been a real murder. This is real life, not fiction.''

''How much do they have on your Mr. Nichols?''

Claire ignored Tillie's deliberately chosen *your*. Romance was always on the sixty-year-old spinster's mind. ''The trooper who drove me to the station said there's a lot of physical evidence linking him to it. They found his fingerprints on the bottle the girl was drinking from before she was shot. And one of his cigarettes was found in the ashtray. Of course if the tests on his gun match up to the bullet . . .'' Claire's voice trailed off.

''This thing is as confusing as one of our mysteries.''

''You're certainly right there, Tillie. And we've got to unscramble it, not only for Tony's sake, but for the reputation of Cauldron Press, as well.''

''Did you talk with him again before you left?''

''No. He didn't say a word to me when the police gave us both a lift out to his place. I just got my bag and stuff out of his car and the trooper took me back into town.''

"They must believe Tony Nichols is your boyfriend." Tillie's voice was strained. "You'd better explain to them you just met the guy."

Claire shook her head, slightly embarrassed at the disapproval in Tillie's expression. Her assistant was conservative, from the sensible rubber-soled shoes she favored to her love of Ronald Reagan.

It was pointless to try to hide from the fact that her feelings for Tony had ruined her ability to think clearly. "I did tell them I was in town to see Patricia Snow about a manuscript. None of the rest of it came up, although it probably will."

"Of course it will. Surely Nichols will voice his suspicions about Cauldron."

"I don't know about that. He hasn't yet."

"That's odd. Why would he jeopardize himself?"

"I don't know, Tillie, I don't know. But somehow I think Tony has his doubts about Cauldron Press's being the culprit. He mentioned Billings Newcastle this morning. I think he might have some evidence that implicates him in all this. Unfortunately he wasn't about to share it with me. He hates me, I think." Claire's voice had grown faint.

"I'll bet." Tillie's voice made it clear she thought nothing of the sort. "You don't believe Tony Nichols murdered that girl, do you?"

Claire didn't hesitate a second. "No. Of course not— I was with him at the time she was shot. But someone has gone to great lengths to make it look like he did. Which proves more than anything else that his story about Patricia's manuscript is at least partially true."

Tillie's manner was guarded. "Which part?"

"She told the truth about showing the manuscript to someone. I think she must have sold it to someone.

Someone who doesn't want that fact proved. Why else would she end up murdered?''

Tillie shook her head as she turned onto Claire's street. "Beats me, honey. But don't worry about Mr. Nichols. All the police will have to do is locate this Pearl Loney, and he'll be in the clear, fingerprints and cigarettes notwithstanding. It's you I'm really worried about. Do you have any idea why someone would shoot at you?"

"The more I think about it the more I'm sure they'd intended to get Tony. The door of his place was open when I woke up, and I'd bet that whoever was shooting at me had been in the house. They could have killed me then if that was their true intention."

Riding the horn to move a stubborn taxi away from the curb, Tillie swung her battered Oldsmobile into a space in front of Claire's apartment building. "I'll bet Tony Nichols shows up at your door as soon as they let him loose."

Claire shook her head. "The police said he had to stay in Rhode Island. I may never lay eyes on the man again."

Inside Claire's apartment, Tillie left the younger woman sitting on her bed while she ran her a bath and made tea. Leaning back, Claire closed her eyes, racking her brain for the answers to the questions that seemed too numerous to address.

Quite suddenly she saw Tony in her mind's eye, blowing out the lit match as he'd stuffed an unsmoked cigarette into his pocket that night at Patricia's.

How could the police have found a cigarette butt with his prints on it? Someone must have planted one there, after stealing it from his house or office.

"Come on, kiddo, into the tub. Then it's omelet time." Tillie's raspy cheerful voice propelled Claire into the bath, away from all the questions clamoring in her head.

After a meal that Claire didn't taste but dutifully ate, Tillie marched her back into her bedroom and tucked her under the lace-trimmed sheets.

"Now close your eyes and forget about everything. I'll stay here with you and that canine impersonator of yours, then we'll run down Mr. Harrison tomorrow. By Monday this whole thing will be a bad memory."

"Stop being mean about Woofer." Claire smiled at her cockatiel who was soaring around her bedroom. The bird loved to roam free, and he'd been ignored ever since they'd come in.

"Thanks for taking care of him while I was gone, Tillie. You don't have to stay with me, though. My watchbird will handle security."

"Are you sure?"

"I'm sure. And don't worry about dealing with Mr. Harrison on your day off. I'll get in touch with him tomorrow, then I'll fill you in on everything at the office Monday. But before you leave, tell me about Roz."

Tillie grimaced, then lit another cigarette, her fifth in the last half hour. "Well, although the rumors are really flying, I can't figure out what she's up to. Everyone says Billings Newcastle sent her over Thursday morning with the contracts that would cement the sale of Cauldron Press to Usherwood Publications."

"What? Mr. Harrison agreed to sell?" Tony's veiled accusations about her supposed ties to Newcastle came back to Claire's exhausted brain.

"Now don't get excited. I think it was just Newcastle's usual guerrilla tactics, carried out with fitting ability by Abramawitz. But I'm sure it didn't work, because Mr. Harrison's secretary said she heard a lot of screaming and yelling coming from his office. When Roz left, she shouted, 'You'll be sorry you ever tried to pull this off, Vincent!' and slammed the door."

"Why would Newcastle entrust Roz with something that important?"

"Rumor has it she's been promoted to editor-in-chief at Usherwood. When I called Damien yesterday, he asked me straight out if it was true Mr. Harrison was selling Cauldron. He also asked me how you made out with Tony Nichols. It's obvious he suspects we're up to something with the guy, although he thinks Nichols is going to try his hand at mystery fiction instead of cookbooks."

Ruefully Claire shook her just-washed hair. She still had so many questions, and she wished Tony was with her now.

"What *are* you up to with this guy, Claire?"

There it was. The direct question Claire had been dreading. Carefully she framed her answer. "I believe him, Tillie. I have no proof that his wild claims are true, but after spending some time with him, I believe him."

"You're going to try and prove Sarah Winesong stole *The Poison Pen Pal* from that poor dead girl?" As she spoke, all the life drained from Tillie's face. She looked like a doll made from a dried apple.

"I just want the truth, Tillie. If Winesong did steal it, or buy it, or hire someone else who did, we won't be able to publish the book."

Silently Tillie pushed her half-frame glasses back up her skinny nose and stood up. Her shoes squeaked against the hardwood floor. "You have to keep me informed of what you find out, Claire. I don't want you doing this alone."

"I'm glad I can count on you."

After Tillie let herself out of the apartment, it was a while before an uneasy sleep claimed Claire.

Tony had been knocked out, twice. She'd been shot at after being chased through muddy woodland. A girl had been murdered. Were these events all the work of one person?

Claire closed her eyes tightly. It was too horrible to think how far the ring of deceit could widen among people she knew.

Chapter Ten

Tony doused the headlights and sat back to light a cigarette. The street was deserted except for a lone figure heading toward the entrance of Claire's building. The person, bundled in a long raincoat and black hat, continued on past the entrance, and Tony relaxed.

Whoever shot at Claire could return for another try, but everything looked peaceful for now.

Studying the windows of the graceful, hundred-year-old building, Tony counted up three stories. All Claire's lights were out. Well, what did he expect at four in the morning? That'd she'd be sitting up with candles burning, pining for him?

These silent questions increased his remorse over his behavior yesterday. Shaking his head, Tony cursed and flipped the butt of the cigarette out the window.

If only he'd not been such a jerk to Claire at the police station. If only he'd asked her to stay and talk a little more before she left his house. If...if...if... His behavior tormented him. In an attempt to keep his personal history from repeating itself, he'd done to Claire what he'd accused her of.

He'd judged her, didn't keep an open mind. Because of his animosity toward Billings Newcastle, he'd never given Claire the benefit of the doubt.

Flinging the Volvo door open to the crisp chill air, Tony stepped out and slammed it behind him. It was time to put prejudice aside. Claire Kennedy was everything she seemed: honest, forthright, principled.

He was going to tell her that. If she was asleep, he'd just sit in front of her door until daylight, then pound on it until she let him in.

But would she be interested in anything he had to say? The question slowed him down, and with his head cocked to one side in his distinctive manner, he kept walking. Maybe. At any rate, it was time to stop pushing aside his feelings for her because of the damned complications of Patricia Snow and Cauldron Press.

Crossing into the light shining on the sidewalk, Tony smiled at a trio of young toughs walking toward him. They glared back, but he didn't mind. Even with the possibility Claire would slam the door on him, he couldn't wait to see her.

CLAIRE MOVED STIFFLY around her apartment, her sore muscles mementos of her flight through the marshy woods. Chilly in the scant lace teddy, she removed her favorite silk shawl from the back of a dining-room chair and wrapped it around her shoulders.

Though it was barely four in the morning, she was wide-awake and restless. Pausing in front of the hutch that housed her VCR, she considered a movie. No, she decided, walking into her darkened kitchen, she'd do something quieter.

Like eat. Maybe food could numb the ache that gnawed at her ever since she'd left Rhode Island.

Staring into the refrigerator, Claire was shocked to see most of the shelves empty. This was something she rarely let happen. Though she usually had to put dinner off until ten or later, Claire enjoyed well-balanced, home-cooked meals. *Just like Mother never made.*

Sighing over that little zinger from her childhood, she opened a bin. A brownish onion and a shriveled tomato rolled toward her. She'd not shopped on Thursday. On Thursday she'd been in Rhode Island.

With Tony.

Merely thinking his name made her miserable. This is impossible, she told herself. Everything that happened between them was touched by anger and mistrust. Two ingredients fatal to love.

Love? Claire shook her head and reached into the freezer for the double-chocolate-chip Häagen-Dazs. Dishing out half of it into a blue china bowl, she grabbed a spoon and returned to the living room. Collapsing into the overstuffed chair, she dug in.

Suddenly she heard measured, careful footsteps outside her door. She waited. The footsteps moved on, steadily growing fainter until they were completely gone.

Giddy with relief, Claire got more comfortable. She wasn't one to be skittish about living alone, but tonight she wished she had a roommate. *A black-haired, broad-shouldered roommate.* Ignoring that thought, she dug into the ice cream again.

As the cool sweet comfort melted down her throat, various plans of action skirted across her consciousness. It was too early to call Mr. Harrison. And, though the telephone beckoned, making her hand tingle at the thought of the rich vibrations of Tony's voice, she couldn't call him, either.

He'd made it clear he didn't want to speak to her.

Depressed by the thought, Claire rose and crossed the shadowy room to Woofer's cage. She rubbed the cool antique brass. Like most of the things she collected for her apartment, this had been carefully chosen. After a childhood without permanent furnishings, she'd become a veritable pack rat about acquiring things, especially solid heavy chairs or anything chintz-upholstered.

Her ex-husband hadn't fought her attorney's plan to buy out his interest in the condominium apartment, and she'd never regretted it.

It was home. Her first, and she loved it.

Fighting unexpected tears—"Good, old self-pity," she scolded herself aloud—Claire removed the flowered cover from the cage. "Wake up birdbrain. I need company." Her greeting netted her a playful bark and growl from her green-and-yellow friend, who hopped up and down restlessly to be let out. "Okay, okay. But you can't have my ice cream."

The bird jumped through the cage door, then soared up to the valance above the sheer lace drapes. Watching Woofer's antics, Claire sat back and continued eating, her brain racing.

She should have asked Tony about Damien Laurent's story. Was the Greek woman who sued him for plagiarism the same one he'd lived with, but never married?

As she pondered that, more questions sprang to mind. What about Roz Abramawitz? Would Mr. Harrison have any chance at all against Newcastle if Roz made the connection between Winesong and Snow?

Fat chance, she thought. Roz would broadcast to the whole publishing industry that Usherwood had been sent a manuscript identical to *The Poison Pen Pal* by one unknown, now dead writer.

Quietly Claire scraped the last mouthful from the bottom of the bowl. Plagiarism was the worst sin imaginable to people who took pride in the creative process. As an editor, she'd been crushed when Tony had leveled his charges against Cauldron.

It must have killed him to live through his trial and conviction, she realized. The cockatiel landed on her shoulder, and she made kissing sounds at it. "The worst part of it is, Woofer, that until Tony found that damn letter I stole, he believed me." Woofer cocked his head and soared off.

A noise from the direction of her door diverted her attention. Turning her head, Claire stared through the shadows. Now what? She listened, hoping not to hear the sound again.

But she did. A tiny squeak of wood followed by the rotation of metal against metal.

Someone was turning the knob.

In a quick glance Claire noted the door chain hanging unengaged. And she hadn't noticed before that the dead bolt was open. *Oh no, I didn't lock up after Tillie left last night!*

Claire slowly lifted the china bowl off of her lap and put it and the spoon on the floor. Clutching her shawl, she tiptoed toward the bedroom, but then stopped. The rattling was getting louder, the grinding serious now. Whoever was in the hallway was trying to jimmy the lock.

The gunman from yesterday! she thought. Claire's skin was damp with perspiration, her stomach a frozen ball of fear. She glanced around for a weapon. In the umbrella stand next to the desk, an English, marble-headed cane gleamed in the half light of the room.

Claire grabbed it and changed direction.

There wasn't time to call the police, but she'd scream her lungs out if she had to. Surely one of her neighbors would hear.

Her hand gripped the cool heavy stick as she waited. The noise at her door had stopped. Had the person outside heard her? Were they poised, waiting to break the door down and attack? For several minutes she didn't move, the tension making her arms tremble.

No longer able to stand the suspense, she moved the last three feet to the door. With stiff fingers she engaged the bolt then jumped back, raising the stick higher.

Instantly footsteps approached, followed by a soft knock. "Claire? Are you awake?"

Incredulous, she lowered the stick and stared blankly at the partition separating her from a man whose voice she'd instantly recognized. "Tony?"

"Yes, it's me, Claire. Open the door."

Relief flooded through her, nearly making her nauseous. She was going to have to invest in a king-size bottle of antacid if she had much more to do with Tony Nichols!

She fumbled with the dead bolt, then pulled the door open. Above her, Woofer began yapping, his Doberman pinscher impersonation in top form as he buzzed down from the draperies toward the man she let in.

"What on earth are you doing here?"

"This," he replied, enveloping her in his arms and crushing her against him. Claire was too surprised to struggle against his kiss, and after a moment she joined in wholeheartedly.

As Tony tightened his arms around her, Woofer dive-bombed from above, barking madly. "Ow! That damn thing pecked me." Tony ducked his head and took a swipe at the attacking bird.

Claire started to giggle, because he'd missed the bird by several feet. They both began to laugh, leaning against each other for support. Finally Claire wiped her eyes with her left hand, realizing she still clutched the cane for protection.

"Where in the world did you get that?"

She smiled and put her weapon down. "Damien Laurent gave it to me last Christmas. He collects them. I carry it with me when I jog. It makes a great show of force."

"I'll bet." Tony slipped his arm down around her waist, seemingly content to stand in her entryway forever.

"What were you doing out in the hall?"

He pushed his curling hair off his forehead. "I'm sorry. I was going to wait until you were up, and I was just checking to be sure your door was locked."

Claire immediately sobered. She moved away from Tony into the living room to snap on a table lamp, then met his eyes. They glittered like agate. "Why did you come here, Tony? You're supposed to stay in Rhode Island." A sudden hope sprinted into her mind. "Did they find Pearl Loney?"

"No, they haven't. I came to see you because I wanted to apologize."

"You're lucky I didn't shoot you."

"Do you also have a gun? I'm glad I live in Rhode Island."

"No. But you didn't know that." Claire felt vulnerable all of a sudden as Tony's eyes roved over her body silhouetted in the soft light. "What do you have to apologize for?"

"I was a jerk yesterday. I shouldn't have kept accusing you, badgering you like I did. You were the one who was being chased all over the place by some jerk with a gun."

She remembered a quote she'd read attributed to Ernest Hemingway: "You can tell the size of a man by the size of the thing that makes him mad." Claire understood Tony's anger at her yesterday; it was the same she'd had for him the day they'd met. "It's okay. But aren't you getting yourself into even more trouble by leaving the state?"

"Yeah, probably."

Claire pulled the shawl off the floor where she'd dropped it and swung it around her shoulders. She motioned for Tony to sit down. Her own legs were weak, both from the aftereffects of adrenaline and that welcoming kiss Tony'd delivered. "How did you make it past the doorman?"

"That clown? He was asleep. I buzzed him from the outside and he never even woke up. Since the lobby door was wide open, I just came upstairs."

Hearing a door creak in the hallway, Claire saw that hers was still standing open. She rose and went to close it, venturing a peek into the hall. Her neighbor, Mrs. Heinz, was leaning out of her apartment, her hair net pulled down over her eyebrows. "Are you okay, dear? I heard something...."

"Yes, thank you, Mrs. Heinz."

"Are you sure? I can call 911. They'll be here in an hour or so. Or I can call Mr. Mason. He has his World War II sword, you know."

Suppressing a smile, Claire used her most persuasive voice. The last thing she wanted right now was another interview with a policeman. "Really, I'm fine. But thanks again." With a friendly wave, she locked the door behind her and turned back to face Tony. "Well, at least

you didn't get attacked by my neighbors. You're lucky—
one of them has a sword."

"He should replace your doorman."

"It's obvious someone should. Maybe they'll hire me
when Cauldron Press closes down." Though she was sitting several feet away from him, Claire saw Tony flinch
at that remark.

"Maybe we can keep that from happening, Claire." He
stared at her a long moment. "I know you didn't steal
that manuscript from Patricia Snow. And I know I didn't
murder her. I was hoping we could work together and
prove it."

"Thanks for finally believing in me, Tony. And for
your information, I've decided to tell Mr. Harrison we
can't publish the Winesong book until all your accusations have been answered."

Tony patted his jacket pocket for a cigarette. "How do
you think he'll take that news? I thought he wanted
everything kept quiet."

"He did. But that was before—" suddenly the memory of Patricia's lifeless body sizzled through her mind
"—before all the violence. Mr. Harrison is, above all, a
reasonable man. He'll see we have no other choice."

"Are your instincts about people always right?"

A tiny smile accentuated the single dimple near Claire's
mouth. Slowly she nodded her head in the direction of
the front door. "Usually. Although I never would have
guessed you'd do such a convincing impersonation of a
watchdog."

"I guess you bring out the beast in me. Speaking of
beasts, where's that idiot bird?"

On cue, Woofer barked twice, then growled from the
direction of the bedroom. Claire felt her excitement grow.
Not just because Tony finally believed she had integrity,

but because he must care a great deal to come and see her. Had he even forgiven her for stealing Roz's letter?

Claire put off asking about that. "He's guarding my bedroom. He won't hurt you anymore."

"Where'd you get that thing? Trade in your pit bull?"

"He was an inheritance from my dad. He won him playing poker with a man who trained Dobermans."

"Hell of a pot." Tony glared at Claire, then for want of something better to do, ran his fingers along the stubble on his face, thinking he probably looked like those young hoods he'd seen outside on the street.

"He's a nice companion."

Chewing on the inside of his cheek, he nodded. "Interesting, anyway. So, what's next? Have you talked to Harrison?"

"Not yet. But I've got some things I want to check out at my office this morning."

"Yeah? Like what?"

As much as she trusted Tony, she didn't want to make any statements she couldn't back up with action. But she'd decided to get ahold of Sarah Winesong's address and go see her before Monday morning. "I'll let you know. Promise," she added, as a wary look crossed his face.

"Okay. I'll go with you. Until the police find who killed Patricia, I'm going to stay in New York."

"Why?"

"To protect you."

"Protect me? That's very sweet, but unnecessary."

Even to his own ears the words sounded corny. But he meant them. He wasn't going to let her out of his sight until Sarah Winesong, or whoever was behind all the mayhem of the past few days, was locked up. "I disagree. Like you said, I'm a great watchdog."

"No."

"No? What do you mean, no? You are the most stubborn—"

"I'm stubborn! What about you? You're supposed to be in Rhode Island. Until the troopers find the justice of the peace and get her corroborating story, you're under suspicion for murder. They're not going to take kindly to your disappearing act."

Lighting the cigarette he'd held in his hand for several minutes, he shook out the match, looking in vain for an ashtray. "Too bad. I'll prove they can trust me."

"Do you always decide to do your own thing, regardless of the law?"

Stiffening, Tony flushed. "What do you mean by that?"

Claire drew a deep breath, a little afraid to bring the topic up. "I'm talking about A. A. Nichols, the cookbook author. I'm talking about a lawsuit for plagiarism. Which you lost. Etcetera, etcetera. I'm talking about all the things regarding Patricia Snow you've probably decided not to tell me."

Tony sat immobile, his eyes looking off into the distance. "How did you find out about that, Claire? Who told you?"

"What difference does it make? All that matters is that *you* didn't."

The seconds stretched into minutes, and Claire began to shiver as Tony sat and smoked. Finally, unbuttoning his jacket, he sat back. "Okay. Let's talk."

Claire's heart pounded. Now that it was time to finally hear his side she had an urge to run.

"Several years ago, in the late seventies, I did a series of cookbooks. Recipes and gardening tips, natural-food lists, and things like that. All my years traveling around the country with my folks, I did the cooking. After college my experimenting paid off. I made a lot of money from my cookbooks, then went to Europe to play a while. I'd always wanted to try my hand at some other kind of writing, so I began researching a kid's history book. Outlined it, roughed up a hundred pages of character sketches of leaders, saints, outlaws.

"Not dry dates and battle stuff, but action pieces that could get a kid interested in the characters, not the historical-significance crap they try to give you in school." Tony paused, his eyes staring across the room.

"That's when you lived in Greece?"

"Yeah. Met a woman in Kornos whom I got involved with. She was a journalist, and she helped me type and did some editing for me. She was real supportive of the idea. I made plans to go to Paris to do some research, then on to London, but she didn't want to come with me, so we parted. I sent my book around and got a couple of bites, then a contract offer. The week after I signed, I was hit with a plagiarism suit. The book was never published, and she won her case."

Claire could almost taste Tony's humiliation. "But how could she win? How did she prove it?"

"She produced several drafts of my book, which she'd helped me type, and claimed they were hers. That, along with the expensive lawyers Billings Newcastle paid for, they did me in."

"Billings Newcastle!" She drew the silk shawl more closely around her at the mention of the man who was so famous for his underhand tactics. "Why did he get involved?"

"He was buying out the publishing house I'd worked with on my cookbook series. He'd made me an offer the year before to reprint for half my royalty fee, and I refused. Evidently this was his way of paying me back."

They both sat silently, waiting for the other's next words. Finally Claire spoke. "So that's why you've suspected Newcastle is connected to this scam. Did he set Patricia up to ruin Sarah Winesong and Cauldron Press?"

"Who knows? I was suspicious as soon as I heard the rumors a month ago that he was interested in buying Cauldron from Harrison. Then, when I got the galley copy of Sarah Winesong's manuscript to review and saw it was Patricia's, I thought, whammo, Newcastle strikes again."

"No wonder you were so angry."

Tony did not move his eyes away from Claire's as he recalled their first meeting. "I was a creep to you then, too. But for all I knew, Newcastle put you up to buying Patricia's book. It wouldn't be the first time he'd paid someone off inside a company to ruin it. That's his modus operandi. Then, when those notes on Newcastle were among the stuff stolen the following day, I was sure you had some part in it."

"I appreciate your telling me this, Tony. We've got to tell Mr. Harrison about it, too. He'll be better able to defend Cauldron Press against Newcastle if he's warned."

Tony shook his head, tossing the cigarette into the cold fireplace. "It may be too late, Claire. You're forgetting about Roz Abramawitz's letter. If Patricia sent a copy of her manuscript to Usherwood Publications, Newcastle has Vincent Harrison in a legal death grip over the rights to the book. You said yourself your contract and legal departments have no correspondence from her. Unless we can come up with the IOU Patricia told me she signed,

Cauldron may have no claim at all on the book. Which might be what Newcastle's planned all along."

"If Newcastle knows about the debate over which woman wrote *The Poison Pen Pal*, doesn't that prove he's the one who murdered Patricia Snow? To shut her up?"

"It's a sound theory, but I can't prove it yet, and neither can you. Once we find out who manipulated Patricia, either for a real manuscript or to blackmail Cauldron Press, we'll be a lot closer to proving who murdered her."

Claire buried her head in her arms, trying to think clearly for a moment. Billings Newcastle. She'd never even met him, and she wanted to kill him herself. Except there was something a little too pat about the whole thing, something she couldn't put her finger on.

A piece of the puzzle sat just outside the scope of her reach. The only thing clear about this mess was that Tony trusted her.

Didn't he? "A case could also be made, a lot more logically," she said, "that someone inside Cauldron murdered Patricia just to keep the scandal from being made public. Are you sure you've finally changed your opinion of me?"

Standing up, Tony walked over to where Claire sat, arms folded across her breasts, and picked up a strand of her golden hair. Rubbing it between his fingers, he spoke gently. "Nothing's changed. Not since the first instant I laid eyes on you."

Claire shook with a tremor of anticipation, wanting his touch, but holding back. "That line is too old to work in any book, Tony. Despite the fact I stole the letter from Mrs. Snow's, you don't think I'm a thief, or worse?"

"No. I think you are the most sensitive, highly principled, sexiest woman I've ever been bashed over the head by." Tony drew her out of the chair to her feet, his hands scalding her arms.

Claire backed away a step. "I'm sorry—"

"Don't be sorry. Be quiet." Tony pulled her closer until Claire was pressed fully against him, her lips only inches from his.

His gaze remained even with her wide brown eyes as he slid his right hand underneath the heavily fringed shawl, up her bare arm to her neck. Burying his left hand fully in the soft thickness of her hair, he kissed her.

As the seconds passed, Claire responded, her lashes finally closing with abandon as a groan escaped from deep within Tony. She held him hungrily, her slim fingers reveling in the luxurious thickness of his hair, the broad smoothness of his neck.

Breaking the kiss, Tony's smile faded to one of deeper need. He tossed the shawl onto the floor, reclaiming her mouth as more minutes passed. He moved to her cheek, murmuring. Then his tongue smoothly began to explore her lips, the curve of her cheek to her ear. Claire could barely restrain herself from dragging him down onto the floor.

But despite her jagged breathing and wobbly legs, Claire knew she and Tony should stop. There was so much to do still, the future of so many people in their hands.

Gently pushing her hand against his chest, she looked into his eyes. "Tony. Please stop."

For a second his eyes brimmed with confusion, then a curtain of impatience slipped halfway down. "Do you really want to stop, Claire? I will, but only if you tell me you really want to."

"I can't tell you that, because it would be a lie. And I hope never to lie to you, Tony. But there's so much between us still. Someone's framing you. Someone tried to kill me. They're ruining my company, and the livelihood of several people hangs in the balance. We need to decide what to do next."

"I thought that was pretty obvious a minute ago."

Ignoring his direct look at her bare thighs, Claire picked up her shawl and covered herself. She sat down in her chair in front of him. "We need a plan of action. Once we get the proof we need, we'll give all the evidence to the police. Then we'll be free to get involved with each other, Tony. If you still want me."

For several seconds he just stared down at her. Claire knew that their future together was riding on his answer. "I'll always want you."

She waited another second for the light to come back into his eyes. It did.

Tony smiled and reached down to wipe away a wisp of hair stuck to her lip. "But you'll have to help me. Go put some clothes on, and lock up that damn bird. Then maybe I can concentrate."

Somehow she found the strength to stand and smile. "I'll be right back. Don't start without me."

"Not a chance."

She leaned forward to brush a kiss on his lips when an explosion blew the silence and peace of the Sunday morning outside into a million shattered pieces.

They rushed to the window that overlooked the street and saw Tony's Volvo—or what was left of it. It had been blown to bits. Red and blue flames leaped higher by the second, and black smoke began to foam through the morning air.

Two teenagers were running down the street, their clothes tattered. If the ghastly form on the charred remains of the driver's seat was what Claire thought it was, the kids had left a friend behind. Dead.

Chapter Eleven

Damien Laurent's red silk robe was tied securely at the waist, a satin sleep mask pulled up over his hair. His bloodshot eyes bulged slightly at the sight of Claire and Tony standing at the front door of his brownstone.

"Claire. My God, it's not even nine o'clock! And Sunday. What's happened? What are you doing here?"

"Damien, can we come in? I'm really sorry to be so rude as to drop by without calling beforehand but Mr. Nichols and I need to speak with you."

Damien cast his eyes over Tony, then glanced at the box of pastries from the Pierre Hotel bakery in Claire's hand and bowed slightly. "Of course, love, come in. Do I smell a story for my column, as well as breakfast?"

Claire took a step, but Tony reached for her arm to stop her from entering the lavish foyer. "Mr. Laurent, before we take any of your time, we need to ask that whatever we tell you be kept off the record, and out of circulation, for a few days. If you can't promise that..."

Startled, Damien drew back. After a moment he smiled. "Oh, come in. Of course, I'll be as quiet as the proverbial church mouse." The critic winked at Claire as she and Tony stepped into the foyer. "Really, Claire, however do you find them?"

Her whisper was conspiratorial, but her attempt at good spirits sounded forced. "Just lucky, I guess."

Damien took the pink-ribboned bakery box and nodded for them to proceed into the living room. "Why do I have the feeling something bad has occurred, Claire?" His voice rose an octave. "Has something happened to Vincent? Or Aunt Tillie?"

"No, they're both fine. But Tony and I had a close call this morning. A bomb went off in his car, Damien, and a boy was killed."

Taking her arm firmly, Damien ushered them into his dramatic living room. "New York is really a challenging city to live in these days. Sit. Both of you. I'll get something to fortify us all."

As he disappeared into the kitchen, Claire exchanged a glance with Tony. "I hope I've made the right choice getting Damien involved in this."

"You said we could trust him, Claire."

"I'm sure we can, Tony, but what if he won't help us?"

"Then we'll go to someone else."

Claire drew in a shaky breath, then sat back into the cushy softness of the black suede sofa. This was no time for an attack of nerves, she told herself. "We need Damien's help, Tony. He can track down the Newcastle connection without drawing attention to Cauldron Press like Tillie or I would. But I don't want to put him in any jeopardy."

"He strikes me as a businessman who can take care of himself. What are you going to offer him in return for what he can do?"

"I'll offer him an exclusive scoop on a soon-to-break scandal, complete with cops, murder and mayhem. I'm sure he'll bite. Though I probably should clear this with Mr. Harrison first."

Tony gripped her hand, his lean face intense. "You haven't talked to him for two days. If we wait until tomorrow, it may be too late. We've got to act fast to get the goods on Newcastle. My car getting bombed proves it."

Claire gulped, remembering the grotesque sight.

"Whoever's behind this," Tony continued, "is no longer content with having me rot in jail. If that street punk hadn't hot-wired my car, I'd have been permanently silenced."

Realizing he was right, Claire shivered. She and Tony had gone down to the street and listened on the sidelines when the authorities showed up. The police said it was probably a homemade gasoline bomb, wired to the ignition.

One cop had interviewed her and asked if she had any idea whose car it was. She'd lied, adding yet another felony to her hit parade. "Let's not think about that now. We'll hope the murderer sees the story in the paper and assumes he got you."

"He?"

"Or she, okay?" Claire knew he was testing her resolve to find the truth, but she couldn't stop her knee-jerk loyalty to Sarah Winesong. Until she talked to the author herself, she'd hang on to her diminishing hope that the woman wasn't involved.

Claire searched in her gray tweed jacket for a Tums. "That's one of the things I'm going to check when we get to my office, if I can only find—"

Damien's return cut short her comment. "Here we are, darlings, java and croissants. The only civilized reason to be up before noon." Their host set an ebony lacquered tray down on the table in front of them, the china clinking merrily. As he passed around napkins and dishes, he studied them.

Claire took a cup and tried not to look nervous. "Your home is gorgeous since you had it redecorated, Damien."

"Thank you. Just like me after my chin tuck, right?"

As Claire chuckled, Tony fought the urge to leave. He wasn't totally comfortable with Damien. Though he found him likable, it seemed to him Laurent was trying to camouflage something.

"Well, Mr. A. A. Nichols, does this visit have anything to do with your reentry into the world of culinary literature?"

Tony shook his head. "No. Cookbooks are behind me, Mr. Laurent. Although my past association with a certain member of the publishing community is part of the reason I've come to you."

Damien wiped his mouth with the silver-bordered napkin and stared at Tony. "And which member is that?"

"Billings Newcastle."

Claire's stomach tightened. They could blow it all if she'd misjudged Damien's friendship. Fear wafted around her like stale smoke as she watched the two men weigh each other.

After several seconds, Damien sat back. "Mr. Newcastle is a very important man, Mr. Nichols. Just ask Claire. I understand the company she works for is about to become the latest jewel in his crown of publishing houses."

"That rumor is wrong, Damien," Claire shot back. "You know Mr. Harrison will never sell. Cauldron Press means too much to him."

All three were quiet for a minute as Claire's emotional declaration sank in. Finally Damien nodded. "You may be right. Vincent did tell me when he started out that once he got a few name authors, Cauldron would be strong enough to compete with anyone. With Sarah Winesong, his vision was realized."

"Until now." Tony leaned forward. A faint shadow of beard on his strong jaw was heightened by the theatrical lighting above.

"Cauldron Press is really in trouble, Damien," Claire said, nervously folding and unfolding her napkin. "And we think Newcastle has set up a series of events to force Mr. Harrison to sell out or have his business ruined. There's even the possibility of murder...."

Damien's gaze remained steady. "You mean the car bomb? It sounds to me like the police will call that an accident. New York street dopers trying to blow the car open, probably." He sipped his coffee.

"I'm not talking about Tony's car. Another person, a young writer, was murdered two days ago," Claire replied.

"A writer? Anyone I know?"

"No."

All three drank their coffee. "I see," Damien finally commented. "Not killed, murdered?"

"Complete with bullets, blood and the cops, Mr. Laurent. Which is why Claire and I need you to find out whatever you can about Newcastle's plans to acquire Cauldron, particularly the price he's paying, and if it's a fair market value. It's important that he not be tipped off. We don't want him to know we're on to him."

Damien raised an eyebrow. "Of course. I assume you have some reason for me not to go directly to Vincent for this information?"

"Yes, I do," said Claire. "Please, Damien. I want to help him. He's kept some financial dealings from me, and I can't put any more pressure on him now. But I need to know what we're up against with Billings Newcastle."

"You can help the publishing world rid itself of a piranha by helping us unmask Newcastle, Mr. Laurent."

"Even piranhas have their place in the scheme of things, Mr. Nichols. They clean up the refuse." Damien smiled coolly at Tony, clearly pleased with himself.

Claire ignored the gibe, and the jousting men, to get to the finish line. "We also need to know if Roz Abramawitz is part of the offer," she said.

"Your good friend Roz?" Something made Damien flinch, and he sat forward quickly. "Well, the plot thickens."

Claire knew the powerful critic well enough to see he was intrigued indeed. All she needed to do was persuade him it would be worth his while to help.

After a moment he stretched his long arms, cracking his fingers. "I can understand our dear Ms. Kennedy's instincts to protect and preserve Cauldron Press, Mr. Nichols. Next to Aunt Tillie, I'd say she loves that company more than anyone. But I don't quite understand how you fit into the picture."

"Let's just say my priorities are to help Ms. Kennedy."

The critic's laugh was sharp. "Ah, love. How refreshing. It is April, isn't it?" He turned to Claire, whose freckles were standing out prominently. "Why, Claire, I do believe you're leaving out a certain element in this story line."

She ignored his insinuation. "With your help, we can probably save Cauldron Press, Damien. You know Mr. Harrison will be grateful."

Damien blinked. "Oh, I'll make Vincent pay for my help, of that you can be sure. Okay, I'll find out what I can. Call me tomorrow at my office, in the afternoon. Even I need a little time, Claire."

"Thank you, I will." Kissing Damien lightly, Claire held hands with him as they walked to the door. She glanced back at Tony, who followed.

He was frowning, fighting the sense of foreboding that had grown since he'd pressed Laurent's doorbell. Had they made a mistake talking to Damien? What if he tipped Newcastle off?

As the door shut behind them and they descended the steps to the sidewalk, Tony linked his arm with Claire's. "Well, what do you think, Claire? Will he keep things confidential?"

"I'm sure he will. He loves idle gossip, but knows how valuable a story like this could be to his career. And he's been very loyal and supportive of Mr. Harrison for years. We don't have to worry about Damien. When he agrees to do something, he does it."

"You know him better than I do." Kissing her gently, Tony wrapped his arm tightly around her slim shoulders. She was so tough and businesslike, ferocious even, when it came to protecting her company. But lurking under the surface was someone as vulnerable as he was.

"He guessed we're involved, though. I hadn't planned on that," Claire said.

"So what? I can't wait to see the hot story about an ex-cookbook hack and the most beautiful lady editor in New York City being an item. It'll do wonders for my reputation."

Claire felt a rush of emotion. "Mine, too. Tillie will be delighted once she meets you." Nuzzling his shoulder,

Claire smiled. "Come on, let's go to my office and make some calls."

They moved off to hail a cab, and neither of them so much as glanced back.

Relieved, the person watching them from the shadows of the house next door to Damien's walked toward the critic's front door. With a black-gloved hand, the visitor pressed the buzzer insistently and waited, all the while tapping a silver-tipped cane against the concrete stoop.

"So THIS IS WHERE you spend eight hours a day."

"Make that twelve. Yeah, really great, huh?" Claire wrinkled her nose at the clutter and barely controlled crisis of manuscripts stacked on her desk. She gestured toward the small window behind her. "But there's this great view. Makes up for everything."

Tony walked behind Claire and gazed out at the bright green leaves of spring lightly scattered over the trees in Central Park. "It's beautiful. But with all the work in here, I'd wager you seldom get a chance to look out."

"You're right. Now, tear your eyes away from the view, come over here and sit down. We've got a lot to do."

Suddenly Claire felt Tony's warm lips on the back of her neck. His hands circled her waist in a possessive gesture.

"You're the view I can't take my eyes off."

Nestling into Tony's embrace, she savored his warmth a moment, then lightly pushed against him. "Behave, Tony, or I'll sic Woofer on you when we go back to my place—"

"Oh, no, anything but that!" With his hands raised in mock surrender, Tony laughed and released her. He walked around the ink-stained desk and faced her. "What's first?"

"Well, we need to ferret out Roz Abramawitz's home address."

"I love your idea of going to see her, but if you two don't get along, why do you think she'll see you on a Sunday?"

"I'm counting on shock value. Hopefully she'll be so surprised she'll let something slip about Newcastle's connection to Patricia Snow's manuscript."

"Yeah, let's hope the surprise isn't on us."

Claire pursed her lips thoughtfully, hearing the warning in Tony's words. Their plan to confront Roz with their hunch that Newcastle had defrauded Patricia Snow by posing as a representative of Cauldron was a big gamble. And they had no ace in the hole.

If Roz knew what her boss had done, they'd have to convince her to turn against Newcastle. On the other hand, if Newcastle had pulled all those strings without letting Roz in on it, she might be ticked off enough to want to expose the publishing czar.

Either way, Roz could be very dangerous. "Tony, do you want to wait and see what Mr. Harrison thinks about all this first?" Claire watched as he got that same hard look she'd noticed on their first meeting.

Turning away from her, he raised his hands. "I don't know what I think we should do next. It's dangerous to be charging around, sniffing for clues about Newcastle, but I'm doing it and you're right beside me. I think maybe I should just leave and go off on my own for a bit. After all, it's me the murderer is after."

"Don't be a nitwit, Tony. I was the one who got chased through the woods, remember? And who knows who that bomb was meant for? Damien might have been right, and it wasn't you at all. It could have been those kids, or it could have been meant for me."

"You?"

"I heard footsteps fifteen minutes before you showed up at my door this morning. Maybe it was someone who'd planned to leave a calling card for me."

He slumped against her desk and crossed his arms. "Okay. Let's charge ahead, but we've got to use some caution."

Pulling open the top drawer of her desk, Claire smiled. "Caution is the downfall of all the best poker hands. If you wait to raise the stakes, some shyster always takes the pot. We're going to go see that barracuda and find out some things. Today!"

Tony's rich swelling laughter filled her small office. "On that note, let me just add that I can't wait to get you in a good game of strip poker."

"I'd have you down to your underwear in three deals."

"Maybe. But not because I'd have a losing hand, Claire." His hungry glance rested on the softness of the gray cashmere sweater, then perked up. "Okay, what first?"

"I'm going to call Tillie."

"And I'll call my editor at the *Times*. He may have a bead on where Abramawitz lives, since she's not listed."

"Good idea. I should have thought to ask Damien. He knows where everyone sleeps." Claire felt Tony's eyes on her as she bent to reach for her purse. What, she wondered, would happen when *The Poison Pen Pal* real-life mystery was solved? Would Tony go back to Rhode Island? After a couple of months of weekend visits, would his ardor cool? Would hers?

A flash of loneliness overtook Claire as she realized that solving all the mysteries around her might mean the end of her relationship with him.

Leaving Tony dialing the phone at her desk, Claire marched out to the reception area to use another phone. She'd be ready to dump all the intrigue and maze of wrongdoing back in Mr. Harrison's lap once they'd found something solid on Newcastle.

She gave each of the drawers in Tillie's file cabinets a quick yank. Locked. "Damn," she muttered under her breath as she punched in Tillie's familiar phone number. "Hi, Tillie. Yes, I'm fine. Thanks again for being so good to me yesterday. Look, I'm at the office. I've looked in your Rolodex and mine and there's no information on Abramawitz's home address. Who can I call to find it?"

"Are you alone?" Tillie's tone was full of suspicion.

"Why are you asking?"

"Is Mr. Nichols okay? Is he there with you now?"

Frowning, Claire kept her voice calm. "Yes, he is, Tillie. Did you hear what happened this morning? Is that why you asked if he was okay?"

"I asked you that because you were so worried about him last night. What happened this morning?"

Briefly Claire told her about the bomb. "So, since things have escalated a bit, I'm going to try to go see Roz."

Tillie rattled off four names and numbers, paused, then said, "Maybe you should let the police handle this, Claire. They'll follow the trail and come up with a culprit."

"Yeah, but I'm convinced it wouldn't be the right one, Tillie. For that reason I need to ask you one last favor.

Where's the key to your file cabinets with all the writers' correspondence?''

"Why?"

"I want to check something. Don't worry, I won't mess anything up.'' For some reason she didn't want to tell Tillie she was planning on contacting Winesong. Tillie was so protective of her job as liaison with the recluse that she'd want to be the one to call. But Claire had no intention of letting Tillie into the line of fire.

"I've got it with me. Can it wait until tomorrow?"

Claire shrugged. The contract only carried Winesong's mailing address, which was a post office box, she remembered. And there'd be no way to check for a home address today because it was Sunday. "I guess so.'' She thought fast, then decided to risk hurting Tillie's feelings. "Where do you keep Sarah Winesong's phone number?"

The silence lengthened. "Tillie?"

"What are you going to do, Claire?"

"Nothing. Not right now, anyway. But I may need to call her soon, and I just want to have the number handy.''

"We don't have a number. She always calls us. Always, like in the three calls a year she makes. If we want to get ahold of her, we have to write, then she calls us back. All I can do is give you the names of some people who might know.''

Tillie sounded strained as she spoke. The sucking noise told Claire she was inhaling deeply on a cigarette. "Damn, I'd forgotten that little eccentricity. Okay, well, see if there's anything you can dig out. I'll see you in the morning.''

Claire hung up, irritated at this turn of events.

"What's wrong, Claire?"

"I won't be able to reach Winesong today." She told him about the system for contacting Sarah.

"Okay, so get the contract tomorrow and we'll check with the post office for a home address. I know you have to supply one to get a box. Did Tillie have any idea where Roz lives? My guy at the *Times* is out today."

"No, she didn't. But she gave me the names and numbers of a couple of people to call." Claire tore her small list in half, handing the bottom part to Tony. "You call these. Say you're with the *Wall Street Journal* or something. Doing a story on Newcastle's purchase of Usherwood Publications."

"Boy, you're good at this," he said, smiling. "I'll do it, but first I want to bring up one other thing."

"Yes?"

"You do know that your own high ethics may not be shared by other people close to you?"

Claire felt herself stiffen against the hardness of the door frame. "What do you mean?"

"I mean that, no matter what Roz tells us, we can't totally clear everyone of complicity with Newcastle in the manuscript swindle, or Patricia's murder."

"I know that. But I've seen no proof that anyone at Cauldron has done anything wrong. And I'm sure none of them would go so far as to conceal evidence from the authorities in order to protect Winesong from prosecution."

Tony clenched his fist. "I just don't want you to forget something. Someone tried to kill you, and frame me, because we're getting too close to some facts that person wants kept hidden. After all, even Tillie or Vincent Harrison could have—"

Tony's words were interrupted by a shocked voice from the outer doorway. "Claire! Mr. Nichols! What are you doing here?"

Her face burning, Claire turned to face Vincent Harrison. He was standing in the small outer office, clutching a large cardboard box, staring at the two of them with surprise—and, she was chagrined to see—more than a shade of suspicion.

TONY WENT DOWN to hail a cab, leaving Claire alone with Mr. Harrison. She'd accompanied her boss to his office in silence. The guilt she felt was ridiculous, she told herself. But she still felt as if she'd been caught red-handed stealing from the school milk fund.

"So, Claire, tell me what you and Mr. Nichols have accomplished? Did you ever find Patricia Snow?"

"Yes, we did. But something quite awful has happened, Mr. Harrison. The girl is dead."

"What!" Vincent Harrison stopped removing the stack of typewritten pages he'd been sorting through to stare at Claire. "What happened?"

Claire filled him in on the events in Rhode Island, from Tony's bonk on the head to the murder and her own close encounter with the gunman.

He looked most shocked when she repeated what Tony had told her about Patricia's charges. That she'd been approached by someone who'd paid her a retainer fee on behalf of Claire Kennedy.

The early-morning car bomb she left out, unwilling to even think about it again. "So the Rhode Island state troopers arrested Tony," she finished. "Because it was his gun that was used in the shooting, and maybe even in the murder. He's up to his neck in trouble. We didn't tell them about finding Patricia's body, which turned out to be a mistake in light of the fact they can't locate Pearl Loney."

"Pearl Loney?" he repeated.

"The justice of the peace at Benton Convent. Anyway, speaking of trouble, Tony's not the only one in it. So is Cauldron Press."

"Why? Has someone accused us of complicity in the girl's murder?"

"No. I don't mean that kind of trouble. I mean that with all of this, we can't publish *The Poison Pen Pal* as scheduled." Claire sat in a heap on the sofa, exhausted. There, she told herself, she'd finally said it.

After several moments of silence, she looked up to find Mr. Harrison looking at her with eyes that seemed focused a million miles away.

"It's too dangerous for Cauldron Press, Mr. Harrison—"

"Just a minute, Claire. So the police suspect Mr. Nichols. Then why the devil is he here with you in New York? He didn't hurt you, did he?" Harrison rushed to Claire's side and put a hand on her shoulder.

She felt a shudder tremble through his slight form, and she found herself patting his hand, as if he were a child. "No. On the contrary, Mr. Harrison, he's been really good to me. As a matter of fact, I'm sure he's been set up. And I think that situation may have something to do with the fact that Billings Newcastle is trying to buy Cauldron Press from you."

Standing erect, Mr. Harrison blinked his pale blue eyes rapidly. "Claire, there are a lot of things I haven't told you before that I'm going to now."

He took a deep breath, folding both hands behind his back as he paced in front of his desk. "With the Winesong book set to go, I really thought my financial difficulties were past, but now that this scandal has broken around us, I may not be able to do anything about Newcastle."

"Don't say that! If I can prove he's criminally involved in all this activity, we can bring the book out. After all, Cauldron is privately owned. Newcastle has no stockholders to intimidate and—"

"No. But he owns the bank that has extended me considerable credit this past year. And he's threatened to foreclose on the loans instead of rolling them over again if I don't sell to Usherwood Publications."

Claire watched as Mr. Harrison went back to his desk and sat down. He was partially hidden by the cardboard box in front of him, but his words rang out clearly. "I didn't tell you because I didn't think it would ever come to this. But if we don't go ahead with the Winesong book as scheduled, there's nothing we can do to save Cauldron Press from being taken over by Newcastle."

"You can't give up now. We'll find a way."

He surprised her by chuckling dryly. "Well, I thought until five minutes ago that these bundles of paper would be the answer to our prayers, but now that you've said you think we should halt production on the book . . ."

Claire forced herself to stand and walk over to the desk. "We can't publish *The Poison Pen Pal* while there's a remote possibility that Sarah Winesong stole the book. We need to be able to prove who wrote it."

Harrison nodded toward the stacks of paper in front of him. "We can do that now, Claire. Here are all the original copies of her various drafts of the book, complete with margin notes and corrections. If this doesn't prove she wrote it, then nothing will."

"Where did you get these?" Claire's surprise was edged with disbelief. Numbly she looked down at the copies in front of her. If they did have all the drafts, they could prove that Sarah Winesong wrote the book.

And that Patricia Snow hadn't!

"They were delivered to me by messenger this morning. This note was with them." Harrison handed Claire a folded sheet of paper. Sarah Winesong's familiar spidery hand covered the sheet. It read:

Dear Vincent

I've heard, from a very reliable source, of our problem with this young woman, Patricia Snow. I'm sending you this note so you'll understand a bit of the background of my book, and how this whole story has been orchestrated by some very industrious criminals.

For the past two years, Patricia Snow did typing and research for me. My health, as you know, has been quite fragile, so I placed an ad in the Immaculate Sisters College paper in Rhode Island, not too far from a retreat I occasionally go to.

A few months ago, I discovered Miss Snow had a severe drinking problem. I had my associate, a lovely woman who has helped manage my affairs for twenty-five years, terminate Miss Snow's services, but we allowed the poor child to stay in a small house I inherited from my cousin, Marielle Chancon.

Miss Snow did no writing or research on my manuscript *The Poison Pen Pal*, though she did type it.

I hope this information will put your mind at rest, Vincent. Please give dear Miss Kennedy my love and tell her I still look forward to meeting her in the near future.

"So, Miss Winesong thinks Patricia stole her book and passed it off as her own out of spite?"

Vincent nodded energetically. "Yes, and it makes perfect sense. Snow and Nichols set up the plot to blackmail us, then the poor drunken little fool must have double-crossed him and sent it off to Roz Abramawitz to try and sell it to her, too!"

Her mind reeling from all the new information, Claire picked up one of the piles of paper and glanced down at it. It was the opening scene of Chapter Three of *The Poison Pen Pal*.

"So Newcastle may not be involved at all. Tony and I were so sure...."

"Who knows? I'd say he's not. But you can bet he'll tie us up in court for years if we don't immediately publish *The Poison Pen Pal*. If we keep to our schedule, the advance orders will let me pay the bank off, Claire, and he'll have no other hold on us other than that letter the poor demented Miss Snow sent to Roz Abramawitz."

"She also sent a manuscript. Don't forget that little problem, Mr. Harrison."

"I haven't. But these drafts will prove that Patricia just doctored Sarah's story and made a copy of it. It's very believable, Claire. People will do anything when they're as desperate as that girl was."

Uneasily Claire shook her head as if to clear it. "But who told Sarah about all of this? Did you?"

Vincent smiled. "No. But I'd be willing to bet you've told every bit of this to Tillie, and as I expected, she took things into her own hands and contacted Winesong."

"Tillie? Mr. Harrison, I know you didn't want me to bring her into this, but—"

"Claire, dear, it's okay. Really." Vincent walked around the edge of the desk and took the manuscripts from her hands. "The only thing you need to be concerned about now is Mr. Nichols."

"Tony? What do you mean?"

Vincent Harrison stared at her for a long moment, apparently weighing his words carefully. "Since it seems that Patricia Snow did in fact steal the book from Sarah Winesong, only one mystery remains."

"I don't understand...." Claire sat down in the same chair Tony had used a few days ago when he'd made his dreadful allegations about Cauldron Press.

"My dear, someone murdered that girl. Most likely to keep her quiet about something. And the only person I can clearly see benefiting from that silence is Mr. Nichols."

Her stomach churned and tightened as he finished his thought. "Tony is not a murderer," Claire whispered.

"But who else would have killed her, Claire? Who else? After all, wasn't he involved in something like this before?"

Claire rose, fury in her eyes. "How did you hear about that?"

He didn't respond, merely nodded toward Tillie's desk.

"He was *framed* on a plagiarism charge. By Billings Newcastle. He's not a murderer, Mr. Harrison. I'd stake my life on it."

Turning slowly, Vincent Harrison gently tapped his fingers together as he walked back to his chair. His words drifted over his shoulder. "If you spend any time alone with him now, you may be doing just that."

Chapter Twelve

"Tony, don't argue. Just go back to Rhode Island. I'll call you tomorrow." Claire shut the cab door, almost slamming it on Tony's arm.

He stared at her for a moment, then opened the door and jumped out. "Get in, Claire. I'm not going anywhere until you tell me what happened with Harrison."

"I don't want to talk about it right now." Turning away, she hurried down the sidewalk, joining the dressed-for-church Sunday crowd. Bitter tears burned behind her eyes.

Had she been a fool? Again? Had she actually made the mistake of believing in a man whose dark side made it impossible for him to be a giving, honest person?

A hand grasped her elbow. "Don't run from me, Claire." Tony's eyes blazed with anger and pain. "This is adolescent and unfair. Every time something happens that throws you, you run off like a sulky child. Now stop for a minute and tell me what's eating you. I thought we were working together."

"So did I!"

"And just what is that supposed to mean? What did Harrison say to you? Tell me, right now, or I'll go up there and bash it out of him."

Claire knew Tony meant what he said. Glancing around, she made a quick decision. Ignoring the scathing curses the swarthy cabdriver yelled at them, she took Tony's arm. "Come on. Let's walk."

Tony fell into step beside her and fought down his exasperation. How could everything be all right one minute and sheer hell the next? "Was Harrison shocked at all the news?"

"He was shocked at a few things. Then he shocked me right back with a few tidbits of his own."

Tony jostled two kids who tried to walk between them, and pulled Claire closer to him. "Oh, yeah? Like what?"

"Like he got a surprise package this morning, too. Special delivery from Sarah Winesong. Along with a letter admitting she knew Patricia, she included all her draft copies of *The Poison Pen Pal*."

Incredulous at this news, Tony's face hardened. "Well, what else did the letter from the mysterious Miss Winesong have to say?"

"Quite a lot." She summarized it, closing with, "So it appears Sarah *did* write the book, Tony."

As the muscles in his face tightened more, Tony recognized the hollow sound in Claire's voice. Shock. More had happened in Vincent Harrison's office than she was telling him. "The drafts don't prove anything, Claire. They could be the ones stolen from my office, for all we know."

"I don't think so. I recognized the handwritten corrections on them. They're Sarah's. The only thing she said Patricia Snow did for her was type."

"Damn right she typed that story—while she composed it."

"That's doubtful. Tony, I know this is hard for you to hear, but I really think you've been duped. According to

Miss Winesong, Patricia Snow didn't *just* go to work for her six months ago. She said she's been paying her for over two years.''

Tony cursed as the crosswalk light blinked red. "What else did you expect, Claire? If she's trying to cover up the truth—"

"Oh, stop it! Stop it right now!" Claire wrestled her arm free and brushed a tear from her eye. She seldom cried, and this outbreak promised to make up for it.

Tony's hand rested in the middle of her back as they stepped down together from the curb. "Claire, let's go back to your place now. Then you can tell me everything that happened. Why be so upset?"

"No." She halted, surprised when she looked up to see they were standing in front of the Waldorf Astoria. It seemed a million years ago that she'd met him there. She felt like running, but knew she owed it to Tony to tell him what was on her mind.

"I'm still going to check out things with Roz," she said. "But I want to go see her alone."

Both hands rested on his hips, his knuckles white from the pressure. The clip-clop of a horse-drawn carriage in Central Park echoed off the walls around them, then faded. "Why alone?"

"She'll tell me more if I'm by myself. Don't argue with me, Tony. I'm going by myself. Go back to Narragansett." With that she headed for a cab at the curb. It would mean a trip back to the office first to run down Roz's address, but at least she'd have some time to think.

She also needed to confront Tillie and ask her when and how she'd gotten hold of Sarah.

Tony let her get about ten yards before he yelled, "Claire! Wait."

But she didn't. And he didn't call her a second time.

As he watched her climb into the cab, Tony noticed two park policemen, mounted on impressive chestnut-colored horses, toward his left. They were talking and looking at him, one of the horses pawing the ground. *Great. Now I'll get slammed in jail for leaving Rhode Island, and then never get to the bottom of this.*

Casually he crossed into the park, oblivious to the joggers and cyclists, couples and fat-cheeked babies in strollers. It took all his energy to control the pain that savaged him. He was sure Claire would be safe for a couple of days, as long as she stuck to her apartment and office. Besides, no matter how that Abramawitz woman was connected to things, she didn't look the type who'd physically attack someone.

It was time to take the situation into his own hands, Tony decided. He was tired of playing by the rules. No one else had.

SITTING AT HER DESK at eight-thirty Monday morning, Claire kept her head down as Tillie burst through the door.

"Well, well. What did you and Mr. Nichols do all night?"

"I slept. If he has a shred of sense, he did the same thing. Back in Rhode Island."

Tillie stared at the top of her boss's head. "I see. What did you find out yesterday? Did you speak to Roz?"

"No, I never even found out where she lives. I tried calling you until one o'clock this morning." She looked up. "Where were you?"

Tillie bent and tied her sneaker. Her voice was hoarse. "I told you I have a sick neighbor. She's worse, so I baby-sat."

"When did you find time to call Sarah Winesong, Tillie?"

A gnarled hand grasped the corner of Claire's desk as Tillie struggled to stand. She took her pack of cigarettes out, removed one and lit it, then sat down across from Claire. "She called me. Out of the blue, the minute I stepped in after leaving your place on Saturday. She said she'd heard a rumor Vincent was in trouble and wanted to know what she could do to help."

"So you told her the whole story? How did she sound, Tillie? I wish you'd told me this, or told her to call me!"

"She *is* going to call you. She asked for your home number and told me she was going to call you there tonight about nine."

"What did she say when you told her about the plagiarism charge?"

"She didn't sound the least bit surprised, Claire. 'Vincent can take care of all this. I'll send him some things to help him put an end to this foolishness,' she said. Then she hung up without a goodbye."

"You're sure it was her?"

"It's the same woman I've talked to for twenty-five years, Claire. I'd swear to that. But how did you find out I talked to her?"

Claire shielded her eyes with her hands, then shook her head. It was obvious Tillie didn't know about the package Mr. Harrison had received. Well, if Sarah did call her at nine tonight, she'd be ready for her. "It doesn't matter, Tillie. Let me thank you for taking things into your own hands. I know you did what you think was right. We'll get through this. Now—" Claire met Tillie's nervous gaze and handed her several pages of correspondence "—get someone in the typing pool to do these today. Also, please find out if Damien is free for cocktails tonight, and let me know when Mr. Harrison comes in. I'm going to the art department to approve book covers.''

Brushing past Tillie, she chanced a full-faced look at her assistant, hoping the swelling around her eyes had gone down.

The older woman's expression showed it hadn't. ''Next time you cry all night use cucumbers on your eyelids.''

''There'll be no next time.''

''Never say never,'' Tillie said, standing and nodding to the closed door. ''The art department is going to have to wait. Roz is outside.''

Claire stopped with her hand on the doorknob, her heart lurching at the news. ''Is she here to see Mr. Harrison?''

Before Tillie could answer, the door opened and Roz Abramawitz marched in, all of her four-foot-ten inches of spite and malice dressed in canary-yellow shantung silk.

''Well, the vagabond Claire Kennedy is back in the Big Apple. How was your vacation, dear? Not much sleep, according to those bags under your eyes.''

''Hello, Roz. Excuse me, but I didn't hear your knock. Can you give me a moment to take care of my scheduled appointments?''

Ignoring Claire's pointed look toward the outer reception area, Roz sank onto the chair by the desk and pulled out her cigarettes and lighter. ''But, of course, dear. Go right ahead and outline dear Tillie's chores for her. I'll just wait right here. It'll be convenient.''

Claire stared at Tillie, who made the gesture of a knife being drawn across her throat. Claire shook her head and rolled her eyes. ''I'll handle things in here, Tillie. Will you please call up to art and tell Pete to wait for me? I'll be there in ten minutes."

Reluctantly Tillie left, leaving the door ajar. Roz kicked it closed with the spiked heel of her alligator pump.

Claire walked around her desk and sat down, carefully folding her hands in front of her. Remembering that her father always told her to look at a spot just behind the person you were playing against for a big pot, she focused her eyes on the coat hook on the back of the door. "Okay, Roz, what's behind this party-crashing scene?"

Roz looked annoyed at the question. For some reason, this terrified Claire. She wanted Roz out of her office, but with all the unanswered questions about what part Usherwood Publications played in the Patricia Snow affair, it was too dangerous just to throw her out.

After inhaling deeply, Roz deposited her ashes in Claire's coffee cup. "Is this a party? Things seem more like a wake around here."

"Get to the point, Roz. I have a tight schedule today."

Smiling sweetly, Roz's tiny teeth glittered in the fluorescent light. "You have been a busy girl, haven't you? So where's Mr. Nichols?"

Though it seemed as if the oxygen had been sucked from her lungs, Claire managed to keep her breathing even. "Who?"

"Tony Nichols. The hunk you had cornered at the Waldorf the other day. I must say, Claire, I never expected the cool Ms. Kennedy, with ice water in her veins, to run off for a couple of days with such a hero type. Damien Laurent wouldn't tell me why he looked familiar to me, but he did say he was shocked at your behavior."

The knot in her stomach doubled. Damien. She and Tony had trusted Damien. Had he told Roz everything? With a sinking heart, Claire asked the question that could end her tenure in the publishing world forever.

"When did you see Damien, Roz? And what did he tell you about my business with Tony Nichols?"

"So direct, Ms. Kennedy! My goodness, will you never learn the finer points of thrust and parry?"

Claire's palms were sweating. If Damien had betrayed her, then Newcastle was probably covering his tracks at this very moment. "I don't know where this is all leading, Roz. What's your point?"

"My point is this. When I'm the editor-in-chief here at Cauldron Press, I'll expect you to concentrate more on business and less on your little *liaisons dangereuses.*"

"You'll never be my boss." Unflinchingly Claire burned that bridge, then risked all her remaining cool by allowing her voice to carry a threat. "I asked you when you talked to Damien Laurent?"

Roz squirmed in the hard chair. "Oh, Damien and I had drinks when I stopped by yesterday to see him. He was in a snit, said he'd been besieged with unexpected Sunday company, but you know how Damien exaggerates. When I made mention of you, he got into a lather. I don't know why. Something, I think, to do with the mysterious Tony Nichols."

Roz dropped her smoldering cigarette into Claire's cup, nodding at the sizzling sound it made. "You're never going to get anywhere, Claire, unless you're nicer to the influential people who run our business."

As Roz continued to rattle on, Claire began to relax. It looked as if Roz was here just to antagonize her, not because Damien had spilled the beans. But then she almost hyperventilated herself unconscious when Roz brought up a new topic.

"What did you say, Roz?" she asked.

The sudden interest was not lost on Roz. "Oh, now you're paying attention. Well, that's good, Claire, but you can forget about trying to steal her away from me. This young college girl from Rhode Island sent me the most delicious manuscript I've ever seen from an unpublished writer. I told Mr. Newcastle on Friday that if she didn't call me this week, I'd go see her personally, just to get ink on a contract before some other house snaps her up. Her name is Snow, Patricia Snow. Remember that name?"

The nausea began to build in Claire, and blood rushed to her head. She must not faint. Only Victorian heroines and spinsters fainted. Claire gulped some air and stood up. "I have to go see Mr. Harrison, Roz. I'll see you later. Thanks for dropping by."

Roz remained sitting. She stared quizzically at Claire, whose face was feverish, her usually sparkling brown eyes dull and flat. "Certainly, Claire. Call me. We'll have lunch."

Claire gripped the desk for support. She had to get to Tony, warn him that Roz was headed for Rhode Island. Just as she reached her pale hand toward the phone, it shrieked on the cradle. Claire lifted it and whispered, "Yes?"

"Claire? This is Vincent Harrison. Please come up here and tell me what's going on with that dreadful Abramawitz woman."

Claire sighed. "I'll be right there."

SITTING FULLY DRESSED on her bed in the growing darkness, Claire stared out the window. Woofer glided gracefully from room to room, emitting his usual string of Doberman pinscher imitations to break the silence. Normally amused, Claire felt weighed down. She wanted Tony. Wanted to see his tall, remarkable form fill the doorway. Wanted his warm laugh to pour over her and distract her from just waiting for the phone to ring.

She eyed it nervously, then checked her watch. Six-forty. A long time to wait. But as soon as Sarah called, she would insist on a face-to-face meeting—tonight, if possible. Mr. Harrison wouldn't be able to stand the stress of many more days like today.

He'd nearly choked when she reported Roz's conversation about hearing from Patricia Snow.

"Roz can't go to Narragansett, Claire. Once she discovers the Snow girl is dead, the papers will pick up the whole thing. You know how Roz loves to involve the press. She and Damien Laurent are out twice a week with that crowd."

"I don't know how we can stop her unless we tell her about our problem."

Harrison had exploded. "That's it! I've done everything I can to protect Sarah from bad publicity and the buzzards that will zero in on this story. I'm calling the police now."

He sat down and dialed, as Claire leaned on the sofa beside him. While he waited to be connected, he handed Claire a folder.

She'd opened it and read the startling advance-order report on *The Poison Pen Pal*. Their original press run was to be 100,000 copies, and they had orders for twice that number.

"It's already a bestseller, Claire." She looked up and met Mr. Harrison's eyes, then stood and depressed the phone.

"Let's wait until I talk to Sarah tonight."

She'd taken his silence as agreement.

Harrison's final words had been another warning to stay clear of Tony Nichols.

Now she sat and stared at the stack of manuscripts sitting on the dresser. Mr. Harrison had begged her to take them home and look through them. He wanted her to be as sure as he was of Sarah's innocence.

Tony needed to see these, she thought suddenly. Maybe then he'd begin to see why she believed in Winesong. Maybe then he'd forgive her for hurting him yesterday. Tears filled her eyes at the memory of their last moments together, before he'd fled north.

Slowly Claire removed her shoes and stood up. She switched on the light on the antique server she used as a dressing table and removed her jewelry. Her mirrored image looked back at her forlornly. All the makeup in the world couldn't hide the fatigue, or the tension pulling at her mouth. She ached to hold Tony just one more time.

"USHERWOOD PUBLICATIONS. Roz Abramawitz."

"Miss Abramawitz?"

"Yes. Who is this?"

The voice was hoarse, tinny, aged. "Miss Abramawitz, this is Sarah Winesong. The novelist. I wonder if I could ask a big favor of you?"

Excitedly Roz jumped up from her desk, wrapping the rubber spiral telephone cord around her wrist. "Miss Winesong! This is such a surprise, and such an honor. Of course. Anything."

After listening for a moment, Roz wrote down the address and repeated the directions. Nodding her head, she hung up, then stood for a moment and savored the conversation. Who'd have guessed, she thought to herself, this twist of fate?

Grabbing her yellow coat, she darted from her office. Her smile was one of victory, the type a cat might feel as it tastes the warm flesh of a mouse.

IN HER BLACK leather skirt and slouchy red T-shirt, Claire felt much more comfortable. She locked her door, thought about going back in for a coat, then decided the April evening was mild enough. Waving to her doorman, she stood on the stoop for a moment, looking up and down her block. Chinese? Tai? A hamburger?

She still had almost two hours before Sarah called, so she'd decided to go out. Unable to decide which local joint would offend her stomach the least, Claire walked briskly across the street, heading for the deli on the corner. She had to get to the grocery store, too, before she died of ptomaine poisoning. A burgundy mustang, with faded paint and no headlights, pulled up next to her.

"Hey, gorgeous. Come here."

Keeping her eyes straight ahead, Claire fought the instinct to yell at him to get lost. Just what she needed, she thought. Kids with hot pants and the inability to see she wanted to be left alone.

"Claire. It's me."

She almost stumbled at the sound of her name. Glancing into the car's interior, her appetite vanished. Tony sat there, a navy wool fisherman's hat pulled down low on his forehead. He looked rakish, criminal—and thoroughly desirable. "Where did you get that car?"

"Rental. Come on, get in. We've got an appointment."

He double-parked the Mustang while she ran around the front of the car and got in.

After slamming the door, Claire turned and drank in the sight of Tony. He was wearing a faded orange soccer shirt, with white piping, and tight white jeans. She felt flustered while he spent several seconds staring at her black-stockinged legs and short leather skirt.

Folding her hands on her knees, Claire shifted forward, causing her T-shirt to fall off her left shoulder. While a hundred non sequiturs and inane sentence fragments ran through her mind, Tony leaned across the seat and kissed her lightly on the chin.

Burying his strong hands in her silky blond hair, he pulled her closer still, plunging his tongue into her melting mouth, both of them instantly feeling mounting desire. A low wolf whistle from the sidewalk and the catcalls of some boys broke their embrace.

"Tony, I—"

"Ssh, don't talk yet. Just let me look at you some more."

"The way you've been staring at my leather skirt, I feel like a poacher caught red-handed with the illegal goods."

"It's not the skirt I'm interested in. It's the lady inside. How are you? Better after a day without arguing with me?"

"I've been terrible. I'm sorry I ran away from you yesterday. But so much had happened—"

"I understand. Really."

Claire felt tears running down her cheeks as she now reached out for him, crushing him against her, kissing him a hundred times. "I know this has been devastating for you, Tony. Tonight I'm hoping to put the last pieces of the puzzle together. Sarah Winesong is—" Pushing suddenly away from him, Claire's brown eyes widened in fear. "But what are you doing here? Why didn't you go back to Rhode Island? I thought we agreed it was much more sensible if you—"

Tony hushed her by pressing a finger to her lips. "We didn't agree on anything. And for the first time in a few years, I went ahead and did what I thought was best without worrying about the consequences. Which is why I'm driving this car. We're going back to New Jersey."

"To Benton Convent?" Shifting back in the seat and putting on her seat belt, Claire heard the undercurrent of anger in Tony's deep voice.

"No. Parsonage. It's about thirty miles north, quite close to the house where we found Patricia."

She unbuckled the seat belt. "Let me out of the car, Tony. I can't go. I have to go home to get a call at nine."

"What I'm taking you to see is a lot more important than a phone call. I followed Roz Abramawitz around town all day, unbeknownst to her, of course. After she left Cauldron Press she went shopping, then returned to Usherwood. Roz left work and met Damien Laurent in the Russian Tea Room for cocktails."

The same sense of foreboding she'd had in her office returned. Damien. Had he told Roz about the true nature of their interest in Newcastle? "You eavesdropped on Damien? Did he see you?"

Tony gunned the car and shot through a light, then screeched to a stop to avoid several pedestrians. "I borrowed a waiter's hat and coat and hung around the tables behind them. Neither saw me."

"Well? What were they talking about?"

"It seems Roz feels she's about to pull off quite a coup. You see, she's going to Parsonage tonight, also."

"Tony, knock off this suspense routine. Who is Roz going to see?"

"Why, Sarah Winesong. Who else?"

Chapter Thirteen

"Roz is meeting Winesong! My God, what for?" The night was beginning to take on the unreal quality it had when they'd found Patricia. Claire shuddered, unable to shake a mounting sense of foreboding.

Tony took the expressway toward New Jersey. "To lure her away from Cauldron Press? To blackmail her about Patricia's letter to Usherwood? To pay her off for killing Patricia? Take your pick. There are lots of possibilities."

"But how did Roz find out where Sarah lives? All we have on our contracts is a damn post office box number."

"Winesong called and gave her the information. According to what I heard her tell Damien, Winesong's asked her for help."

"Help?"

"Yes, ma'am. Damien asked if she'd checked with Newcastle, and Roz claimed she didn't need to get his approval on anything. It sounded like Laurent wanted to go with her, but she wouldn't agree."

Claire's mind raced toward the confrontation ahead, then ricocheted back to her earlier one with Roz. She filled Tony in on what had taken place in her office that morning. "Maybe Winesong wants to see Roz because she found out Patricia Snow had contacted Usherwood Publications."

"We'll find out tonight."

"What do you propose we do once we catch up with them? Break in on their meeting?" Claire liked that idea, and her excitement grew.

Tony silently chewed the inside of his right cheek. "I think we have to play that one by ear. But I want to say something to you, before you get too gung ho about cornering a rat."

Catching her breath, Claire turned and watched him closely. "I'm listening."

Tony kept his eyes on the road. "From now on I'm going to keep after you until you learn to let go. Of the past, of your absorption in your job, of whatever it is that always pulls you away from me when we start to get close. I think if we try we can make something important of our feelings for each other, Claire."

She was breathless at this unexpected turn of events. In the dappled light from the expressway, Tony's well-sculpted profile was gorgeous, and unbelievably dear to her. "I don't know what to say, Tony."

Tony's voice was husky, full of passion but edged with tension. "Say what you feel."

Suddenly it was all very easy. "I may be falling in love."

"With anyone I know?"

"E. A. Poe. Dark, brooding type."

He squeezed her hand tightly. "You editors all go for those literary types."

"Especially ones who are desperadoes."

A tiny word of caution brushed against her happiness for a moment, but Claire dismissed it. Mr. Harrison was wrong. Tony was everything she thought he was, and more.

She reached for his arm and, leaning over, grazed his cheek with her lips.

The car drifted a little toward the oncoming lanes of traffic, which made them both laugh aloud. "Take it easy on me, okay? I've got a lot of driving ahead."

"I'll behave."

"Good." Claire Kennedy was what they called solid in the military. Well-balanced and ready to meet life head-on, she'd be able to withstand the shock of what he feared waited for her in Parsonage, New Jersey. He hoped.

MONDAY-NIGHT TRAFFIC was skimpy, and it took only a little over an hour to reach the part of New Jersey they wanted. Above them, the night sky was bereft of stars, and a heavy, late-spring fog swirled in a gray haze across the road. Tony kept the headlights on low as he crossed a covered bridge, then hit the brights to read the directional sign for Benton Convent. It was several miles ahead, but their destination was fourteen miles to the east.

Neither mentioned the proximity of Sarah Winesong's home to where Patricia Snow had been murdered, but both thought of little else. Even with the car's heater blowing full blast, Claire still felt chilled.

Tony rubbed his hand up and down her opaque black stockings, and though his touch warmed her, Claire shivered. Wrapping her arms around her chest, she directed her thoughts to places other than Tony's hands. "I'm glad to see you haven't had a smoke for the last couple of hours. Finally giving it up?"

Slanting his eyes toward her, Tony nodded. "I'm trying. Are you flattered?"

"Yes, if it's on my account. If it's not, I'm just plain happy. I've been thinking about that cigarette the Rhode Island police found at Patricia Snow's house. I saw you put the one you started to smoke back in your pocket that night. I can't imagine how they found one that had your fingerprints all over it."

"We'll probably never know."

Claire was silent for a moment, several little fragments of information clicking into place, though the puzzle still needed to be completed. "Someone got your cigarette from somewhere, that's for sure. But who? And when?"

Turning into a heavily overgrown drive, Tony stopped and shone a flashlight through the car window onto an iron mailbox. Two Sycamore Court was neatly lettered on the side, the same address Roz had so happily shared with Laurent. Tony shut off the headlights and slowed to a five-mile-an-hour crawl. "We're here."

Anticipation sent goose bumps along Claire's arms and down her back. Tony's hand reached out for hers, his strong squeeze reassuring. The car continued creeping down the private road, though after several moments she still saw no trace of a house. "Are you sure this is the right place?"

"It's the address Roz had."

"What time is it, Tony? Maybe we're too late."

"No. It's only ten to nine. Roz said Winesong was expecting her at nine. Damn!" Suddenly Tony swerved the Mustang off the paved road. It bumped up and down madly as he headed for a small clearing between the sycamores and elms that lined the drive. When he slammed on the brakes, Claire flew forward into the dash.

"Claire! Are you hurt?"

The warm taste of blood surprised her as she licked her top lip. With his hands on her arms, Claire reached down for the seat belt. It had popped out. "I'm not hurt, though I now have a fat lip to go with your bumps and gashes. Why in the world did you swerve off the road and stop like that?"

Glancing out the rear window, Tony hugged Claire close to him and pointed. "I'm sorry. I really am. But look, there are headlights back there."

A car was approaching down the same road they'd just left. The fog bank marched solidly behind it, as if protecting the vehicle.

Claire held her breath as the car rolled even with them, then past their darkened huddle. The car's taillights pulsed like gashes against the dense, smoky fog. Claire whispered, "What are we going to do now?"

He pulled off his jacket and handed it to her. "Here, put this on. We'll go the rest of the way on foot. The house can't be that much farther down. We'll just follow the line of trees. Come on."

They got out, and the car door creaked as Tony pressed it shut. Linking his fingers in Claire's, they started off in a run in the direction of the house. The taillights of the car that had passed them were still visible a hundred yards up the road. With a glance behind her, Claire whispered, "I don't see any other lights coming. That must be Roz."

Claire kept her eyes glued on the twin red glows ahead. After a minute or so she realized they were gaining on the lights. Then suddenly the lights blinked off.

Pulling up, Tony guided Claire off the road again. "The house must be close. The car's stopped." The muffled echo of a car door closing reached them.

With his arm wrapped around her, they stayed close to the woods as they stealthily approached the unknown. A breeze began to blow from the sand marshes to the north, and ghostly ribbons of fog swirled among the treetops. Almost magically the house at Two Sycamore Court materialized.

It was a dramatic structure of granite boulder and massive thick walls covered with an accumulation of moss and ivy, formed over the years. A clump of trellised rose vines climbed around the doorway, sprouting leaves, but bare of blooms.

Roz Abramawitz stood on the front steps, one hand on the heavy wrought-iron knocker, as an overhead light revealed the garish yellow of her clothes. Holding a fur car coat, she was reading a note that she must have pulled from the door. She seemed ill at ease, and she turned suddenly, staring in Tony's and Claire's direction. Fortunately they were hidden by the fog.

As she and Tony continued to watch, Roz turned back toward the house and placed a tentative hand on the doorknob.

It opened and she peeked around it. Her nasal voice called out, "Miss Winesong?" After a few seconds, Roz went in, leaving the door ajar.

"What do we do now, Tony? We won't be able to find out a thing if we stay here in the woods." Claire's teeth were chattering, and she experienced a pang of hunger. She'd not eaten since the night before.

"I know." Tony was worried about Claire's safety. Until now he hadn't given any consideration to the possibility that they'd been set up. Had Roz seen him and recognized him when he'd followed her to the Russian Tea Room? Had Damien Laurent?

Tony turned and took Claire's face in his hands, gently brushing her lips with a kiss. "Why don't you go back to the car. I'll stay here and risk a run across the yard. Once I figure out what room they're meeting in, I'll pry open a window or something."

"I wouldn't leave you alone here for all the bestsellers in the world."

He paused and smiled. "Okay. Let's go."

Together they moved swiftly across the circular yard and then pressed themselves against the damp ivy-covered walls. Claire smelled the moldy odor of decay of last year's leaves as her boots sank into the mud along the foundation. Slowly she and Tony crept toward the front door.

Barely ten feet from it, it was thrown forcefully shut from inside. A second later the front light was extinguished.

Tony and Claire froze. His dark eyes glowed with anxiety as, with a nod, he directed her toward the rear of the house.

A large bay window jutted out onto a porch. Café-style curtains on the lower half of the windows blocked their view of the room. A small chandelier glittered brightly through the diamond-cut panes, offering the perfect illumination for seeing inside—if you were nine feet tall, Claire thought.

No voices carried outside, and Claire noted with alarm that the fog was thickening. The line of trees that stood a hundred yards from the house was now obliterated.

Tony put his cold lips to Claire's ear. "If I give you a boost, you can get up high enough to look in."

Claire's brown eyes widened, her freckles now standing in stark contrast to her fair skin. "What if they see me? Tony, let's go back to the front door and knock.

Maybe if we just confront them we can get to the bottom of everything without all this skulking around. I feel like a character in one of Sarah's books!''

"Confront them? Are you forgetting what happened to Patricia Snow?" As soon as the words were out, Tony regretted their harsh edge. He could see Claire shrink back inside herself.

"Okay, just one look, then maybe we'll go knock," she said hesitantly.

Tony nodded. He needed to know if Winesong and Roz were alone. He had a hunch they weren't. Bending down against the wall, Tony made a cup of his hands. Claire's lithe figure rubbed against him for a second as she stepped into it. He allowed himself a brief nuzzle, then with a single boost, he lifted her up toward the window.

Settling her stockinged feet onto his shoulders, she murmured, "Okay, stand up." Tony stood, raising her the rest of the way.

Despite the fact she was nearly frozen, Claire broke out in beads of perspiration. Slowly she moved her head upward, until her eyes were just above the top of the curtains covering the lower panes.

The room she saw was huge. It was dark-paneled and full of furniture, its walls covered with dramatic pictures of English sea battles.

Anchoring her fingers firmly into the ivy climbing the wall, she leaned closer to the window. A desk in one corner was piled high with papers, and an overstuffed settee sat next to an unlit hearth. On a tea table was a silver service complete with sugar tongs, a bowl of lemon slices and folded napkins.

Then Claire saw Roz.

She was slumped in a green, hobnail-studded wing chair across from the tea service, her head hanging limply on her chest. A faint, wet stain darkened the lapel of her yellow jacket, and a empty cup lay upside down on her lap.

The chair opposite Roz was turned so that Claire could only see the legs of the person sitting in it. And the shoes. Heavy-soled orthopedic shoes, the kind Tillie wore, stuck out on motionless feet. Leaning against this unseen person's chair stood a silver-headed, black-lacquered cane.

Claire caught the scream rising in her throat just as Tony rubbed his hand along her leg. Nearly losing her balance, she looked down and met his eyes. She didn't have to say a word. He lowered her from the window and held her close.

"What is it? What's going on in there?"

"Oh, Tony! We've got to call the police. Something's happened to Roz."

Before Tony could ask her what, there was the crack of a shotgun. Crouching quickly, they looked around. The fog hid everything beyond a five-foot radius. A second shot splattered against the wall above their heads; chips of rock and cement exploded around them.

Tony shielded Claire with his body and whispered, "Are you okay?"

"We have to get out of here!" She squirmed underneath him.

"Just lie still for a moment." Staring into the fog, Tony detected no movement. The night was quiet again except for a hollow rustle of leaves, stirred by a light breeze.

His pulse pounding in his ears, Tony looked around for someplace to hide. Just as he'd decided to make a run for the car, he spotted the basement door. Twenty feet from where he and Claire lay, the heavy wooden door, at ground level, beckoned. "See that door over there? That's where we're going."

"Into the house? Are you crazy, Tony? We don't know who's in there, or what they've done to Roz, or—"

Placing his finger to his lips to get her to lower her voice and get control of her emotions, Tony spoke with authority. "Look, it's our best bet. I'm a lot more worried about the nuts out here shooting than that damn old woman inside. Now, let's go."

Against her will, Claire followed Tony's lead and crept on her hands and knees toward the door. Her skin was bleeding and bruised by the time they reached it. Tony jumped to his feet and pushed her inside, easing the door closed behind them.

The odor of mildew, and a strangely familiar smell Claire couldn't immediately identify, assaulted their senses as they hurried down the stone steps. Pulling the flashlight from the jacket he'd made Claire put on, Tony sent the beam around the room.

It was surprisingly bare. A few cardboard boxes sat in one corner, a chair with ripped upholstery in the other. A bunch of shiny cans stood in a row beneath a workbench, which held a toolbox. The only other item was a freezer. The door of it was propped open with a pole, and a series of puddles radiated from it, leading up the stairway to what was probably the kitchen. There were no windows.

Holding Claire by the hand, Tony led her to the steps on the opposite side of the room. At the top of the landing, the door was locked. Pressing his ear to the wood, Tony heard nothing.

"I bet there's a screwdriver down here. I'll go find one and work on this lock. What did you see inside?"

Claire recounted the story, hugging Tony close.

"Are you sure you only saw an old woman inside with Roz? No one else?"

"No, I'm not sure of anything!" Claire shot back, pulling away. "All I saw was the woman's feet and legs. And I don't know what was wrong with Roz. She wasn't shot or anything, just unconscious. I think she spilled her tea and then passed out. Who else were you expecting to be here?"

Tony looked at Claire for a long moment before answering. "It's been obvious from the beginning that Sarah had to have had an accomplice, Claire. There's been too much physical mayhem. The fact that you saw her inside seconds before we were targets for the gunman outside proves it."

"Do you still think it's Newcastle?" Claire searched Tony's face for the truth, but before she could press him further, his hand shot to her mouth.

"Ssh. Listen."

Claire listened. Then, from across the room, back at the basement entrance, came the sound of metal scraping against metal. As her numb brain tried to identify the sound, Tony ran down the steps toward the door. Before he got halfway across the room the noise stopped.

Seconds later a car engine roared to life, the sound slowly fading as the car headed away from the house.

Hanging on to the stair railing, Claire watched as Tony pushed his weight against the door they'd come in through. He didn't have to say a word. She knew it was locked. "Tony..."

"It's okay, Claire. We'll be okay."

Seconds later he stood on the stairs next to her, helplessly grasping, then releasing the knob.

At that instant Claire identified the other odor she'd noticed when they'd first walked in. "I smell gas. Is there a water heater down here?"

"No. It's probably those cans. Hold the flashlight for me while I look around down here." He jumped down the stairs and began rattling through the toolbox.

Out of the corner of her eye, Claire saw that the fog was now seeping through the cracks around the basement doorway and wafting toward them. Her nose crinkled at a new aroma. "Are you going to smoke now, of all times?"

Tony turned from the bench, shaking his head. "Don't be ridiculous. I just told you those cans are full of gas. I'd never risk lighting a cigarette."

Panic pulsed through her veins as she realized what it was she smelled. It wasn't fog that seeped under the basement's outer door.

As Tony headed back up the stairs toward her, Claire raised her outstretched arm and pointed toward the locked door behind him.

Then came her scream, a one-word nightmare. "Fire!"

Chapter Fourteen

"Take off your panty hose and skirt," he ordered.

Claire trembled as Tony wrapped wet strips of his torn T-shirt around her forehead and neck. Despite the desperate circumstances, she was sure they'd figure a way out.

Holding Claire's clothes in one hand, Tony stripped his pants off and threw all the garments into the freezer. Claire rubbed them in ice. They worked as a team, no words necessary for the task at hand.

After a few seconds, Claire pulled his dripping wet Levi's out and handed them to him. "Put these back on."

"Thanks. You better take your T-shirt off and wet it, too, and dunk your hair. Hurry, Claire. We don't have much time before that gas blows."

Smoke was beginning to fill the basement. It was now pouring through the cracks around the outer door, upward toward the only other exit, which was bolted closed from inside the house.

Claire pulled the red T-shirt off over her head and dunked it into the melting ice. Her face glowed as her full breasts rubbed against Tony's arm.

As her eyes met his, they both broke into nervous laughter.

"You have beautiful breasts, Claire."

Her gaze dropped to the firm silhouette of his buttocks. "And you've got a fabulous rear end, Mr. Nichols."

"This is insane." Tony helped Claire pull her wet T-shirt back on, caressing her briefly through the freezing material. "This isn't the way I'd imagined undressing you."

"You've thought of that, have you? With all that's been going on?"

"Yes."

"Good, I'm glad I'm not the only nut who has fantasies during stress."

"You're not a nut at all, Claire. Now, let's try the door again."

Claire covered Tony's massive hands with her smaller ones. "Having you back in my life, even in this situation, is like hitting the jackpot. Even if we don't get out, I want you to know how much . . ."

Noting the hysteria rising in her tone, Tony stroked her hair, matted to her head and dripping wet. "Ssh, we're going to get out. Right now, as a matter of fact. Are you ready?"

"Tony, what about the people inside? Why don't we pound on the door. Roz may be able to wake—"

"Save your breath, Claire. Whoever locked us in and drove off probably took Roz and Winesong with him— or else it's too late to worry about them anymore." As he walked back toward the stairs, Claire's eyes roamed the dim basement.

She picked out the outline of a door on the far wall, and a light came on in her head. If she wasn't mistaken, she'd found a way into the house. "Tony, come here. It's a dumbwaiter."

Tony followed her to the small open door.

"This is great, Claire. I'll get in and you send me up." They both looked in, seeing at the same time that his broad shoulders would never fit.

"It's not big enough for you. I'm going to have to go up."

Tony looked upset. "Okay. But don't mess around trying to help Roz when you're in there. Go straight to the kitchen, unlock the door and let me into the house."

"Yes, sir." With a small salute, Claire climbed into the cramped space.

Tony saw his own fear and trepidation mirrored in Claire's face. Roughly he pressed a hard kiss onto her lips, handed her the flashlight, then pulled up the wide swatch of torn wet fabric at her throat up to cover her mouth and nose. "You look like a bank robber."

He closed the door on her, and Claire felt the panic of someone about to drown. She struggled to stay calm. A sudden jolting movement, then a swift, somewhat jerky climb began as Tony pressed the lever to send the dumbwaiter upward.

Toward what? An unknown gunman? A deranged novelist? A dead rival?

The possibilities were all too gruesome and frightening to contemplate, so Claire instead concentrated on Tony. Shivering, she yanked on her leather skirt and cursed her tights, which bit into the tops of her legs. Just then the jerking movement stopped. Had she made it? Was she in the kitchen?

Pushing excitedly at the door of the tiny compartment, Claire panicked when it only opened a scant two inches. Shining the light out the crack, she saw a solid wall. The elevator must have stopped before it had gotten completely up to the opening.

Drenched with sweat, Claire banged on the sides of the dumbwaiter, screaming, "Tony! Tony, it's stopped. Tony!"

Below her Tony's voice echoed up the shaft. "Claire, it's okay. The electricity's off, but I'll use the manual crank and get you up the rest of the way. Hang on."

Her stomach cramped painfully and she began to hyperventilate, but after a few seconds her breathing came back to normal. She took deep lungfuls of air and waited. Another sluggish vibration on the hoist rocked the dumbwaiter, then Claire felt herself moving upward again.

After several seconds she came to a stop, and she immediately pushed on the door. It popped open. Craning her neck out, she pulled down the fabric that covered her mouth and drank in the air. The room was dark and smelled musty, but it was so much cooler than the dumbwaiter she felt like a bird set free in a clear spring sky.

Carefully she unfolded her legs and crawled out, shining the light in wide arcs. The room was an office of some kind, books were piled high, and stacks of paper sat next to wooden file cabinets.

Running across the hardwood floor, Claire reached the door and peeked out. An enormous dark hallway loomed in front of her, filled with smoke.

"Dear God, the house is on fire, too!" Not sure which way led to the kitchen, Claire rushed barefoot down the hallway. The smoke was getting thicker, and when she reached some stairs she was greeted by orange and red flames licking at the banisters.

What appeared to be the foyer below her was also full of smoke, and greenish tentacles wafted from the room to the right, back-lit with sparks and a roaring fire. Running down the center of the stairs, Claire looked around, then headed through the smoke toward the rear of the house.

Nearly gagging on the acrid stench of burning fabric, she raced into a room full of sheet-draped furniture. A dining room? Scorching paths of fire gnawed the chairs, like ravenous guests from hell.

Moving a few feet down the hall, she opened another door. It was the room Claire had peeked into from the outside. It was consumed with fire, the smoke black and merciless, blocking all vision. In vain Claire dropped to the floor, and above the crackling roaring fire screamed. "Roz? Miss Winesong? Are you in here?"

Dizzy, her eyes streaming blinding tears, Claire crawled out into the hallway toward the last entrance at the back of the house. Pushing against a swinging door, she nearly yelled in delight. The kitchen!

Smoke obliterated the appliances, but she managed to locate the doorway to the basement.

Crawling, crying and choking, she got up on her knees and pulled on the door. It was stuck. Beating on it, Claire yelled. "Tony. Tony? Are you there? Tony?"

Calm. She had to be calm. Inhaling, Claire ran her fingers over the door's latch, finally finding the dead bolt. After a moment she slid it back and threw open the door. Why wasn't Tony standing there?

At that moment there was a tremendous explosion, ten times louder than the one that had destroyed Tony's car. The shock waves threw Claire several feet across the kitchen and into the wall. Fighting the pain from what felt like a million punches, Claire began to crawl. Flames poured through the basement doorway.

Tears of loss and terror ran down her cheeks. In the distance sirens blared. As unconsciousness pulled on the

edges of her mind, she was scarcely aware of being picked
up and carried from the house. Fighting the blackness,
Claire sobbed, "Tony. Don't leave me now, Tony. Please
don't leave me."

"Relax, dear Claire. It's all over now." The man
holding her staggered away from the house, his arms
aching with her unaccustomed weight. He rued the fact
that he'd left his favorite cane behind.

IN THE THICK SHRUBS, Tony regained consciousness and
shook his head. Rising unsteadily, he started to run
around toward the front of the inferno, but stumbled and
fell against a patch of hacked-away tree stumps at the
edge of the drive.

Clear your head, Tony-boy. What are you doing? Tony
allowed himself a few seconds to rest, as the past several
incredible minutes replayed themselves.

While waiting for Claire to get out of the dumbwaiter
and back down to the kitchen door, he'd had a brain-
storm. By using the heavy metal pole that had propped
open the freezer, he'd managed to pry open the outer
basement door and get back outside.

His only thought had been to reach Claire, but before
he could, an explosion knocked him several yards away
from the house into the trees. *Claire. My God, no!* The
pain in his left leg was overshadowed by a consuming
fear.

"Claire! Claire!" His smoke-damaged vocal cords
rasped, but before he could drag himself more than a
couple of feet, he saw a slight figure carrying Claire toward a blue Jaguar parked well away from the fire.

Her hair hung in blond soot-covered streaks, and her
long legs were gashed. Lunging toward the pair, Tony fell
headlong into the grass. He couldn't move his leg.

Quickly refocusing on Claire, Tony felt a surge of relief wash over him as he saw her momentarily raise her head, then nuzzle back into the man's shoulder. She was alive.

But who was carrying her? As vertigo swept through him, Tony fought to remain conscious. He blinked furiously to wash away the ashes in his eyes, and Claire's rescuer came clearly into focus.

Damien Laurent. *How in the hell...?*

Sirens screamed and the first fire engines pulled into the circular drive. Tony took a deep breath, and his hand clutched the small piece of jewelry he'd found next to the freezer.

He'd recognized it immediately, both whom it belonged to, and what it meant. Things were going to be okay.

It was all over now.

SOMEONE HAD PUT rolls of cotton in Claire's mouth and down her throat. And then beaten her severely with a cast-iron pan. She rolled over onto a shoulder stiff with pain, then opened her eyes. Putting her hand to her lips, she stuck out her tongue and searched her mouth. No cotton. Was all this pain a dream? She tried to sit upright, but a heavy strap held her down on the hospital bed.

In a rush, the room spun into view, then back out again as dizziness overtook her. A pair of gentle, but firm hands guided her head to a basin where she retched, then mopped her face with a cool cloth. The nurse fluffed the pillow behind her, then eased her back against the sheets.

"There, there, Miss Kennedy. Just relax."

"Where's Tony? Tony Nichols. Is he okay?"

The young nurse smiled reassuringly at Claire, then took her pulse. "I'll send in Dr. Waters as soon as we're done here. How are you feeling?"

Claire jerked her hand out of the nurse's capable grasp, and rubbed it furiously. A heavy gauze bandage covered the palm.

Suddenly the vision of the firescape that was Sarah Winesong's house crowded out the antiseptic order of her hospital room. Tears began to run down Claire's cheeks as she fought the horror. She hadn't been able to get to Tony. Was he dead?

The nurse put her hand on Claire's shoulder, urging a glass of water and a small paper cup of pills on her. Without arguing, Claire swallowed them.

She wanted desperately to sleep. To sleep dreamlessly. To not contemplate the fact she may have lost Tony. But she had to find out; not knowing was a thousand times worse than knowing. "Is Tony Nichols okay?" she rasped.

"Just try to rest, Miss Kennedy. I'll send the doctor right in."

For a few moments Claire lay still, the only movement she made a fitful swallow as she choked back quiet tears.

"Miss Kennedy? How are you feeling?"

Opening her eyes, Claire met the kind ones of a young resident. He had an open-necked denim shirt on under his white coat, and merry blue eyes. She wanted him to go away. "I feel lousy. Are you going to tell me where Tony Nichols is?"

Dr. Waters walked closer to Claire, unfolding his arms and dropping his clipboard onto the bed beside her. He reached for his stethoscope, placing his pink fingers on Claire's neck. "If you'll just breathe deeply, Miss Kennedy, I'll get my exam over with quickly and you can go back to sleep."

As the doctor raised Claire to a sitting position, her dizziness returned. She fought it off with deep ragged breaths. "Doctor, either you tell me if Tony Nichols was admitted to this hospital, or get someone in here who can. Then we'll discuss my condition."

A look of pity crossed the resident's face, but before he could respond, another, more familiar voice addressed Claire from the doorway. "Claire, my dear, you must calm yourself. The doctor is trying to help you."

Claire jerked her head toward the speaker, shocked at the pale tired face of Vincent Harrison. "Mr. Harrison! Tell me what's happened. Is Tony okay? What happened to Roz, and Miss Winesong—"

Mr. Harrison put his finger to his lips to quiet Claire, then nodded at Dr. Waters. "Doctor, could you leave me alone with Miss Kennedy for just a few minutes? I think I can get her to cooperate if I impart some information to her about last night."

The doctor smiled and walked out of the room, annoying Claire even more by the pronounced look of pity on his smooth face. The restraining belt around her chest dug into her ribs, and Claire tugged at it. "Do you know why I'm trussed up like this, Mr. Harrison?"

"My dear Claire, you cracked several ribs last night. Please lie still."

Forcing herself to lean back into the pillows, Claire waited. "What's happened, Mr. Harrison? Please tell me everything."

Taking Claire's hand, Harrison sat next to the bed. "My dear, it appears that Mr. Nichols escaped the fire that consumed Sarah Winesong's house last night. At least the police haven't been able to find his body."

Joy flooded through her, and tears of happiness welled up in her sore eyes. "But where is he? He must be hurt, maybe unconscious, or suffering from amnesia. Have they searched the grounds?"

"Yes. There's no trace of him. Or his car."

"His car? He drove away from the scene and no one saw him?"

"It appears that way, my dear. But don't concern yourself—the police won't let him near you."

A roaring started in Claire's ears again as her head began to throb. Something was very wrong with this conversation. She knew a lot had happened, but Mr. Harrison's comments were confusing her. "I want to see him."

"No. No, you don't, Claire. The man murdered Sarah Winesong and Roz Abramawitz. And if Damien hadn't followed Roz out there like he did, Nichols probably would have murdered you, too."

The roaring got louder in her ears as Claire struggled to make sense of Mr. Harrison's words. Roz was dead. Winesong was dead. But the rest... "No. Tony didn't kill them, Mr. Harrison. Someone was trying to kill us. Someone shot at us when we followed Roz to Miss Winesong's. Shot at us and locked us in the basement. Then started that fire. It wasn't Tony."

Harrison shook his head, patting Claire's hands. "My dear, it must have been a trick. Maybe Mr. Nichols had a confederate who pulled those stunts to establish an alibi. Trust me, Claire. What I'm telling you is the truth. He orchestrated everything. Sarah Winesong called me at seven last night to say that Roz and Tony Nichols had called her and demanded an appointment. They were working together, Claire. They were trying to blackmail Sarah directly. They must have murdered that poor Snow girl, too. Damien said he saw Nichols hanging around the Russian Tea Room. He must have been waiting for her.''

''No. It can't be true.'' Tears were streaming down her cheeks. Her energy began to drain away, probably due to some medication she'd been given shortly before she came fully awake.

Before her boss could reply, the young nurse appeared to the left of Mr. Harrison, a look of dismay on her face. ''I'm sorry, sir, but you'll have to go now. Miss Kennedy needs to rest.''

''Certainly.'' Vincent Harrison gave Claire a searching look, then patted her hand again. ''I'll come back tomorrow, Claire. Just rest. It'll all be over soon.''

As consciousness seeped away, the room swirled again, sending Claire into a deeper blackness. But her mind protested even in sleep. ''No. It's not true. Tony. Tony...''

Chapter Fifteen

"And then what happened?" Claire lay back in bed, but crossed her arms in defiance.

"Nothing much. According to this news article, the fire department is investigating the cause of the blaze. It says here they were able to positively identify Roz's body." Tillie pulled the blanket over Claire's feet, then sat down on the edge of the bed and continued reading.

"And Sarah Winesong?"

Tillie swiped at the corner of her eyes, balancing her glasses up on her forehead. "Well, since she had no known relatives or household help, the authorities asked Mr. Harrison to view the second corpse. It was burned so badly he said he couldn't be absolutely sure, but the police are assuming it was her, since it was an elderly woman, and in Winesong's house. They've nicknamed the case *The Poison Pen Pal* murders. I wonder what jerk leaked the name of Winesong's book to the press."

"And there's still no word on Tony?"

Tillie slapped the newspaper onto her bony knees and peered at Claire. "For crying out loud! The man is a fugitive. Do you think he's going to call you and check in? He's hiding from the cops, and three, count them, three murder raps!"

Biting her lip nervously, Claire closed her eyes instead of meeting Tillie's gaze. She knew her friend didn't really believe in Tony's guilt, but was taking a hard line out of sorrow at the loss of Sarah. "You know Tony didn't kill anyone. The story in the paper is ridiculous."

"I don't know any such thing. The guy left you in a burning house and drove off."

Since Monday night, she had completely accepted the fact that Tony loved her. He must have seen Damien Laurent pull her out of the house, or he never would have left the scene. There had to be a perfectly good reason to explain his behavior.

Claire only wished she knew what it was.

Despite the fact she couldn't explain Tony's actions, she believed in him. Warmth spread through her as she savored this new feeling of being a part of another person. She was through with running away when things got rough. "It's ridiculous to argue about this now, Tillie. He's been framed from the first. By whomever Sarah was working with. By her killer."

"You've got her posthumously tried and convicted, huh?"

"I'm sorry if my words hurt you, Tillie. But that's how it looks to me, and I was there. Now I'm going to check myself out of here. It's Wednesday already, and I feel fine. I'll rest at home, and it'll be much easier for Tony to reach me there."

"Claire—"

Swinging her legs off the bed, Claire eased herself into her terry slippers and turned her back on Tillie. "Don't try to stop me. It must be Billings Newcastle who's behind all this. He was probably at Winesong's, waiting for Roz to show up."

Tillie grasped Claire's arm, helping her to the chair in the corner of the room. "You've gone mad. There is absolutely nothing to tie Newcastle to the things that have happened. Besides, he's got an alibi. Damien said this morning his sources told him Newcastle was at a dinner in Manhattan last night. How could he have been running around New Jersey taking shots at you?"

"Sources have been known to be wrong. And alibis are easy to buy when you're as rich as Billings Newcastle." Claire's anger subsided, and she fought the weakness threatening to overcome her as she got dressed. She slipped the hospital gown off her bruised and sore shoulder and gingerly stepped into her jeans, taking care not to pull off the bandages that covered her hands.

Tillie watched her for a moment, then in resignation helped her into her sweater. "Okay. But if you're going home, I'm going with you."

"Fine. You can make tea for Damien. He's meeting me there in an hour."

"Why?"

"Because I think he knows more than he's telling. He's been looking into Newcastle's attempt to force Mr. Harrison to sell Cauldron. I want to know why he followed Roz out to Winesong's, and if he saw something the other night that could help Tony."

Claire's voice broke as she said his name, and Tillie patted her arm. "It's going to be okay, kiddo. If the three of us can't figure out a way to handle Mr. Nichols, then no one can."

Claire managed a grin. "Thanks, Tillie. Remember, though, I don't want Mr. Harrison to know what we're trying to do. The poor man has enough to worry about."

A low whistle erupted from Tillie. "I forgot to tell you. I hear he spent all morning with three men from the bank. Rumors are that everyone's future is riding on the success of Winesong's book—''

"He's not still going to go ahead and publish it?" Claire's skin paled as she waited for Tillie to answer.

"Oh, yes, he is. In fact, Mr. Harrison's going out to the printing plant tonight, to personally check the book covers. Thursday is print day. He said they have to be perfect, the last book from Winesong and all. . . .''

Claire collapsed slowly onto the bed and shook her head, letting her jeans tumble to the floor. "After all that's happened, it's still that damn book that most concerns him.''

"Sarah Winesong made Cauldron Press. And Mr. Harrison is convinced that book is going to save it. The company means everything to him, Claire. And to me.''

"I know, but with her death . . .'' Claire's voice trailed off as she shook her hair out of her face. Though she'd never even met the reclusive author, she'd been stunned at the news of her death. A deep sense of personal loss haunted her—for Winesong, and even for Roz.

Despite their opposing styles, Claire had always harbored a certain respect for Roz's aggressiveness. "I guess all the real-life mayhem that's happened will only mean more sales for *The Poison Pen Pal*.''

"Yep. Freak-show time. People love real scandal even more than 'Dynasty.' The past two days' news stories about fires and murders and dead authors should really whet their appetites.''

"Well, I'm sick of all the fingers pointing at Tony. And I'm going to make sure the papers print the truth in type as big as they've printed their scandal. He's a wonderful, kind, giving man.''

"You're determined to stand by this guy?"

"I have to, Tillie. So go get your car. I'll see you downstairs in ten minutes."

Tillie grabbed her purse and three arrangements of flowers, nearly dropping a pot of white lilies from Damien Laurent. "These look like funeral flowers."

"They could have been." Claire stood and pulled her jeans back on. Stuffing her personal items into her overnight bag, she took another five minutes to lace up her tennis shoes. As she headed for the door, the telephone next to the bed rang.

Staring at it for a second, Claire turned and headed out the door. The well-wishers would have to wait. She had to see Damien. And find Tony.

EIGHT RINGS. NINE RINGS. Ten. On the eleventh, Tony put the receiver back on the cradle and opened the phone-booth door immediately to douse the light. He didn't want anyone to get too close a look at him. His eyes still smarted from the smoke of Monday night's fire.

Claire must be having an X ray or some tests, he tried to tell himself. This attempt to explain why Claire wasn't answering her phone did little to calm him.

Holed up in a dingy twelve-dollar-a-night room on the outskirts of Queens, he'd been frantically trying to reach her. The nurses at the hospital had insisted she was well, but incommunicado. Should he risk going to see her? No, he decided. He'd never escape the police.

Crossing the street, Tony said his hundredth silent prayer that Claire knew he hadn't just abandoned her at the Winesong estate. When the police and fire personnel had pulled out their guns because Laurent, no doubt, had warned them he was armed, he'd seen it was better to slip away than risk explaining his hunch who set the fire and why.

Because then he'd had little proof.

But now he had solid evidence. The small copper Medic-Alert bracelet he'd found in Winesong's basement belonged to Benton Convent's missing justice of the peace, Pearl Loney. And after a day combing through the Department of Immigration files a helpful contact at the library had provided, he knew why it was there.

This thrill of finally knowing who was responsible for Patricia's murder didn't, however, compare with his worry about Claire. He'd admitted to himself several days ago that he loved the woman, but he hadn't been prepared for this gut-jumbling helplessness he'd been feeling since the fire.

He'd gotten back to New York the next morning and called on an old news-reporter friend to find out if Claire was badly hurt. The hospital report said she was critical, but stable. Tony only hoped she'd stay that way until he could hold her in his arms again and kiss each and every one of her beautiful freckles.

At least he didn't have to worry about her tonight. She was safe as long as she stayed in the hospital.

Wincing as he put more weight on his bandaged left leg, he limped over to the rented Mustang and slid in. Time was slipping by. The sky was already dark at six o'clock and the approaching headlights glimmered in twos and threes.

At least his leg wasn't broken. After pulling the knob to flash his own car lights on, Tony reached for a cigarette.

The tobacco burned his tongue, reminding him of Claire's teasing comments about his vice. He tossed the package out the window, then gripped the chrome wheel tightly as he pulled out into the traffic.

The pain from the scattered blisters on his palms actually comforted him. They reminded him of his anger, and the score he was going to settle finally tonight. *You're gonna pay for everything, you heartless bastard.*

As if he could taste the revenge he vowed against the person who'd caused so much misery, Tony swallowed hard.

Roughly changing gears, he took a deep breath and pushed the car to seventy-five. "Miss Winesong's last mystery is about to be solved," he muttered. And the last chapter was sure to have a twist ending.

TILLIE AND CLAIRE sat side by side on the high-backed sofa, staring at Damien Laurent. Tillie's elegant nephew stood poised by Claire's fireplace. The critic's usually perfect hair was intact, but his pink Countess Mara necktie sagged crookedly at the neck.

"I'm absolutely sure, Claire. There's no possibility at all that Newcastle knew about Patricia Snow's claims against Sarah Winesong. If he'd known, he'd have halted all negotiations to buy Cauldron Press from Vincent immediately."

Claire's expression remained shocked.

Tillie blinked, then worriedly patted Claire's bloodless hands. "You okay, Claire? Drink some more tea."

"This can't be true."

Damien shook his head. "It is true, Claire. Vincent sold Cauldron Press to Billings Newcastle Monday afternoon, solely on the strength of the projected sales of Winesong's book. I've seen the contract."

"But he said he'd never sell. He said he wouldn't have to if *The Poison Pen Pal* was published."

"But he did. For the full market value. Which means Newcastle is an unlikely candidate to have been blackmailing Vincent. Vincent made five million dollars on the deal. Personally.''

Nothing was making any sense to Claire. Every time she thought she understood what was going on, a totally new twist of events turned things askew. "Why didn't he tell me the truth?"

"Why should he? After all, Vincent was sole owner of the company, answerable only to the bank. Frankly, Claire, you've been rather intent on proving Cauldron Press's complicity in the Patricia Snow scandal. Vincent was probably worried you would sour his deal in the final stages."

"Why did you follow Roz the other night, Damien?"

He stepped back, surprised by Claire's abruptness. "I was curious. Both about Roz's meeting with Sarah Winesong, and your Mr. Nichols skulking around the restaurant. I am a journalist first and foremost, you know." He tapped his cane on the floor for emphasis.

Claire eyed it closely, realizing it was nearly the twin of the one she'd seen at Winesong's. "I'm glad you're my friend, Damien. And I owe you my life for pulling me out of that burning house."

Beaming, Damien started to accept her thanks, but she interrupted. "Do you have another cane like that one?"

"This?" He waved it in the air, then smiled. "All the canes in my collection are one of a kind. This one is Chinese, though the silver work is Spanish. I had a couple of similar ones, but I've given them away as gifts. Why do you ask?"

"Claire. Did you hear me?" Damien said when he got no response.

Shaking her head as if to clear it, Claire wrung her palm-burned hands together, wincing at the pain. "I'm sorry, Damien, I didn't. What did you say?"

"Why do you ask? About the cane. Are you going to start collecting them, too? We can form a club—Aunt Tillie, you and Vincent. He has nearly as many as I do now."

Something clicked in Claire's mind. A tiny piece of new information caused a domino effect of thoughts and random ideas to fall into line. And the line spelled out an explanation so clear, and so hideous, that it took her breath away. "Who else came by to see you last Sunday, Damien? Roz told me you had a lot of company."

"I did. Let's see...." Damien began to pace, swiping at the air, which was full of Tillie's cigarette smoke. "Well, a writer friend arrived after you and Mr. Nichols left. Oh, yes. There was Vincent. He was in good spirits and had just driven back into town. Wanted to stop and see me before he went home. No sooner did he leave than Abramawitz rapped on the door. My guest list was a progressive potluck on Sunday."

"What is it, Claire? What are you thinking?"

Tillie's questions went unanswered as Claire stood and walked to the window looking down on the street. Woofer, from his perch on the valance, performed his imitation of a dog barking. "I really need to be alone for a little while now. I'm so tired."

Damien and Tillie exchanged glances, then Tillie shook her head and shrugged. Picking up the tea tray, she walked into the kitchen.

Claire turned and looked at Damien thoughtfully. "You've known Mr. Harrison for a long time, Damien. Can I ask you one last thing?"

"Certainly."

"Is Vincent Harrison his real name?"

Frowning, Damien looked down at his feet. "That's an odd question, Claire. I thought you knew Vincent changed his name when he first emigrated from Paris in the late forties. His original name is Chancon. Vincent Chancon. I think he should have kept it. French surnames have so much more élan than anglicized ones."

Chancon. The name on the deed of the house where Patricia Snow was murdered. The name of the person who named Winesong sole heir. Carefully controlling her voice, Claire asked another question. "So why did he change it?"

"Vanity. He said he was so poor in France that he needed a new, strong American name to be successful here. I told him years ago he shouldn't have given it up. It's so musical—pun intended."

"Was he ever married?"

At that moment, Tillie walked back in the room and stood between Damien and Claire. "Vincent's never been married. You know that."

"Yes, he has, Aunt Tillie." Damien smiled as both women faced him. "I met the girl, Marielle her name was. She and her sister, Pearl, came to the States around the same time as Vincent. Their marriage lasted a year, and Marielle died shortly afterward."

"Pearl?" Claire's voice rasped. "What happened to Pearl?"

Tillie sat down woodenly beside Claire as Damien answered, "I don't know for sure. Last I heard she married a small-town farmer and moved to New Jersey. But that was thirty years ago."

"I never knew any of this," Tillie mumbled. "I can't believe Vincent never told me...."

Claire reached toward Tillie and patted her arm. "It seems Mr. Harrison didn't tell either of us a lot of things, Tillie. But I think someone from Mr. Harrison's past has come back to haunt us all. Go with Damien downstairs now. You both need to get some rest."

"It's all gone now, Claire. The company, Sarah, Vincent. What am I going to do?" Tillie looked dazed.

Damien's expression showed his shock at his aunt's pain. He nodded to Claire, then gently helped Tillie to the door. The older woman turned back to Claire.

"You're sure you don't want me to stay the night, because I could—"

"No, Tillie. Thanks. Thanks to you both. Now go. I'll be fine."

Claire closed the door behind them, then engaged the dead bolt. Returning to her chair, she felt bereft of all feeling. The trauma of the past few days was nothing compared to tonight's.

Tillie and Mr. Harrison. She'd never suspected that her assistant's loyalty and devotion extended beyond the professional man. She must be in love with him.

Nor had she ever suspected what now seemed clear as day. Vincent Harrison had betrayed them both.

DeSalvo Printing was a two-hour jaunt across Manhattan to Yonkers' industrial section. By the time Claire walked to the front gate of the warehouse, it was past nine. The taxi driver had not been overjoyed to leave her in the empty employee parking lot.

He'd accepted his ten-dollar tip suspiciously, muttering something in a vaguely middle-European accent about "smarty American women." He'd driven off, glancing back at Claire once to see if she'd changed her mind.

She hadn't. And her normal jitters at being out alone in a strange part of town had fled. She was past worrying about such trifles as muggers. The real dangers in life were much closer to home.

Carefully she looked around the shadowy grounds for a sign of the night watchman or any other employees. No one was visible. But there was the car. Vincent Harrison was still here.

His gleaming black Lincoln sat in the shadows outside the empty guard shack, its car-phone antenna piercing the air above it. Leo DeSalvo, the owner of the printing plant, had only a two man crew on at night. They must be inside with Mr. Harrison, checking the ink colors and picture definition of the cover for *The Poison Pen Pal*, she guessed.

Harrison? Or should she have said Chancon?

Moving quickly, Claire tried the handle of the Lincoln. It opened cleanly. For a fraction of a second she hesitated, then firmly pulled the seat forward and slipped into the back, moving aside the heavy cardboard box next to her.

Her plan was a simple one. She'd wait here for Mr. Harrison, then demand he tell her why he'd sold Cauldron Press. And why he'd never told anyone he was related to Sarah Winesong.

Resting her hand on the box, Claire studied the contents for a moment. Manuscripts.

Lifting out a few pages, Claire impulsively read in the glow thrown by the building's security lights. It was the middle of a chapter, no heading or page number appeared on the page, and a bold childish script had corrected several typos.

After a moment, Claire sat up nervously, her breathing more shallow as her eyes raced across one page, then another. In shock, she realized she was reading from an early version of *The Poison Pen Pal*. One she'd never seen before. The characters' names were different, but the story line was the same.

On the bottom of the second page, a different handwriting appeared. A bold thick script read: "Patty, insert the scene about the lion's-head vase here—it'll work great to prolong the suspense." The note was signed "T."

She recognized Tony's hand from the note he'd left her in Narragansett. Everything came together at that moment, and shakily she put the pages back into the box, then stared out the window.

She was reading a draft of Patricia Snow's manuscript, the version that had been stolen from Tony's office.

With a flash of memory, she also pictured the lion's-head vase full of tulips sitting on his counter at home. It had seemed familiar that day, but she hadn't known why. Now she did.

She'd read it described perfectly as the murder weapon in *The Poison Pen Pal*. A prop from life Sarah Winesong couldn't have ever seen, but one that Patricia Snow had.

Tony had been right all along.

Cauldron Press had stolen the book. Vincent Harrison must have orchestrated the cover-up from the first night he'd met Tony. He'd broken into Tony's office to steal the manuscript, hit Tony, and probably been the one who'd chased her through the woods.

And murdered three women.

As a bone-deep shudder passed through her, Claire saw two men come out of the plant. Vincent Harrison stood with one of the printers, nodding and shaking hands. As the man from DeSalvo Printing walked toward the lone car in the employee lot, Harrison limped toward the Lincoln, where she sat holding the proof of his crimes.

He was leaning heavily on a cane. She'd forgotten until Damien mentioned it that Mr. Harrison also collected them, along with his other antiques. His face was set in lines of fatigue. And something else. From twenty feet away Claire saw a self-satisfied smile of victory etched deeply on his face.

Claire's brown eyes glinted with fury and hate. By trusting Vincent Harrison she'd almost sacrificed the one man she'd ever truly loved.

Well, it was time to call in the markers.

Claire lunged for the door and leaped out. Her appearance startled Harrison, who stopped dead and stared at her in shock, no recognition on his face. Then a smile of relief glimmered, and his voice crackled as he shouted, "Claire, my God, you gave me a start. What are you doing out of the hospital so soon? Did you want to see the book cover? You should have called me. I have one I was bringing to show you."

Walking around in front of the Lincoln, Claire stopped three feet from where Harrison stood. She could barely keep from rushing at him, so badly did she want to beat him with her fists, to dole out some small punishment for his crimes. "What else were you going to bring me, Mr. Harrison? A lethal injection? A poison pill? Or maybe just a careful suffocating with a hospital pillow?"

"Claire, my dear, you're delirious. Come and get back in the car. I'll take you to the hospital."

"You're not taking me anywhere. So just stay where you are. I'm going inside to call the police. And I'm sure they'll be overjoyed to know *The Poison Pen Pal* murderer has been unmasked."

Harrison leaned heavily on his cane, clutching the small stack of book covers in one hand while the other groped deeply into his overcoat. "After all that's happened, you don't know what you're saying, Claire. Tony Nichols betrayed you and now you're upset—"

"Don't say another word! I won't listen to you defame Tony anymore. You framed him from the start, just so you could keep this scandal quiet and get your damn money from Newcastle. You planted a cigarette he smoked in your office at Patricia's. And you broke into his office to steal the evidence that would have indicated Patricia's book was real. There's no use denying it. I just found the manuscript you stole from his office. It's pitiable, Mr. Harrison. You've cheated and lied, just to protect some dried-up old woman's reputation and bolster the selling price of a company you planned all along to turn over to Billings Newcastle."

"Claire, I—"

"No. I'm going to have my say. You used me because you were too weak to let the truth come out about your precious famous author. All you had to do when you found out the truth was publish Patricia's manuscript under her name. You could have kept Cauldron Press, and not murdered that poor girl. But instead you blew it! How could you have been so weak?"

Harrison appeared to cower at her words. His voice was a ragged whisper. "You don't understand, Claire. Without Newcastle's purchase, I would have lost Cauldron Press to the bank. It would have taken years to get Patricia Snow's reputation, and earning power, up to Sarah Winesong's. I just couldn't risk it. There was no time."

"That's ridiculous. Winesong hadn't been published for years, and with the right kind of publicity, *The Poison Pen Pal* would have made tons of money, no matter who wrote it. Why was it so important to protect Winesong? Why? Because you were related to her, Mr. *Chancon*?''

For a moment Vincent Harrison remained motionless, then slowly came to life. He stood straighter, and the pained expression was replaced by one of alert malice. Slowly he withdrew his hand from his overcoat. A shiny, small-caliber gun glinted in the security lights.

''Why? I'll tell you why, Claire. Not because Vincent Chancon is related to the famous Sarah Winesong. Because Vincent Chancon *is* Sarah Winesong.''

''You—''

''Shut up.'' He grabbed her by the arm and pushed her toward the building. ''Now get inside, or I swear I'll kill you right here.''

Chapter Sixteen

As she stood in the hallway inside DeSalvo Printing, memories of a day in French class fifteen years earlier swirled in Claire's mind. *Chanter*—to sing, *chanson*—song. Damien's comment that Harrison's original French name was "musical" sudden became much more than a pun.

Vin for wine, *chancon* for song.

Sarah Winesong was not a real person at all, only the pseudonym used in a deadly game of deceit played by Vincent Chancon.

"The body the police found with Roz? Who was it?" Claire demanded.

"Be quiet." His grim demeanor did not welcome questions.

She spoke again, hoping to distract him enough to get the gun he was training on her pointed in another direction. "Was it Pearl Loney?"

The gun wavered perceptively. "I said shut up."

Halting suddenly, Claire turned to face her boss. Alarm seemed to fill him as he gripped his gun more tightly. "Go on. Why are you stopping?"

"I'm tired of walking. And I want to talk to you."

"Keep walking. Go all the way into the warehouse, then we'll talk."

Warily Claire turned and continued. The heavy scent of acetone and linseed oil clung to the air as the two of them trudged by a row of offices. Ahead of them at the rear of the complex, were the presses and warehouse.

At last they passed through the double doors at the end of the darkened corridor. A single light in the corner bathed the enormous bolts of paper in every color. Against all the walls stood huge racks holding ten-gallon drums of inks and glue. Lined up in the center were filing cabinets holding their precious contents of copper and steel printing plates.

Claire found herself wondering briefly where the plates for *The Poison Pen Pal* were stored. If she had her way, she'd smash each one at Harrison's feet.

Glancing back at him, she started. Shadows flickered in all corners of the huge room. Her attention was pulled to the glint off a ten-foot-tall paper cutter beside the door to the loading dock.

Suddenly Harrison closed the distance between them by reaching out and grasping her left elbow. "Go over there and sit."

Claire walked to the stool that he pointed to and sat, carefully fixing her gaze beyond him. Without moving her head, she moved her eyes in search of any sign of an exit, or the night watchman. Surely someone heard the shot Harrison had fired to open the outside door.

"It's no use looking for a guard. The printer told me the watchman was off tonight because his wife is ill. We joked about the fact that the now notorious *Poison Pen Pal* would be left unprotected."

Flinching inwardly, Claire looked at him, but maintained a passive expression, despite her horror at hearing the news. "But you're here to protect it, right, Mr. Harrison?"

"Very astute, as always."

"But you pose the greatest threat to the book's success."

"Don't play games with me, Claire. Nothing will keep that book from becoming the greatest seller of Winesong's career."

"You mean of your career?" Gently Claire continued, not taking her eyes off Harrison's face. "If you kill me, your book will never be published."

For an instant Harrison looked sick, then a lopsided smile formed on his thin lips. "Why?"

"With more scandal, you can bet Newcastle will back out of the deal to buy Cauldron Press. Patricia's mother will tie up *The Poison Pen Pal* in court for years."

"No, she won't. I'll see to that loose end when I leave here tonight. The only proof left was the IOU, and I burned that."

"If anything happens to me, Damien Laurent will be very suspicious. So will Tillie. She's finally coming to see that you aren't the person we all thought, Mr. Harrison. Are you willing to kill both of them, too? Don't forget, Tony Nichols is still out there somewhere. There are other options."

"Don't try to trick me, Claire. I know your technique of negotiation. That skill is what makes you such a brilliant editor. Sarah Winesong's last work shines because of you."

"Because of Patricia Snow, you mean." Claire knew instantly she shouldn't have said that, but she was unable to keep her anger at bay.

Harrison's features set into a mask of hatred. "Patricia was nothing but a drunken little leech. If she hadn't been so greedy, hadn't gone back on our agreement and sent her whimpering effort to Roz, I wouldn't have had to—" Harrison caught himself. "But you know all that, don't you?"

"I know now that you had Pearl Loney pose as Sarah Winesong for phone calls. I know you misrepresented the talent in Patricia's book to her, and used my name to do it. That's despicable, Mr. Harrison. And you're not going to get away with framing Tony. What I don't know is why you did all this."

With a tiny bow, Harrison moved the gun from his right to left hand, as he put down the cane and book covers on the long table. Grasping the gun with both hands, he cocked the trigger and pointed the barrel at Claire's horrified face. "Why? Because there was no other way. Just like there's no other way to keep you quiet, dear Claire. Much to my dismay."

Steadily Claire held up her hand and covered the gun's barrel. It was a bluff, one that made her knees quiver, but she was desperate to buy time until some plan of escape could take shape in her mind. "But why didn't you ever reveal that *you* are Sarah Winesong? Weren't you proud of all the success you earned as a writer?"

Down came the gun, still cocked. "Proud, yes. Maybe too proud. You see, part of Sarah's mystique was that she was a widowed, wonderful recluse. I couldn't risk revealing my identity. Don't you see? The public would have been disappointed that Sarah wasn't real."

"I think you're selling your public short, Mr. Harrison. They would love you for all the entertainment you've provided them over the years. Why don't you let me help you bring the truth out? I'm sure our business would triple once it was announced that Vincent Harrison is really Sarah Winesong."

As Claire spoke, her eyes drifted to the shelf behind Harrison. A heavy set of shears stuck out, their large circle-shaped handles tantalizingly close. If she could grab them, maybe she could knock the gun from his hand.

Harrison's voice had a dreamy quality to it. "Actually I think everything has really worked out for the best. All those times you rejected my work, Claire, I plotted how I'd get even with you, even though I knew you were right and my books were weak. I thought about letting Sarah Winesong die, rest on her laurels, but then Pearl found Patricia's book. I couldn't resist, and I did do quite a lot to help that story, you know."

He was really losing it, Claire saw. "Put the gun down, Mr. Harrison."

He cocked the trigger again, his voice rising. "It would have worked, if it wasn't for Tony Nichols. How could you choose him over your family at Cauldron Press, Claire?"

"I'll answer that one for you, Harrison. Claire has too much class and integrity to protect a criminal, even family." Tony's voice rang out harshly from the back of the warehouse.

Panic-stricken, Harrison grabbed Claire and pressed the gun to her temple. "Well, so Mr. Nichols has turned up. How fortunate. Come on out, Nichols. Or I'll shoot dear Claire right now."

Claire's eyes strained to detect Tony's whereabouts. Then Tony's voice boomed out again, this time from the opposite direction.

"Put the gun down, Harrison. The cops have Pearl Loney's bracelet, and your prints are on it. She must have lost it when you stuck her in the basement freezer. And now they know she was the one who died in the fire, not Sarah Winesong. After they read the letter I sent them, along with a copy of Marielle's and Pearl's immigration papers, it wouldn't surprise me if they'll look into your young bride's sudden death all those years ago. Left you enough life insurance to start Cauldron Press, didn't she?"

Dragging Claire down onto the concrete floor with him, Vincent fired wildly in the direction of Tony's voice. "You're a dead man, Nichols. When the police show up all they'll find is Claire's body. Who do you think they'll believe shot her? Her deranged spurned lover? Or her boss, who's been so savagely libeled by a psycho ex-writer?"

Terror gripped Claire. She could taste the acrid gun powder, thick in the air. "You killed them all—"

"Yes. I killed them all." Harrison's breath was stale on her face. "And I'd kill them again. Just like I'm going to kill you. You should have been stronger, my dear. Pearl told me it was obvious you were in love with Nichols, said I couldn't trust you. I should have listened and killed you that night in the woods."

"Is she the one who stole the copies of the manuscript for you, so you could concoct the story that they were Winesong's drafts?"

"No. I did that. She searched Nichols's house, but never could find anything beyond some garbage he was working on about Newcastle. I was in Rhode Island when you were, and I did the rest.''

Harrison seemed to realize that Claire was trying to stall. His pupils dilated to their full size in the dim light, and he began to wheeze.

"Let her go, Harrison."

A chill shot down Claire's spine as Harrison's mouth hardened into a deadly smile. If Tony was trying to push him into making a hasty move, she'd have to be ready to run.

She saw him stiffen and again grasp the gun with two hands. "Don't let Tony push you," she said. "I'll help you. With the right incentive, your secret can be safe with me. The police have no hard evidence."

For a moment Harrison looked at her like he had so many times in the past, with trust and respect mingling in his eyes. "What kind of incentive?"

Slowly Claire stretched out her hand and picked up the stack of book covers that had slid to the floor. Though her heart begged her to scan the room for Tony, she forced her eyes to remain locked on Vincent's. "A piece of the sale. A percentage of the royalties. Money, plain and simple. A payoff."

Vincent began to laugh when the words were scarcely out of Claire's mouth. It was a demented cackling sound, like nothing she'd ever heard. "Please, my dear, this is too ludicrous. I would never, ever believe that you could be bought."

His voice changed dramatically, and he pulled the gun back up to her eye level. "And I don't believe it now. Sorry, dear Claire."

As Harrison's fingers tightened around the trigger, Tony leaped from the darkness toward him like a panther. "Get away, Claire! Roll under the table!"

There was a crack of the pistol as Claire rolled to her right, slamming her ankle against the metal table leg. She was momentarily deafened by the noise.

The warehouse was plunged into darkness. The bullet had exploded the light fixture overhead.

Crawling on all fours, Claire scurried out from under the table and circled a pallet of paper. Frantically, she tried to see what was happening.

Harrison appeared to be striking Tony with the gun, while Tony held Vincent's legs, pummeling his torso and trying to knock him down. Both men's breaths came in gulping gasps. Claire crawled closer, yelling, "Tony, get the gun! Throw it this way."

Her voice seemed to energize the combatants, and their movements became more frantic. Suddenly Claire spotted Harrison's cane on the floor. It had fallen and rolled under the table near her. She turned and crawled back around the pallet to grab for it.

The silver head was cold against her hand. As she grabbed it and stood up, the gun went off again. For an instant the night air was quiet, save for the tinny echo of the bullet. Then Claire screamed. With a slicing motion she swung the cane toward the slight figure of Vincent Harrison, who again aimed the gun at her.

As the cane slammed into his arm, another shot rang out. Claire ducked under the printing table, crawling frantically toward the rear of the shop. She didn't know how badly Tony was hurt, but he hadn't made a sound. All she knew was that she had to lure Harrison away from Tony in the hope Tony could get away.

She heard Harrison behind her. "Stop right now, Claire. It's useless to run away. I've got the gun."

Groping in the dark, she picked up a container and stood up. With all her strength, she hurled a mayonnaise-size bottle of ink in the direction of his voice. The shattering noise against the cement told her she hadn't hit her target, though his cursing gave her hope that maybe he'd been slowed by a glass fragment.

Zigzagging under the tables and around boxes, Claire dropped back to her knees and continued crawling. Stopping under the heavy wooden cutting table where the individual pages of a book were trimmed, she slowly turned around. Her ears strained for the smallest clue as to Harrison's whereabouts, but she heard nothing.

For several seconds she held her breath. Just when she thought she'd choke with anxiety, the tabletop creaked. Harrison had crawled up onto the table.

A moan from the floor in the middle of the room told her Tony was coming around. Before she could move toward him, another shot rang out. Then she heard Harrison start to move. The table jiggled and the sound of ripping paper met her ears. His leather soles must have caught on the sheet that hung over the edge of the table.

Suddenly Claire had an idea. As his steps got closer, just above her head now, she slowly placed her hands on the paper and yanked with all her strength.

She heard Harrison cry out as the gun went off again, the bullet ricocheting off the metal ceiling fans. Then it sounded as if the entire ceiling fell on top of the table she was crouched under.

Harrison screamed, then a rushing, sliding crash of metal seemed to shake the whole building. The thudding noise of Harrison's body hitting the ground sent Claire scooting out from under the table and running toward the spot where Tony had fallen. She hadn't counted the bullets fired, but at that point she didn't care if there were any left in Harrison's gun.

When she finally reached Tony, he was on his knees and elbows, blood running down the side of his face. His dark eyes glowed with pain, grim determination apparent in his face. "Claire! My God, are you okay?"

Falling to her knees, she wrapped her arms around him and kissed him over and over, as he hugged her and stroked her disheveled hair. "I'm fine, Tony. But you—did he get you? Are you okay?"

"Ssh, it's okay, darling. The bullet just grazed me."

Quickly Claire turned and pushed out of his arms. She'd been so glad to see Tony, she'd forgotten about Harrison. Now she was engulfed by her returning fear. Was he unconscious? Hiding in the shadows? At this instant was he pointing the gun at them again? Through clenched teeth she said," Where is he?"

Tony sat upright and drew her roughly against his chest, patting her hair with his hand. "Don't even try to see. It's all over now. He's dead."

In the dimness Claire looked into Tony's face. "But how...?"

"The paper cutter. Guillotine for a murderer. The bullet hit the safety cord, and he fell against the lever. I don't know what made him stumble, but when he did, he never had a chance."

Tears of relief and horror rolled soundlessly down her face. "Tony, I'm so sorry. I was wrong about him, about Winesong... Can you ever forgive me?"

Gently cradling her face in his hands, he kissed her cheeks, then her nose, then her salty lips. "We were both wrong about everything but this." He kissed her again, pressing her to him as if he would never let her go.

TONY AND CLAIRE walked hand in hand out of the Waldorf Astoria elevator, waiting patiently while the bellman unlocked their door. Inside, Claire fell onto the bed while Tony handed out a generous tip.

"Thank you, Mr. Poe. Have a nice stay. Ma'am." The young man smiled, then winked at Claire.

"Mr. Poe?" She giggled. "You registered us under Poe?"

He knelt on the floor and rained tiny kisses up her leg and thigh while she shrieked. He'd discovered how ticklish she was the first night they'd been lovers, and he couldn't resist hearing her laugh. "I thought it was fitting."

Pulling Tony onto the bed with her, Claire ran her hands down his face, nibbling on his chin. "Well, maybe you should consider writing some dark haunted prose when you finish your new book."

"If I finish this book, I may go back to teaching. I like all those coeds looking to me for instruction." Tony yelped as Claire nipped him, then met her lips hungrily.

She rolled off the bed and walked to the window, looking down at Central Park. Like a pantomime, taxi drivers gestured soundlessly as their cars moved in the soft summer evening.

"It was really great of Damien to take us to dinner. I think Tillie is going to be okay now. She looked like her old self tonight."

"You look like your old self tonight. I love that dress, but I think you need to take it off now."

Claire turned around and shook her head. "So impatient, Mr. Poe. Haven't you heard that all good things come to those who wait?"

He smiled. "Tillie's a survivor, Claire. Now that you've been named publisher of Cauldron Press, she's got a new sense of duty. She told me tonight she thinks you're working too hard."

"She's the one who's working too hard. Now that Mrs. Snow has finally signed a contract, she's spending sixteen hours a day getting Patricia's book ready. And talking about working too long, what about you?" Claire slid the zipper of her silk skirt down and wriggled out of it, enjoying the tension in Tony's face as he watched. "Ever since you decided to write your book, you don't come to bed until all hours."

"I come to bed *before* I work, or don't you remember last night?"

"Oh, I remember last night very well." She slipped off her blouse, then undid the black-lace garter belt, resting her foot on the bed near him as she slipped off one stocking. "And if you keep treating your editor like that, she's going to have to insist on an exclusive agreement."

"Exclusive?" Tony's voice was thick, an edge of impatience creeping in to it as she draped her other stocking across his shoulder and unclasped her garter belt.

She now stood in the black-lace teddy that did little to disguise the rise and fall of her breasts. "Of course an exclusive. All the work we've done this past month on your technique, and climax of a scene, why, I can't have you sharing all that literary talent with any other editor." Claire slipped the straps down her shoulders, letting the garment fall to the floor. She stood in a naked silhouette against the twentieth-floor window, waiting for Tony to speak.

Without a word, he rose and removed his clothing in fluid motions, then walked toward her and folded her against him.

Claire pressed one hand into the thick matting of hair on his chest, then ran her fingers under the waistband of his shorts. "Aren't you forgetting something, Mr. Poe?"

His voice was suddenly quite serious. "It's not Mr. Poe. It's Tony. Anthony Alessandro Nichols, to be exact. No actor. No con man. Just the man who's loved you from the moment he saw you two months ago. Just the man who wants to show you how you're going to be loved for the rest of your life."

Tears welled up in her throat, clouding her voice as her eyes burned. She reached for Tony's face, pulling his mouth down to hers for a tender kiss. "Thank you, Tony. You've given me so much already. A future. The chance to believe I can have a future that won't disappear the moment I turn my back...."

He kissed her, squeezing her so tightly against him she felt part of him. "There's no getting rid of me, Ms. Kennedy. Not tonight, not ever. Now, have I waited long enough to get some of those good things you promised?"

"Almost. Since this is our special night to celebrate, I need you to do one more thing."

Responding to the huskiness in Claire's voice, Tony lifted her into his arms and plopped her onto the bed. "One thing? I plan on doing a whole lot more than one thing."

"Get rid of these." Claire lay back on the cool satin coverlet, slowly tugging his shorts down to his knees, smiling as he kicked them off onto the floor. "Just what I like. An author who does what he's told."

Pulling her into his arms, Tony nuzzled her neck. "And just what I like. An editor who knows just what she wants."

"All the best stories are a collaboration of effort, remember?"

He lay next to her, stroking his hand upward from her stomach to her neck, then across her breasts. She moved onto her side facing him, her own hands busy. The quilt under him warmed to the temperature of Claire's skin, and he ached to taste her moistness as she wet her lips. "I'd say it's time for a masterpiece of collaboration, Ms. Editor."

"Is that a pun, Mr. Poe?"

They both chuckled as he rolled her gently onto her back.

Harlequin Superromance

**Here are the longer, more involving stories you
have been waiting for... Superromance.**

Modern, believable novels of love, full of the complex
joys and heartaches of real people.

Intriguing conflicts based on today's constantly
changing life-styles.

Four new titles every month.
Available wherever paperbacks are sold.   SUPER-1

Harlequin Superromance

CALLOWAY CORNERS

Created by four outstanding Superromance authors, bonded by lifelong friendship and a love of their home state: Sandra Canfield, Tracy Hughes, Katherine Burton and Penny Richards.

CALLOWAY CORNERS

Home of four sisters as different as the seasons, as elusive as the elements; an undiscovered part of Louisiana where time stands still and passion lasts forever.

CALLOWAY CORNERS

Birthplace of the unforgettable Calloway women: *Mariah*, free as the wind, and untamed until she meets the preacher who claims her, body and soul; *Jo*, the fiery, feisty defender of lost causes who loses her heart to a rock and roll man; *Tess*, gentle as a placid lake but tormented by her longing for the town's bad boy and *Eden*, the earth mother who's been so busy giving love she doesn't know how much she needs it until she's awakened by a drifter's kiss...

CALLOWAY CORNERS

Coming from Superromance, in 1989:
Mariah, by Sandra Canfield, a January release
Jo, by Tracy Hughes, a February release
Tess, by Katherine Burton, a March release
Eden, by Penny Richards, an April release

Harlequin Temptation dares to be different!

Once in a while, we Temptation editors spot a romance that's truly innovative. To make sure *you* don't miss any one of these outstanding selections, we'll mark them for you.

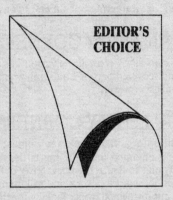

EDITOR'S CHOICE

When the "Editors' Choice" fold-back appears on a Temptation cover, you'll know we've found that extra-special page-turner!

THE *Temptation* EDITORS

Spot-1B

COMING IN MARCH FROM

Harlequin Superromance

Book Two of the Merriman County Trilogy
AFTER ALL THESE YEARS
the sizzle of Eve Gladstone's
One Hot Summer continues!

Sarah Crewes is at it again, throwing Merriman County into a tailspin with her archival diggings. In *One Hot Summer* (September 1988) she discovered that the town of Ramsey Falls was celebrating its tricentennial one year too early.

Now she's found that Riveredge, the Creweses' ancestral home and property, does not rightfully belong to her family. Worse, the legitimate heir to Riveredge may be none other than the disquieting Australian, Tyler Lassiter.

Sarah's not sure why Tyler's in town, but she suspects he is out to right some old wrongs—and some new ones!

The unforgettable characters of *One Hot Summer* and *After All These Years* will continue to delight you in book three of the trilogy. Watch for *Wouldn't It Be Lovely* in November 1989.

SR349-1

Harlequin Regency Romance™

Romance the way it was *always* meant to be!

The time is 1811, when a Regent Prince rules the empire. The place is London, the glittering capital where rakish dukes and dazzling debutantes scheme and flirt in a dangerously exciting game. Where marriage is the passport to wealth and power, yet every girl hopes secretly for love....

Welcome to Harlequin Regency Romance where reading is an adventure and romance is *not* just a thing of the past! Two delightful books a month, beginning May '89.

Available wherever Harlequin Books are sold.